ASYLUM MURDERS

A LADY BLACK MYSTERY

MICHAEL G. COLBURN

ISBN: 979-8-9905420-5-1
ISBN: 979-8-99054203-7 (Paperback)
ISBN: 979-8-99054204-4 (eBook)

Library of Congress Control Number: 2025918805

Any references to historical events, real people, or real places are used fictitiously. All characters, incidents, and dialogue are drawn from the author's imagination and are not to be construed as real.

I.P. Publishing
Burlington, VT

Dedicated to my wife of thirty-two years,
Mary Esther C. Treat, for love and support.
See where one spilled drink can lead?

Contents

PROLOGUE

She'd thought the night would be full of promise—important men, big money. He forced her down a dark alley. When he shoved her to the ground, her head struck something hard. Blood filled her nostrils and slickened her face. She kicked with what strength she had left, but hit nothing. He released her right wrist. Her hand found a hard object on the ground. She grasped it and tried to strike him, but he wrapped his hand around her throat and squeezed. She gasped, struggling for air.

He loosened his grip as he undid his belt with his free hand and shimmied his trousers down. He pinned her with his weight, his face hovering above hers and his sweat dripping onto her skin. Even in the poorly lit alley, violence smoldered in his eyes. Her battered mind screamed, *Why him?*

He squeezed her throat harder as he tried to enter her. He failed. Once again, he tried. *He can't perform!*

It was her last thought before his fist struck her face again. Something in her brain snapped. She had no clue how badly he'd damaged her.

The horse-cart raced toward the Royal Melbourne Hospital. The driver laid her shattered body at the delivery doors. No one knew who had brought the injured woman, where she'd come from, or who she was.

She was breathing—barely. The nurses tended her wounds,

administered pain medication, dressed her in a hospital gown, and settled her into a bed. She slipped into a coma.

The doctor on duty the next morning was Dr. Bran Brookfield, a short, thin man with curly black hair and small, round hazel eyes that bulged from their sockets. Even his Scottish accent sounded arrogant. Brookfield was an import from Edinburgh University Medical School, which he—and others—regarded as superior to Australia's fledgling physician training programs.

He examined the new arrival but failed to elicit a verbal response. He lifted her eyelids, looking for some reaction, but there was none. Pressed for time, he wrote in her chart: *Unlikely to regain full cognitive function. Commit to Kew Asylum, medical ward, for continued observation. Name unknown; assigned Jane Doe.*

THE ORGY

Stepping as silently as he could while carrying the heavy roll of felt cloth, he moved toward the stairs, his brow damp with sweat from the effort. A stair creaked. He froze and listened—nothing. He continued halfway down to a small landing, where he stumbled into a recess containing a plain wooden door. The cloth roll slipped, striking the doorframe, folding in the middle. The bottom end hit his feet, pushing them backward and knocking him to the floor.

He got up, fumbling in his vest for the larger key, and heard it fall onto the stairway behind him. Kneeling, he crept toward the sound.

I didn't drink that much. I should NOT be this fuddled.

He patted the stairs until his fingers touched metal. A burning in his chest made his head throb and his stomach churn. He stood, swaying slightly, and placed a hand over his pounding heart. Leaning his head against the door to steady himself, he reached down, inserted the key, and turned the lock. He slipped the key into his left vest pocket.

I must remember to put the keys back in their hiding place.

Reclaiming his burden, he turned the doorknob and gave the bottom edge of the door a light kick to open it. He stumbled forward toward the center table. *I must hurry.*

He placed his hand on the wooden case on the table, then laid the cloth on the floor and unrolled it a couple of feet. Retrieving the smaller key from his right vest pocket, he unlocked the case, opened the lid, and gazed at the magnificent treasure.

I have to work quickly.

Lifting the treasure, he bent down and carefully set it on the cloth. Using his pocketknife, he cut the fabric to the right length, wrapped the treasure, and left the rest of the roll behind. He hefted his heavy prize and shuffled back to the door. Moving deliberately, he relocked it, turned, and climbed the stairs.

I don't know if I locked the case—and right now, I don't care.

•

The evening began innocently enough—just a few drinks with new and old acquaintances. But now, he wondered how the night had descended into a drug-fueled orgy. He was afraid of losing control—it had happened before.

I need to leave.

He looked around, vision glazed. *Everything is so damn messed up. Nothing looks normal.*

He tried to stand but fell back onto the velvet couch, then sideways into a woman, his head landing in her lap. She stared down at him—with her four angry eyes. She pushed him away with a comment he didn't catch and turned to her companion, who resumed kissing her exposed breasts.

The long pipe came around to him again. He was tired and merely looked at it. An arm rose from the floor and jostled him, reaching for the pipe. He shoved the arm aside, barely maintaining his balance. Then, almost on instinct, he held the end of the pipe over the oil lamp to heat the opium he didn't need anymore. He took a long drag, passed it on, and slumped back onto the couch.

God, he thought, *the women are dancing and singing again, passing that "magic" wand from one to the other. That thing has touched every body part exposed tonight—and there were plenty.*

I need to leave.

Again, he pressed his hands against the couch cushions and tried to rise. Leaning forward for balance, he moved slowly until he was nearly upright. He fixed his gaze on the hallway leading to the door. The singing grew louder. The women were laughing—all of them. He turned his head, and the pretty girl in the green dress he had noticed earlier raised the wand with both hands and pointed it at him. *She chose me. Why?*

She approached him, kissed him on the lips, and placed a hand on his arm. Then she passed the wand to another woman and kissed him again. Her other hand rested on his thigh, just below his waist.

"I'll take care of you," she said.

Her necklace's pendant hung between her breasts. *If only she'd chosen me earlier*, he thought.

She guided him, staggering, out of the room.

CHAPTER 2

LADY BLACK

Lady Edith Black, known as Edie to her close friends, was restless. It had been four years since she and Benji Diamond had married and settled into their cottage outside Melbourne following their adventures on the stolen ship *Ferret*. As she brushed her long, dark hair, she decided that dinner in the city would be a welcome diversion. She put away her brush, considered her approach, and walked to the sitting room, where Benji was reading the paper and sipping a glass of wine.

"Benji, Bart is not here to make dinner, and I haven't planned anything. Shall we go into the city?"

"I'd enjoy that," Benji replied. "Would you like to invite anyone to join us?"

"As much as I love quiet time with you, I need to know if Dutch has learned anything new about Britina. Let's see if he is available."

Edie realized she had not been the best companion in recent weeks. She had been pressing Benji to sell their extensive farm and food distribution business in London, the one that had grown out of their early relationship: running a gang of young thieves and using the farm as a cover. She loved living in Melbourne and knew that if things continued as they were, she would spend half of every year apart from Benji while he traveled back and forth for business.

"I'll telephone Dutch. Where's Bart?" Bart (Bartolomé) and his wife, Carolyn, were Edie and Benji's part-time help for gardening, errands, and cleaning. Bart insisted on cooking a couple of nights a week, recreating the meals his mother had made when he was a child in Guatemala. He made a mess, but the food was excellent.

Edie left the room and didn't answer—or didn't hear.

Benji shook his head and smiled. He had news for her and she'd just set it up perfectly.

After his call, Benji came into the kitchen and handed Edie a glass of wine. "He'll meet us at St. John's Public House at eight. It's a bit of a dive, but with great food, and Dutch has some legal work in that part of the city until late."

"That's a good choice. I certainly won't run into anyone I know," Edie said with just a touch of sarcasm. "They allow ladies, don't they?"

"I'll lend you some trousers."

Edie knew her relationship with Benji was solid and mutual. When they were together, their love and passion grew stronger than ever. To Edie, he was still tall and handsome, though somewhat quieter than the energetic young man she had first known. He kept his curly brown hair neatly trimmed now, with a few scattered gray strands—though he was only thirty-four. He didn't appreciate it when Edie pointed them out. She also knew she wanted more than being a "wait-at-home wife," and she still hoped for a child, though time was running out.

•

The three friends chatted comfortably near the flickering

fireplace of the public house, mugs of ale in hand, and bowls of piping, spicy stew with just-baked bread on the table. After eating, Edie turned to Dutch and leaned in closer. "Have you had any luck reaching Britina at the convent in London?"

Edie hadn't had any contact with her best friend, Britina, in over three years. The police's destruction of Benji's illegal stall market had led to Britina's arrest. Afterward, the judge had released Britina to the care of a convent, where she would study to become a novice nun—but the Mother Superior was strict, and didn't allow contact. The convent had cloistered Britina with the other novices and returned the letters Edie had sent.

To secure the release of everyone arrested that day, Benji, the leader of the gang of boy thieves and the stall market that sold stolen goods, had turned himself in and was sent to prison. Mrs. Hill, Edie's crime boss, owned the market; she'd bought his freedom. He and Edie hadn't reunited until the *Ferret*'s theft.

Dutch looked sad. "Edie, I'm sorry. They rejected my approaches as well. After I'd sent three letters, the Mother Superior wrote to me and told me to stop. She said that the order expects postulants and novices to renounce worldly ties and dedicate their lives entirely to religious devotion," he said. "I've petitioned the judge who oversaw the deal that sent her to the convent, asking him to reach out to the Mother Superior. The agreement stipulated Britina's transfer to a work assignment in Australia after three years of supervision—it's been nearly four. We should have an answer in a few weeks."

Edie reached out and put her hand on Dutch's arm. "Thank you. That's promising news." She paused. "What's a postulant?"

"It's when all the nuns and novices judge a person to see if she's suitable for religious life."

"Poor Britina," Edie said.

Benji and Dutch exchanged glances.

Dutch took the lead. "I'm your lawyer, each of you personally as well as jointly. By law, I have to maintain confidences. I know each of you has something to share with the other. Who wants to start?"

This surprised both of them. They stared at Dutch, then at each other.

CHAPTER 3

BRITINA

LONDON, ENGLAND, OVER FOUR YEARS EARLIER

The bobbies stormed into the stall market at a full run, tipping over carts and grabbing at the women and boys who looked to be part of the illegal market. Customers and stall ladies scattered, and Britina bolted from the chaos, darting into the nearest alley between the warehouse and an adjacent vacant building. Just ahead, she spotted Specs—Benji's money manager—running a few hundred feet in front of her. So far, no bobbies were in pursuit. Britina pushed herself to catch up.

Britina saw Specs scrambling up the ladder of a two-story building, clutching a metal box under her arm. It held the reserve funds they kept hidden in the cart ladies' warehouse residence. At the top, Specs tumbled over the wooden balustrade, the box clattering onto the rooftop. She crawled back to the ladder and started pulling it up to secure her hiding spot, but spotted Britina and lowered it.

Britina sprinted toward her. Behind Britina, two uniformed officers rounded the corner, arms pumping, heads down in effort. They hadn't spotted her yet, but they would if she tried to climb Specs's ladder. She waved her arms frantically, signaling for Specs to raise the ladder.

Specs quickly pulled it up and lay flat on the roof. The bobbies hadn't seen her.

Britina ran past and turned into another alley. It dead-ended—no escape. She dropped to her knees, face buried in her hands. Her jet-black hair fell over her bronzed face as she sobbed.

Breathing heavily, the two officers approached. Britina panted for air, her eyes brimming with tears. She brushed her sweat- and tear-soaked hair back from her face.

"You're under arrest," said the larger officer, pausing to catch his breath between words.

She looked up at his splotchy, crimson face. "What for? I've done nothing wrong."

"Then why were you running?" the second officer snapped. He was younger and trimmer than the first bobby, but still winded. He grabbed her arm and yanked her to her feet.

"Ouch!" Britina cried out as he pulled her arm back farther.

They cuffed her hands behind her back, the metal biting into her wrists. The bobbies marched her past Specs's rooftop hiding spot. Britina rolled her eyes upward and saw Specs watching through the wooden balusters. The younger officer gave her a shove, turning the corner back toward the destroyed market.

Britina's heart throbbed as if someone were squeezing it in a fist. She whispered a silent prayer for the safety of her stall mates. Her world had unraveled in a matter of minutes. Years of hard work she and the others had poured into this market now lay in ruins. She saw trade goods being heaped into a horse-drawn police cart, shattering the livelihoods her stall mates had worked so long to build. More officers moved between the stalls, collecting money from each one.

The sergeant who had led the raid spotted Britina and turned. He carried a long wooden truncheon, which he slapped against his palm as he strolled over.

"Good job, men! We've already sent a few of these criminals to the lockup."

He leaned in close to Britina's face. His breath was foul. She turned her head away.

"What's your name, Cocoa Pie?"

She glared into his bloodshot eyes. "Britina," she snarled.

"Isn't that an Irish name?"

"Jamaican."

"In truth? Are you legal?"

"What do you mean?" Britina snapped, fury rising at this fat, dumpy creep of a man.

"I want to know if you belong in this country." He slapped his truncheon into his palm again, this time holding it near her face. "Answer me!" he growled.

"I had an English father, and I came here legally."

"Had?" the sergeant asked.

"He died of smallpox. My mother, too."

"Sorry to hear that," he said without a hint of sincerity. "How old are you?"

"Almost seventeen."

"Tell me where your criminal boss, Benji Diamond, is, and I'll let you go—if we catch him."

She refused to dignify the swine's question with a response.

The sergeant waited. Britina stared back into his bloodshot eyes, teeth clenched, nostrils flaring, saying nothing.

Finally, he straightened and turned to the other officers. "Just like the others. Take her to the lockup. We'll arraign them all in the morning."

•

They arraigned six stall women, including Britina, and seven young men from Benji Diamond's gang the next morning. A judge released two boys, both under fifteen, with warnings. The authorities held the rest in the lockup to await a trial date. During the arraignment, the judge—seeking confirmation of what he already believed—asked each person to name the organizer and owner of the stalls, but no one spoke. At the request of counsel for the city police, the court issued a warrant for the arrest of Benjamin "Benji" Diamond.

•

A steady stream of water trickled down the stone wall beside Britina's cot, carrying with it the stench of a cesspit. She shivered and pulled the thin blanket tighter around her shoulders, but it did little to ward off the chill.

"Britina Myers," a harsh voice called from the cell door.

She looked up to see a uniformed guard holding something in his hands—something that looked like her Bible from the market stalls. Heart quickening, she stood and approached the bars, daring to hope.

"This was left for you by some religious teacher," the guard said, his tone gruff. "Came with a note."

He opened the pass-through slot and handed both items to her. Speechless, Britina extended her hands and took them with trembling fingers.

The note read: *Stay strong, make good decisions, and trust your instincts.*

She instantly recognized Edie's handwriting. The message was signed by Marie-Nicole.

A wave of warmth spread through her, chasing back the cold. Edie had been here—and her Bible was back in her hands. Her heart swelled with comfort and gratitude.

Clutching the Bible to her chest, she hugged it tightly, as if embracing Edie through its worn pages. Tears pricked her eyes.

Could this incarceration be an answer to my prayers? she wondered. *A step toward the purpose I've been asking God to reveal?*

She bowed her head and prayed silently, asking for Edie's safety—and for strength to face whatever lay ahead.

•

Sister Mary Abel made a routine visit to the lockup three days after the arraignment. It was her custom to tend to any injuries or illnesses among the prisoners awaiting trial. She also offered to pray with anyone who wished.

When she approached Britina's cell, Britina moved slowly to the bars, keeping her eyes fixed on Sister Mary Abel's. Clutching her Bible to her chest, arms crossed over it, Britina knelt and pressed her forehead against the cold steel bars.

"You wish to pray, child?"

"I do, Sister."

Sister Mary chose a passage from the book she carried, pausing after each sentence so Britina could repeat the words. When they finished, Britina said, "I'm not familiar with that prayer. It's very beautiful."

The sister studied her face. "I'm Roman Catholic, a Sister of Mercy. That verse was from the Book of Common Prayer, used by the Anglican order—but I still choose to use it. Were you raised Catholic?"

"I wasn't raised with religion, Sister. I began studying on my own after I learned to read." She lifted her Bible slightly. "I've read the Bible four times."

"I believe yours is a King James version, child, which is good. But we read the Catholic Bible ... which is better," she added, glancing up at the ceiling. "If you'll forgive me, Lord."

"I would love to read it," Britina said.

Sister Mary Abel made a quiet decision. "I'll lend you my copy of Common Prayer."

She returned the next day, bringing a well-worn Catholic Bible for Britina as a gift. "I'll need the prayer book back after your trial," she said gently. "It has special meaning to me, and my Mother Superior doesn't exactly approve."

Britina read the Catholic Bible every day in the week leading up to her trial, but she found it more difficult to follow. Its many footnotes and references to doctrine made it dense and sometimes confusing. She found herself drawn more often to the Book of Common Prayer. When it was time for her trial, she brought both Bibles—and the prayer book—with her.

•

Britina clutched her stomach and bent forward, rocking gently as she waited for her turn before the judge. She was unrepresented, facing charges of receiving and selling stolen goods. The jailers had warned her—people had faced hanging for the same offense. Sister Mary Abel sat quietly in the back row of the courtroom. Britina asked a clerk to bring the sister the prayer book.

As instructed, all defendants stood when the judge entered.

When her name was called, the judge looked down at her and asked, "How do you plead?"

Britina opened her mouth, but no words came. She exhaled, then inhaled, swallowed hard. Finally, her voice trembling, she blurted, "I didn't know the goods were stolen." She paused, then added, "At first." *I don't want to lie—it's a sin.*

The judge frowned. "Guilty or not guilty of receiving and selling stolen goods. One or the other, Miss Myers."

She hesitated, heart pounding, wanting to explain. But the judge scowled and tapped his fingers impatiently on the bench. What could she do?

"Guilty, sir," Britina said, her chin trembling, eyes glistening with tears.

After all the detainees from the stall raid had entered their pleas, there was a long delay. The judge conferred with the prosecution and members of the London City Police. When they finished, he banged his gavel, called for order, and addressed the defendants.

"The court received a proposal. I have accepted it. Benjamin Diamond will surrender and receive a seven-year hard labor sentence. The court will sentence young men and women under twenty-five to transportation and labor assignments in Australia. You will travel in steerage and your work contracts will require you to contribute to Commonwealth society. As for the older women, you will serve twelve months assisting the poor, sick, and injured under the supervision of the Sisters of Charity and under the watchful guidance of this court's friend, Sister Mary Abel."

Surprised, Britina turned and looked at Sister Abel.

The sister stood and addressed the judge. "Judge Rankin, I have a request."

"Of course, Sister," the judge replied.

"Would the court consider changing the sentence for Britina Myers? I would like her to train for the sisterhood. After spending time with her, I believe she can be of great service to our work. After two to three years of living with us and learning our ways, we will then assign her to service in Australia if it pleases the court."

The judge accepted the arrangement. He placed Britina under the supervision of the Mother Superior at the Sisters of

Mercy convent for three years and then assigned her to assist the needy in Australia for four years.

A jolt ran through her body; she felt as if she were floating. *Has God just answered my prayer—to give me a purpose?*

•

Britina entered a highly structured and disciplined life for the first time—and she didn't take to it easily. Mother Superior seemed to resent her presence and hadn't spoken a word to her during the first weeks of her service. A woman in a habit, addressed only as the novice mistress, gave Britina assignments, told her where to be and when, and instructed her on when she could speak and when she must remain silent.

The novice mistress gave Britina one set of plain clothes—not a habit, but something more like work attire—and began referring to her as "postulant." Britina didn't know what the word meant. She assumed it meant "laborer" because she received endless tasks.

At the beginning of the fifth month, the novice mistress informed Britina that the Mother Superior wished to see her in her private study. There was no time for her to wash or change. She was expected immediately.

Britina stood in the doorway. Mother Superior pushed a stack of papers aside on her writing desk and said nothing. Britina bowed her head respectfully. The room was tidy, with two chairs for visitors, a Bible on a stand, a wall of books, and a private altar for prayer and reflection. Religious items filled every space. Mother Superior didn't invite her to sit, and she wondered if the barn where she'd been working made her smell bad—or if she simply lacked the right to sit in Mother Superior's presence.

"Postulant Britina," Mother Superior began, "the reports on you are satisfactory. I have my concerns, but you have been respectful and diligent in your work, and I hope you will continue to be. It is still many months before we decide whether to accept you as a novitiate. However, I've decided you should begin your spiritual and theological training. This will include learning the rules of the religious order, studying scripture, and taking part in regular prayer. I encourage you to spend time in contemplation and meditation, reflecting on your duty to God and how you will serve."

I wonder where I'll find the time for all that with my chores, Britina thought.

As if reading her mind—which unsettled her—Mother Superior added, "You will find the time to accomplish all assigned to you. I will visit with you again in a few months.

"In the meantime, you will have no contact with anyone on the outside. Show me you have given your life to God and have relinquished all worldly desires."

Britina nodded and left.

CHAPTER 4

VISITS TO McELROY

"Wot's dat?" Sammy pointed at a white shape drifting swiftly down the Yarra River on its journey through Melbourne into Port Phillip Bay. He and Ralphie were combing the tidal mud for treasures they could sell or trade for their daily earnings.

"Don' know," his older brother Ralphie said. "Don' look right."

"It'll come closer to the bank up ahead. Let's try to stick it." Their 'tools' were long branches with nails hammered through the ends.

They ran ahead to a bend in the river where the current pushed debris closer to shore.

"Sammy, try to get your stick out in front of it. If you can slow it, I'll grab it with mine and pull it in."

Sammy slowed it just enough. Slipping in the mud, Ralphie slammed the nail into the top of the parcel. Sammy followed suit, and together, they dragged it toward the bank. Sammy dropped to his stomach, grabbed the cloth, and hauled it up onto flat ground. The fabric peeled away, revealing a severed human leg—bloated and rotting.

"It stinks!" Sammy cried. "I'm gonna honk."

"You baby. This could be our treasure. We can wrap it up and take it to the police—there might be a reward."

Ralphie had Sammy take off his outer shirt, and they wrapped the leg as best they could, the foot and part of the calf hanging out at one end.

"I'll never wear that shirt again! Mum'll kill you if we don't get a reward."

"Why me? It's your shirt."

They started walking toward central Melbourne and the police station, carrying their gruesome treasure.

At the station, Frank, who manned the front desk, knocked on Chief Inspector McElroy's office door.

"Two young men to see you, Chief. Can you come down to the desk?"

Chief Inspector McElroy smelled them—or their "treasure"—halfway down the stairs.

"What you got there, men?"

"Severed leg," Sammy said. "I think it's a woman's. Pulled it out of the Yarra. Any reward?"

"Probably a murder," Ralphie added.

"Perhaps. I'm glad you brought it to us. Are you down by the water a lot?"

"Most low tides during awake hours," Ralphie said.

"Good. Constable Frank here will take a brief statement of where you found this, your names, and where you live. Stay alert for anything else that might interest us. Frank, get a constable to take this leg to the coroner. Have it photographed first."

McElroy reached into his pocket and handed each boy two shillings.

"Sir, can we have a little more? I need a new shirt." Sammy pointed at the cloth wrapped around the leg.

McElroy smiled and handed over two more shillings.

•

After his daughter's Australian husband had been brutally murdered, leaving her alone to raise their eighteen-month-old child, Chief Inspector Raymond McElroy had applied for a transfer from the London Police Force. He'd arrived to a less-than-enthusiastic welcome. Aussies preferred their own people to fill positions of authority.

McElroy was tall and athletic, with neatly styled, thick, sandy hair, a mustache that was always impeccably groomed, and a close-cut beard. His square jaw gave him the look of someone who could hold his own in a boxing ring. His easygoing manner led some to mistake him for a pushover—until they crossed him.

Anticipating his first official visit of the day, Raymond paced his office. He had met Madam Annie Wilson before, though not in a professional context. She lived extravagantly and frequented high-society events, mingling with Melbourne's elite. She owned Boccaccio House, a high-class brothel in the city's red-light district, Little Lon. It was one of the most luxurious and refined establishments in the area—second only to those run by Madam Brussel. He wondered what had brought her to headquarters.

"Miss Wilson to see you, sir."

"Thanks, Frank. I'll come escort her."

He left his office and descended the wooden stairs behind Frank to the building's entry, where a constable directed visitors—some toward appointments, others to the holding cells.

"Madam Wilson, a pleasure to see you again." Raymond remembered enjoying a conversation with her at one of the city's gala events. She'd been strikingly candid in the stories she shared. "I believe this is your first visit to police headquarters."

Madam Wilson was short—perhaps four foot seven—with narrow shoulders and a square-shaped head that looked almost too large for her frame. Her hair was receding at the forehead, styled in ringlets combed back and falling to her shoulders. Her small, round eyes were a piercing black, and she carried herself with unmistakable sophistication. She extended her gloved hand.

"Oh, Raymond, there was a time or two before I had my home when I visited," she said with a slight bow. "But they didn't invite me upstairs then."

Raymond chuckled. "Well, that was before my time. Please, join me." He offered his arm, and Madam Wilson took it. Together, they ascended the stairs to McElroy's office, sunlight spilling through the tall windows.

He gestured toward the wooden chair beside his desk. "May I get you tea?"

"No, thank you. I've many errands before the night's work begins."

"How may I be of service?" McElroy asked.

"Raymond, you know I run one of the most respected brothels in Melbourne. My ladies are professionals. They stay off the streets. They don't cause trouble. I treat them like my own children, even though I'm far too young to have adult children, of course."

They both smiled, fully aware she wasn't as young as she claimed—and that some of her "children" were not as old as she claimed.

"My ladies don't leave, at least not without my blessing. They live in luxury in my home. I fear something's happened to one of my best and most attractive girls, Heather Stone. A lovely young woman, originally from Scotland. I was hoping you might have her locked up."

Raymond paused, taking a moment to process Madam Wilson's information. "No, I'm afraid we don't. When did she disappear?"

"Four nights ago. Last I saw her, she and a few of my other ladies were entertaining some prominent gentlemen, having drinks in my front parlor. I wasn't feeling well that evening, so I went to bed early. By morning, Heather hadn't returned to her room. At first, I thought she might've taken on an extended engagement, but not this long."

"Who were the gentlemen"—he put just enough weight on the word—"sharing the room with your ladies that night?"

"Raymond, you know I can't give names. I have a business to protect—and reputations, too."

"I suppose not," he said. "Still, we'll need some details. Wait a minute—I have an idea. I'll be back."

McElroy left his office and descended two steps to the main floor, where a dozen desks were spread wall to wall, corner to corner. He made his way to Petty Constable Jonathan Penn's desk.

"Please come with me, Penn. I have an assignment for you," he said.

Penn, still new and not yet indoctrinated into the "hate McElroy" camp, responded promptly. "Yes, sir." He stood at attention without hesitation.

Back in the office, McElroy introduced Madam Wilson and Constable Penn, who remained stiffly upright, clearly unnerved at meeting a real house Madam—especially one of such high reputation.

Addressing her as "Annie" for the first time, since she insisted on calling him "Raymond," McElroy said, "Constable Penn will need a very detailed description of Heather Stone and everything you know about her—including what she was wearing when you last saw her. She was dressed, wasn't she?"

"Yes, very smartly."

"He will then check the hospitals, hotels, and—I'm sorry—the morgue to see if we can locate her. He'll also need to interview all of your ladies who were in that room that night."

Penn turned a bright shade of pink. Madam Annie frowned.

"He will not take full names," McElroy assured her, "and they won't appear in the final report unless they provide evidence of something criminal."

McElroy noted Penn's discomfort but considered it part of seasoning a new recruit. He led them to a small conference room where Penn could begin the investigation.

•

Chief Superintendent Cartwright had demanded a meeting at eleven sharp, and Raymond wasn't prepared. He was fairly certain Cartwright was the one stoking the hostility directed at him and his position. Cartwright had tried to install his own candidate as Chief Inspector, but McElroy came with strong backing from London and far more experience than Cartwright's pick. On top of that, Cartwright owed favors to the very people who had championed McElroy. Still, that hadn't stopped him from waging a quiet campaign to undermine him.

Superintendent Cartwright appeared at McElroy's office exactly at eleven. Cartwright hadn't summoned McElroy to his office, which would have been the usual protocol. That alone made McElroy suspect Cartwright wanted an audience—he wanted the men in the pen to see him scold McElroy, maybe even shout him down.

"There may or may not have been a murder," Cartwright began, his voice already raised, "but human limbs are turning up without bodies. Something is going on. We look like fools. The papers are having a field day—top of the fold, two days in a row. They love painting us as a pack of baboons." He slapped a photograph down on the desk in front of McElroy. It showed two severed arms.

"You know who found these? A young woman. She fainted on the spot and had to be taken to the hospital. The arms were just lying there in an abandoned lot."

Cartwright dropped a second photo on top of the first and jabbed his finger at it. This one showed a leg partially wrapped in a torn scrap of cloth.

"Ugly! Where was that found?" McElroy asked, recoiling slightly. The limb was already decomposing, turning white and green.

A throbbing vein stood out on Cartwright's forehead as he leaned over the desk. "Several kilometers from Hawthorn, in Fawkner Park. A dog dragged it there. As my lead investigator, this is something you should already know."

"Do we know if they're from the same person?"

Cartwright's voice rose even louder. "McElroy, we know nothing because you haven't done your job. We don't need any additional claims of incompetence thrown at us! This'll be front page in the papers tomorrow and we need to get to the bottom of it—quickly. I expect some answers."

Cartwright stood tall, back straight, every movement sharp, his glare unwavering. McElroy had learned to read his temperament by how many veins were showing and just how red his face got. He wasn't happy now. He wasn't looking for a reply, only action. Without another word, he turned and headed for the door.

"Superintendent," McElroy said, holding back a smirk, "you should know—I had a delivery earlier. Two young men found a severed leg in the Yarra while they were mud fishing."

McElroy felt a flicker of satisfaction—one piece of information Cartwright didn't have. He'd already received the report on the earlier limbs and had signed the order, sending them to the morgue. But pointing that out wouldn't do any good now.

Cartwright turned his head, shot McElroy a glare, said nothing, and slammed the door behind him.

McElroy figured the police commissioner was breathing down Cartwright's neck. The man needed someone to blame—and that someone was him.

He stood there for a moment, then walked to the door and threw it open. "Kernot!" he called out. "My office. Constable Roland Kernot!"

Kernot glanced over and rubbed the back of his neck, muttering under his breath. He stood slowly and made his way to McElroy's office. He'd been Cartwright's pick for the chief inspector job and didn't hide the fact that he had no time for McElroy.

"Constable Kernot, you're a fine investigator. Can you shift any of your caseload to the other investigators? I want you full-time on a critical investigation."

Kernot stood up straighter, a questioning look on his face.

"It's possible," he said, knowing he had little choice. "What's the case?"

"Probably murder." McElroy handed over the set of photographs and described the morning's discovery. "Limbs have turned up in three different locations. Since the latest was found in the river—and a dog dragged one—I assume all of them were in the river at some point."

Kernot grimaced. "This has been front-page news for two days. No one's on it yet?"

"We're waiting on the morgue report. You know how heavy our workload is. I was hoping to free you up for it. I want you heading the investigation."

Kernot was barrel-shaped—not out of shape, just solid.

His cropped brown hair and shifty brown eyes, a bit too close together for McElroy's liking, gave him a wary look. His thin lips barely moved when he spoke. McElroy stood to tower over him.

"If all the limbs belong to one body, we need to find the torso and head to ID the victim before we look for the killer. If they're from different bodies, we've got an entirely different problem. You'll go to the morgue, speak to the coroner, and have him examine all four limbs. I'll send word; he'll meet you there first thing in the morning. In the meantime, we need to find out if anyone is missing, other than one of Madam Wilson's girls. These don't look like a young lady's limbs.

Kernot's face tightened in disgust.

"Start by identifying all the missing persons' reports. Judging by the condition of the flesh, let's go back three, maybe four weeks. It's a stretch in this weather, but the victim might've been preserved somehow. Also, check the hospitals—and Kew and Yarra Bend asylums. And if you come across a young lady named Heather Stone, let me know immediately."

Kernot, still standing, gave a sharp nod, cutting off the beginnings of a smirk, and left the office without a word.

McElroy knew Kernot had orders to report anything remotely incriminating against him straight to Cartwright. There was no doubt in his mind—the superintendent wanted him out and replaced with one of Cartwright's men, probably Kernot. *Let him chase down dead body parts*, McElroy thought. *He can't do much harm there. And if something goes wrong, he'll be right in the thick of it.* Still, he'd keep a close eye on the investigation, just in case.

Cartwright had been wrong about the headlines. The newspaper mentioned the severed limbs below the fold—three days old and already fading from public concern. What stole the spotlight was a far more personal affront to the people of

Victoria: the theft of the Parliament Speaker's Mace. A national treasure stolen right from Parliament House.

They'd finally released the news to the press just in time for the morning papers, after keeping it quiet for four days.

The gold-plated scepter wasn't just ceremonial—it stood for the constitutional rights of every Victorian and the authority vested in the Speaker of the Legislative Assembly. The sergeant at arms carried it into the chamber at the start of each session, removing it afterward to locked storage. Its absence wasn't just a scandal; it was a wound to the heart of the institution. To Queen Victoria's image. To the people's sense of order, tradition, and pride.

McElroy folded the paper. The people of Melbourne would want answers—above the fold and below. *I need help I can trust.*

CHAPTER 5

DEPARTURE

Unlike the other sisters at the convent, Sister Mary Abel seemed to do as she pleased. Britina turned to her for help.

"Sister, I work hard to do as I'm asked. I desperately want to advance to novitiate. Will you help me?" She paused, then added, "Again."

Mother Superior believed Britina still had much to learn about caring for and counseling those in need. She also needed to deepen her relationship with God. So, once again, Mother Superior declined Sister Mary Abel's request.

Still, Britina continued to perform her duties day after day. More and more, she found herself daydreaming about Edie—wondering what had become of her as she moved through her chores. She longed for friendship, for someone to talk to. Her thoughts drifted often to the others, from the market stalls to Specs and to Benji. Would she ever see any of them again? She did not know where any of them were or if they knew where she was.

Britina completed another year of prayer and training at the convent before Mother Superior finally relented under Sister Mary Abel's persistent urging.

Now a novitiate, Britina entered an even more intense year of service—twelve hours a day of prayer and care training at St. Bartholomew's Hospital. Her faith and desire to follow God's will hadn't changed, but the balance had been off—too much prayer, not enough care. That shifted at St. Bart's. By the end of each day, she was utterly exhausted, but for the first time, she truly felt she was serving those in need.

•

When the time came, Sister Mary Abel accompanied Britina to the docks to see her safely on her way and to wish her well. The court had assigned Britina four years of service, providing physical and emotional care to the impoverished, the sick, the insane, and the dying at institutions near Melbourne, Australia. She would live at the Sisters of Charity home in Kew, just outside the city.

This next chapter of her life excited Britina; she longed to see parts of the world she'd only heard about. Australia felt unimaginably far away, and while she had heard grim tales about the hardships of a steerage crossing, she was still eager to move forward, to begin again. At the Sisters of Charity home in Melbourne, she'd have at least a little time to herself. Maybe, just maybe, she could locate Edie if the supervision wasn't too strict. She wasn't sure exactly where Edie was, but she'd learned that the *Ferret* had ended its journey in Melbourne with Edie on board. There'd been no mention of her arrest in the news—so perhaps she was still out there, somewhere in the city.

The pier buzzed with chaotic energy—people rushing in every direction, shouting, laughing, carrying luggage, or herding children. After the silence and strict routine of the convent, Britina found it exhilarating. Everything felt new, wild, and unpredictable.

The steerage passengers were to spend two nights in a depot, preparing to board in organized groups. As she climbed the steps and entered through the enormous main doors, Britina stopped dead in her tracks, stunned.

The massive room stretched out before her, lined with two to three hundred wooden boxes topped with thin mattresses—crammed along the walls and down the central aisles. Her eyes widened. Could it really be that all the passengers—men, women, and children alike—were expected to sleep together in this one vast room?

A wave of horror swept over her.

•

Britina looked around for someone in charge. Seeing no one she could identify, and with the pandemonium only growing, she decided it was best to claim an unoccupied bunk while she still could. Everything she was bringing fit into a single large canvas duffel, which she placed in the center of an empty cot to mark her space.

A round-faced official came scuttling toward her—a balding man with an enormous belly, his apron pockets bulging with papers.

"Wait, young lady! All bunks are assigned! Do you have your papers?"

Britina quickly produced her travel documents and handed them over.

"It says here you're a nun. You're not wearing a habit."

"I'm a novitiate—a novice nun. The habit is optional. I only have one, and I've packed it away."

"In your trunk or your bag? I'll need to note the trunk number on your paperwork."

"I have no trunk. Everything I own is in this bag."

"I see." He glanced over the papers again. "Your name is on the passenger list. Your bunk is number 238—back wall, on the far side. Did you bring utensils and bedding, as instructed?"

"I did, sir." She was eager to settle in.

"That bag's quite large for someone your size. I'll take it." Without waiting for a response, he hoisted the bag over his shoulder and led the way.

When they arrived at the assigned bunk, another bag was already sitting on it.

"Whose bag is this?" the official barked.

"Oh dear . . . sorry!" came a voice. An older woman bustled over. "It's my sister's—we were just getting settled. These are our bunks, right here." She gestured to the two beds to the left of Britina's.

She reached out and clasped Britina's hand in a firm shake, her arm swinging exaggeratedly up and down.

"I'm Marian," she said. Her round face and short, patchy gray hair gave her the look of an aging cherub—minus the wings. She wore a green Vichy-check dress that hung to her ankles, its large white collar sitting slightly askew. Despite the mild weather, she also wore an insulated wool coat buttoned all the way up.

"My younger sister is Mattie. She's around making some arrangements."

Mattie returned a few minutes later, and just like Marian, she stuck her arm out at full length and pumped Britina's hand in greeting. Marian's younger sister was a smaller version of her: shorter, not as heavy, but with the same round face. Her hair was still brown and full, and her voice was noticeably higher-pitched. She dressed almost identically to Marian, except her gingham dress was slightly shorter and patterned with larger red and white checks. Both sisters wore lace-up boots. She, too, had on an insulated wool coat. She caught Britina glancing at it.

"It sometimes gets cold on the crossing—and sometimes very hot. We need to be prepared for all occasions."

The sisters exchanged a knowing look. Then, in perfect unison, they said, "And we must be prepared to take care of each other." They paused, then again, together, added, "And our friends."

•

On the day of boarding, Mattie huddled close with her sister and Britina. "The moment we walk out that door, we'll enter a world of chaos. I suggest we hold hands if we can manage it—and carry all our bags."

Britina had barely slept the past two nights. The constant coughing, sneezing, and shuffling sounds made it impossible to sleep. It was nothing like the tranquil silence of the convent, and she felt exhausted. Still, she was grateful not to be facing it all alone.

Marian led the way, towing them behind her as they navigated through sailors rushing in every direction, loading hundreds of crates filled with supplies, furniture, and travel trunks. What startled Britina the most were the crates of live animals—chickens, sheep, goats, even milking cows and pigs. The noise and odors were overwhelming.

"There!" Marian finally shouted, raising her voice over the cacophony as they skirted a large crate filled with hissing geese.

They pushed forward to the pier, where a peaceful queue had formed. As they reached it, the line began to move. One by one, they stepped onto the gangway.

Despite the morning chill, a thrill ran through Britina. She took in the tall masts she'd only ever seen from a distance, the spotless wooden planks, the shining metal rails, the massive ropes—lines, someone had called them. It felt real now. She was going to sea.

She hadn't expected private accommodations, but below deck, many women were sent to a narrow space at the very front of the ship—someone mentioned it was the "bow." Rows of double-deck bunks lined the walls, with long tables and benches running down the center. The purser guided them in, explaining the accommodations and rules in a hurried, practiced tone.

Marian, undeterred, took Britina and Mattie by the hand, brushed past the purser, and marched them toward the far end of the space.

"Stop," the purser commanded.

"This is our second crossing, Purser. We'll get our bunks," Marian said, dragging her bags behind her.

Most of the bunks were about three feet wide, and two adults were expected to share each one. Marian quickly assigned Mattie and Britina to the top bunk and claimed the bottom for herself, piling their bags beside her before lying down.

"When the purser comes, let me do the talking," she said.

The purser moved steadily down the row, assigning bunks—two adults per bed, regardless of relation, and sometimes three or four children to a bunk, depending on their size and age.

When he reached Marian, she shifted, spreading herself wide across the bunk and putting on the most pitiful face she could muster.

"I remember you, Purser. You were kind to us on our previous crossing."

"Was I, now? How so?"

"I am not well—not sick or contagious—just aging. I require a bunk for myself. My mates are doubled above."

"I remember you as well, Miss Marian. And once I recognized you, I allowed you to pass and take your bunks. But you're no more frail than I am. I'll expect compensation for this privilege."

Marian reached into her bag and produced a cloth-covered container, which she handed to the purser.

"Thank you, Purser."

Britina eyed the extra bag Marian carried, full of small, cloth-wrapped shapes.

"You are welcome, Miss Marian. I'll call on you for further help as the trip progresses."

"And I you, Purser."

"What was that all about?" Britina whispered to Mattie.

"It was a bribe," Mattie replied. "With promises of further transactions from both parties."

"Is it legal?" Britina asked, frowning.

"Of course not," Mattie said. "But before the next few weeks are over, it will serve us well."

Britina wondered why these strange ladies were making a second crossing, but was thankful to be their companion. They seemed kind and clever—and likely to be helpful.

As dusk fell, a steward moved through the space, lighting the lamps. Around them, passengers busied themselves, making final preparations and settling in for the night. The purser returned, issued a few curt instructions, and then extinguished the lights at eight sharp. Still, the low hum of voices continued long into the night.

The next morning, the atmosphere shifted. First-class passengers arrived on the dock, finely dressed, surrounded by friends and relatives who had come to see them off. Sailors scurried about, unfurling the ship's massive canvas sails and preparing the vessel. They lifted the anchor from the riverbed, and the ship glided away from its mooring.

Britina slipped up to a higher deck to watch. Long ropes attached two towboats, guiding the large ship carefully out of port. Her heart raced.

I'm off on an adventure, she thought, a sudden lightness lifting her chest. She felt energized and ready. Despite the tight quarters, she had slept well.

She was on her way to a new life.

She whispered a quiet prayer, thanking God for placing Marian and Mattie in her path as travel mates—and, as always, asking Him to keep Edie safe.

CHAPTER 6

THE ASSIGNMENT

Raymond McElroy tossed the newspaper onto the pile on his desk. He stood up, walked to the window, and looked out from his second-floor office at the Victoria Police Station as Lady Edith Black crossed Russell Street. She wore her long black hair elegantly piled atop her head, pinned beneath a black Derby-style hat adorned with a diamond hat-pin. Her pleated, navy-blue skirt, just short enough to reveal her gracefully shaped ankles, fluttered in the breeze.

She chooses her own style, he thought—not one to conform to the more constrained garments of the day. As she stepped carefully, navigating the uneven cobbles, she looked less like an elegant lady and more like a little girl tiptoeing across a stream. He smiled at the image.

They had met while sailing to England, after he had applied for the position of Chief Inspector. At that time, he was still with the force in London. They dined together onboard the ship, and once they'd landed, he had looked her up and invited her to dinner. She seemed pleased to see him, and after a second evening out, she gently set the record straight.

Her real name was Edie Black, she'd explained, and her heart belonged to another—Benji Diamond.

They agreed that friendship was best, and over time, it evolved into something meaningful to both of them. She trusted him. She'd even shared the story of her invented title—how she'd fabricated a marriage to a Scottish laird to become "Lady Black." He'd laughed, told her it was her future, not her past, that mattered. As they grew closer as friends, she shared her past as a thief and master criminal. It didn't matter to him.

Since her return to Melbourne and her marriage to Benji, the three of them had grown close. Not just the three of them—but McElroy's daughter Ruth and little Elizabeth, too. Benji and Edie doted on the child as if she were their own.

•

As she climbed the stairs to McElroy's office, a constable hurrying down to the main floor rudely bumped her into the stairway wall. He didn't offer her an apology, and she dismissed the incident as a minor slight, not worth obsessing over.

"Good day, Lady Black," McElroy greeted her.

"Raymond, you know the title is only for formal instances when it's useful. Now give me a kiss and call me Edie."

He gladly did as instructed, kissing one cheek in Scottish fashion.

"I'm curious," McElroy said. "How did Benji react to your news?"

"It was an interesting evening, Raymond. Benji had news of his own, and Dutch set us up to bare our souls to each other. Benji listened to me tell him I couldn't sit home and wait while he was gone six months of every year, so I'd started a business of discreet investigations and would work with you and Dutch on crime solving."

"Actually, Edie, as I explained, I can't put you in the position of solving crimes or doing serious police work. But I can use help to gather information."

"I know. Benji questioned it, but he ended up being supportive. He said he knew I needed to be applying myself to something meaningful, and crime is what I know best. Then he trumped me. He and Dutch have been working with the largest food distributor in Great Britain for months, and finally, last week, they presented an offer of purchase for an amount well above what Benji expected."

"To buy the business? That's great."

"Mostly great. Benji has to make a few trips to Adelaide to meet with executives of their office there, then one last trip to England to tour the buyers through the farms, meet our boys, ah, men and families, and inspect all our records. He'll be in England for an extended time, but this will be his last trip alone."

Raymond thought for a moment, sat back, and ran his fingers through his hair. "Edie, I have something I need help with. It's delicate. My men aren't fully supportive of my leadership, and I need some information gathered that could be very sensitive. Did you read the paper this morning?"

"Sorry, no, I don't get a delivery."

He handed her *The Argus* and pointed to the headline: "Priceless Parliamentary Mace Missing." The article continued: "The most extraordinary robbery ever heard of in the Commonwealth."

"What's a mace?" Edie asked.

"The mace was originally a weapon for bludgeoning," McElroy explained. "It's a club, comes in different sizes for battle, and has been carried by soldiers for centuries."

"Ghoulish!" Edie said.

"Yes. However, it's now a symbol of authority in parliaments worldwide. Ours symbolizes the constitutional rights of the

Victorian population. This modern version is ceremonial and far more valuable—gold-plated silver adorned with jewels. I need to gather all the information I can as quickly as I can."

"I'll do it, of course, Raymond. Thank you . . . although gathering information doesn't sound like the adventure I envisioned. I need to start somewhere and appreciate your trust in me."

"Gathering information is what solving crime is all about; information gets pieced together like a puzzle, and then the picture becomes clear. I'll give you a letter from me to carry in case you need to prove you're official."

He walked to his desk, picked up an envelope, and handed it to Edie.

"Here are some details and a list of names. I suspect you'll get cooperation from the sources I'm asking you to visit, but if it turns more dangerous, I'll take other steps—and you'll back away. Understood?"

"Yes, boss. And thank you."

He fixed his look, staring unblinkingly into her dark green eyes. "I mean it. Don't take unnecessary risks!"

"I appreciate that you worry about me." She hesitated, recognizing his sincerity. "Alright."

"The sergeant at arms, George Chaloner, is the custodian of the Mace. He carries it into the chamber to start each day's parliamentary session, carries it out, and locks it away after each session. Find out what you can. We want to discover who took it, but recovering the Mace is our goal. We've issued a reward notice to all the police districts in Victoria. A copy is in the envelope. The envelope also contains the letter I mentioned. Also, it's curious they chose not to report the missing Mace for four days—find out why."

"I'll get started in the morning," Edie said.

"Start with the sergeant at arms—George Chaloner."

•

In a cab on the way home, Edie read the reward notice.

PARLIAMENT HOUSE — Stolen on the ninth of October: the Speaker's Mace. It is approximately five feet long, beautifully engraved with the English and Victorian coats of arms, the Maltese cross, and other details, and gilded. It contains approximately 217 ounces of silver. The Government offers a reward of £100 for information leading to its recovery and identification of the thief.

•

"I'm excited to be working on a police case, Benji," she exclaimed during dinner.

"Edie, you know I support you, although I'm not sure this is the best way to add excitement to your life. I agree with Raymond—you shouldn't take unnecessary risks. Promise me that. Please."

"Of course."

CHAPTER 7

MARIAN AND MATTIE—THE CROSSING

During the first three weeks, Britina was sick most days and nights; her stomach ached, and violent vomiting and diarrhea followed every effort Marian and Mattie made to get her to eat. She had a fever and could barely speak.

"We saw this on the first crossing," Marian commented. "I must bribe the purser to let her rest and excuse her from cleaning. I suspect it's the food or the water in the barrel."

"Some others are sick, but some aren't—and we're not," Mattie said.

"It could be the shot of vinegar and herbs we take daily. Mum always said it would kill all the bad things and keep us healthy. We should try to give some to Britina."

"I have an idea—I'll be back after cleaning with fresh water if you can deal with the purser."

"If you are to care for the sick and poor, we better get you to Australia alive," Mattie whispered in Britina's ear. She spoon-fed the water, vinegar, and herb mixture to the ailing patient.

Mattie wore a blousy bonnet tied under her chin. She carried a cloth knapsack, which she always kept with her while cleaning her area of the ship. "You never know what valuables you might find cleaning decks. I need a place to store them," she'd explained when Britina asked.

"Don't drink the water from the common barrel," Mattie warned. "I'll bring fresh water daily. It won't be much, so we'll sip it through the day and keep the container hidden in our bedclothes."

Where she got clean water for the three of them each day was a mystery. Most of the bodies below deck seemed sick, and all drew their water from the barrel—replenished occasionally but never cleaned. Yet it seemed only Mattie had access to a truly fresh source. Britina didn't want to know how.

The sisters had prepared for this. They exploited the lessons they'd learned on their first crossing south, carefully booking the same ship and crew. They were familiar with the layout, knew the storage locations, and knew which crew members could help them. Marion had brought along dried fruit from their farm, which they had sold before this return trip. The farm had grown apples, peaches, and berries for the market. She also packed hardtack and advised Britina to nibble on it throughout the day to soak up bile and ease the hunger pangs.

Over a few days, the vinegar, herbs, and fresh water seemed to help. Britina felt grateful. Her role was to sacrifice her life in service to God, helping the poor, caring for the sick, fallen women, and the insane. *And now—here I am, being cared for by these two women who cared enough to look after me. Is this a lesson from God, or am I simply not strong enough for my assigned task?*

The supply of vinegar and herbs ran out a week before their arrival. On the night before they were due to reach port in Sydney, after seven weeks at sea, Britina was weak, and her thoughts had grown irrational. It felt as though God had either abandoned her or was testing her, and she couldn't focus. Looking around the ship, she saw many passengers were sick or dying—several had died during the voyage, including a small child, and she'd been powerless to help. She felt hopeless and abandoned by God. That night, the fever took hold.

Mattie and Marian sat beside her. They had moved her to Marian's lower bunk, and Mattie had been sleeping with Marian. Britina was shivering so badly that they laid one of their heavy coats over her. Then, with their hands beneath a blanket, they brought out some dried fruit. They had carried a wedge of cheese with them, trimming off the mold. Mattie split it between the three of them.

After the meal, Marian rummaged through her bag and pulled out three small pottery cups and a jar with a cork topper, the same kind she had given to the purser several times. She pried off the cork and poured the liquid into the cups. She handed one to her sister and one to Britina, who offered a short blessing.

"What is it?" Britina asked, her voice shaky.

"Apple juice from the farm," Mattie said.

"Drink it in one swallow," Marian added.

Other than a few sips of beer—which she hated—Britina had never had an alcoholic drink before. The brandy burned her throat, and she felt it hit her stomach. Then, a gentle warmth spread through her body, bringing a sense of calm and comfort. She lay back in her bunk and was soon asleep. Around midnight, the chill and shivers returned.

Mattie gave her another cup of brandy, held her hand, and whispered to her, but Britina only mumbled incoherently. Marian dipped a rag in the water barrel to cool her forehead.

"We must find her a doctor when we disembark," Marian said.

"Do we have enough money?" her sister asked.

"If not, we'll offer apple brandy and fruit—and if necessary, we'll call in the family. She can recover at the family homestead. She's special; we have to take care of her."

CHAPTER 8

THE SERGEANT AT ARMS

As Edie's hansom cab approached Parliament, the unease and worry over her pending interview dissolved, replaced by calm energy and growing confidence. The cab pulled into the discharge area opposite the Parliament Building. Edie had requested a meeting with Mr. Chaloner by early mail, stating she had a matter of importance to discuss and would arrive at 1:00 p.m.

After paying the driver, she paused to admire the building's grandeur. A stunning example of neoclassical architecture, it reflected the wealth and power of the city. The exterior sandstone gave it a regal, majestic appearance, with a façade adorned by tall, slender columns and intricate carvings. She felt a rush of pride as she gazed up at it.

Crossing the street, Edie climbed the grand staircase to the entrance portico, where a uniformed attendant greeted her.

"Welcome, Madam. May I direct you?"

She stood erect and smiled at the guard. "I have a meeting with Mr. Chaloner at one. I'm a little early."

He guided her through a spacious foyer decorated with marble statues of notable figures, frescoes, and murals illustrating moments in Australia's history. She promised herself she would return to study the murals and explore the grounds during her leisure time.

The attendant asked her to take a seat along the side wall and left to contact Mr. Chaloner. He soon returned and informed Edie that Mr. Chaloner would be with her shortly. When asked, he explained that the parliamentary chambers were on the upper floors of the building—the Legislative Council in the western wing and the Legislative Assembly in the eastern wing. Edie wasn't familiar with the distinction but made a mental note to learn the difference soon.

A husky, slightly harsh voice interrupted her thoughts. "Miss Black, I presume?"

She turned to see a bulky man in work clothes and suspenders, speckled with wooden shavings and drops of concrete. Edie introduced herself as Edie Black on a special assignment from Chief Inspector McElroy. She would keep her married name private.

"Please excuse my sloppy appearance. We're working on construction in the basement. I'm supervising, but I can't resist getting involved in the physical work."

"It doesn't bother me, Mr. Chaloner. I think it's admirable." She gave him an approving look and a nod.

"Thank you. You've come to ask questions about the Mace?"

"Yes, and thank you for allowing me to interrupt your day."

He led her to a small but well-appointed office close to the entrance portico.

"As I'm sure you understand, this is a dreadful blow to Victoria Parliament and the Australian Federation."

"Mr. Chaloner," Edie skipped the small talk, "I understand you're the custodian of the Mace. Will you describe what this entails and when you last saw the Mace?" A rush of adrenaline flowed through Edie's body. *I'm officially investigating a crime.*

"Miss Black, I don't know all the doings around this missing Mace, but I don't think investigating it is a task for a woman."

Edie's face burned, and her fists tightened. She hoped the man didn't notice her reaction.

"Why is that, Mr. Chaloner? And it's Mrs., not Miss."

"Then your place is at home, and investigating a theft could be dangerous."

I hope that wasn't a threat, Edie thought.

"I have a couple of homes in London and Melbourne, and perhaps you should address me by my title—Lady Black. And Mr. Chaloner, this is an official police enquiry. I represent the chief inspector of Melbourne. Your cooperation is required, not requested."

His face registered surprise, turning a shade of crimson to match Edie's. He shifted his tone and demeanor. "I apologize, Lady Black. This episode has me on edge. I am responsible for the safekeeping of the Mace, and somehow, I've failed."

"If you tell me what you know, I believe I may be of help. I have training and a background in crime. Perhaps you can answer my questions."

"Yes, Milady. As I recall, it was just before nine on Friday the ninth, and Parliament had just wrapped up a somewhat disagreeable session. My assistant, Mr. Donavon, was helping me."

"What is his first name, Mr. Chaloner?"

"Ralph."

Edie added the name and position to her notes.

He continued, "We took the Mace and locked it in its box for safekeeping until the next day. It was twenty minutes to nine in the evening when we put the box away in the small room designated for its storage."

"Mr. Chaloner, when did it go missing?"

"Well, I don't know exactly, but when I went to retrieve the

Mace the next day at 1:00 p.m., the box was in place. But when I unlocked it and opened the lid, it was empty—except for the supports the Mace sits on."

"Mr. Chaloner, who else has a key to the Mace box?"

"I am the only one."

"Is it with you at all times?" Edie asked.

"Well, no. I have a lot of keys. I keep them in a key lock in my room."

"What about the room where you keep the Mace? Who has keys to it?"

"Let me see." He put his hand to his chin, thinking. "Building maintenance workers are allowed to use my keys when work is required." He hesitated. "Oh, and Thomas Chester—he's a carpenter, workman, and electrical engineer for Parliament. He has keys to all areas. He's currently finishing a basement extension in the north wing of Parliament House."

"Are contractors given their own keys?" she asked, surprised.

"He's trustworthy, Lady Black. He's one of the Parliament regulars."

"I'll need to speak with him. Does he use additional workmen?"

"Only occasionally. I can check."

"I'll ask him, Mr. Chaloner. Is he here now?"

"No, he's scheduled to be back tomorrow early morning. Sometimes, he sleeps here, but not last night."

"Was there anyone remaining in the building when you left that night?"

"Oh, I don't leave when Parliament is in session, Milady, except for errands. I sleep upstairs, and the Speaker has the bedroom next to mine. The doorkeeper locks the house as soon as the Speaker and the others staying during the session go upstairs."

"Who is the doorkeeper, Mr. Chaloner—full name?"

"Anton Watson," Chaloner replied.

"Sir Matthew Drew is the current Speaker. Is that correct?"

"It is, Milady."

Edie was getting sick of the "Milady" handle, but it was serving its purpose.

"The night of the ninth, did you and Sir Drew retire at the same time?"

"We don't all go upstairs together. No, I didn't see him retire. Perhaps Herzbrun, my housekeeper, did. He's not here now, either."

"First name of your housekeeper, Mr. Chaloner, please?"

"Henry, ma'am."

"I will need to interview him as well. I trust you can arrange these interviews for tomorrow?" Edie didn't pause for an answer. "Mr. Chaloner, please show me the storage room where you keep the Mace."

From the look on his face, Edie could tell that Chaloner had had enough of her by this point, but he didn't object. He turned and led her to a narrow door at the side of the foyer that opened onto a cramped staircase.

She watched him closely for any telltale signs of nervousness.

Chaloner turned to her. "This staircase is dark, and the treads are narrow. Step carefully."

They descended half a flight to a landing with a recessed, plain wooden door. Mr. Chaloner fiddled with his keys and inserted one into the simple lock. He turned it and stepped inside. Edie noticed how he kicked the door at the bottom edge, where it stuck against the floor.

Chaloner lit a lantern. A small table, draped in a white cloth, stood centered in the tiny room. Edie wandered slowly around, not sure what she was searching for—only that she should pay attention to the little things others might miss.

The wooden Mace case lay open on the table, lined with blue felt. She examined the lock and hinges. There were a few scratches around the lock, but nothing unusual—no sign of forced entry.

"You say you found the box shut and locked when you came to retrieve the Mace, Mr. Chaloner?"

"Yes," he said after a pause. "I'm certain."

He doesn't look certain.

"Mr. Chaloner, you stated you entered the room and unlocked the case to find the Mace missing the next day."

"That's correct."

"If yours is the only key, and perhaps the thief picked the lock, how and why would the thief bother to relock the box?"

Chaloner fidgeted and shrugged, refusing to meet her eyes.

She picked a small piece of cloth from the left hinge. Making sure Chaloner noticed, she wrapped it in her handkerchief and slipped it into her pocket. She wasn't sure it meant anything, but the move looked professional—and that might prove useful.

"Mr. Chaloner, where do the stairs go?"

"It's an old emergency exit from the building and a door to the cellar spaces. Both padlocked now."

"May we look?"

"I don't mean to be impolite, but I really must get back to my duties, and I don't have the keys with me."

"Tomorrow then," Edie said, already heading up the stairs ahead of him.

At the top, she stopped and turned. "One more question, Mr. Chaloner. Why did it take four days to report the missing Mace to the police?"

He hesitated again. "The decision wasn't mine to make. It's quite embarrassing to all of Parliament, and the hope was we could locate the Mace in the building and avoid any publicity."

"Whose decision was it?"

"I'm not at liberty to say, Lady Black."

"Mr. Chaloner, check with whomever you need to, but I want an answer to that question tomorrow."

She didn't wait for a reply. She turned and headed for the door. *I may be new at this, but I know when someone's being evasive. I don't trust this man one bit. He's cagey. He resents me being here, questioning him—and that I'm a woman. I make him uncomfortable. Good.*

CHAPTER 9

BRITINA ARRIVES

Britina was incapable of functioning the morning they docked. She mumbled constantly, her words incomprehensible.

"Perhaps prayers," Mattie said. The sisters looked at each other, questioning what to do.

The sisters packed her belongings, dressed her, and tried to get her to eat or drink some water, but she refused everything. They draped her arms over their shoulders and dragged her upright down the gangplank for steerage passengers.

Steerage passengers were often documented by name and nationality as they disembarked. Today's group had to be processed by a single customs agent at the end of the plank and inspected by a nurse, part of a new protocol to prevent diseases—particularly cholera—from migrating from London to Australia.

Marian found a letter of introduction and assignment from the Sisters of Mercy in Britina's bag and presented it along with their own papers. The document included Britina's assignment details in Melbourne, but that would have to wait.

"What's wrong with her?" the officer asked.

"We celebrated arrival this morning!" Marian exclaimed,

offering the apple brandy. "And she's never had any alcohol before. She's drunk."

The agent grinned. "I'll have to confiscate this, of course."

"Of course," Marian said with a smile.

"And she'll need a medical exam to receive her papers."

The nurse inspector began examining Britina after briefly checking the sisters.

"Has she been vomiting or had diarrhea?" the nurse asked.

"Earlier in the week," Marian replied. "She was weak but seemed to improve. Many of the passengers suffered in the vile conditions."

The nurse looked into Britina's eyes and ears and checked her skin and pulse. She placed a hand on her forehead, then pressed a wooden stick down her throat. Britina gagged but didn't vomit.

"She has a slight fever now but doesn't show symptoms of cholera or scarlet fever," the nurse reported to the customs inspector. She handed Britina a flask of water with powder stirred in. Britina, still fuzzy-brained, stared at her. The nurse winked. Britina drank the flask dry and handed it back, feeling better almost instantly.

"She'll need to see Dr. Thaddeus Snow and receive treatment before she can be cleared for entry. His office is up Thames Street, over there," the agent said, pointing. Then, addressing the sisters, he added, "I'll keep your papers. Bring back a certificate of health from Snow for your friend, and I'll stamp them."

The sisters escorted Britina up the street to a brick building with a white scroll-cut shingle hanging from a metal bracket. It read: *Thaddeus Snow, Anatomist and Doctor of Diseases.* The nurse's powder and the fresh air had revived Britina somewhat, but the sisters still supported her as they walked.

"I can't go back," Britina said to one of them.

"Drink all the water you can right now," Mattie replied.

Before they entered the offices, Britina took a large gulp from the water the sisters offered her. Inside, Dr. Snow himself greeted them. He was aptly named—his hair, a long mass of white curls, was the whitest Britina had ever seen. His sideburns, beard, and mustache matched, all white and curly. But his eyes were strikingly dark, deep as inkwells.

"I have to use the toilet," Britina announced as the water caught up with her.

Snow pointed to a room. "I need a sample anyway. Go in there and urinate into this," he said, handing her a container.

"I'll have to inspect you," he said when she emerged. "It's two pounds. Do you have the money?"

"I only have one pound to my name," Britina lied.

"Hmph!" Snow snorted. "And you, ladies?"

"We have only a few shillings to spare," Marian replied.

"It'll have to do. Hand it over."

Britina, more alert now, dug into her satchel carefully, making sure not to reveal its contents. She felt around and extracted a pound coin, passing it to Snow before quickly heading into the room with her container. Marian took three shillings from her bag and handed them to the doctor.

When Britina returned, she handed Snow the bowl of urine. He looked her over.

"I'll take her into the examination room."

"Not without us, you won't," Mattie said firmly.

Snow glanced at the sisters, then back at Britina. He yielded to their resolve.

The sisters helped Britina undress, wrapped a sheet around her, and laid her down on the exam table. Snow examined her neck and throat, held the back of his hand to her forehead, then cupped one hand over her chest and tapped it with the fingers of the other, his ear close to her mouth. He frowned at the sounds in her lungs.

He had her sit up, rolled a paper tube, and pressed it to various spots on her back, each time placing his ear to it and listening closely. Between placements, he asked her to take deep breaths.

"I think it's influenza," he said. "I'll treat her throat and provide medicine. Once she's settled, give her a few days of mustard plasters. Keep her isolated and hydrated. You two should take precautions as well."

Snow painted Britina's throat with a reddish-orange liquid, using a bit of cotton on a wooden stick. "Iodine," he explained. "Wonderful medicine." He handed over a small vial containing a brownish liquid. "Give her this twice daily, just two drops. It's mead wort and willow bark oil to fight the fever. Wash your hands often."

He pulled a paper from his desk drawer and asked for her full name.

"Britina Myers."

He signed the release form and handed it to Britina; Mattie took it. "I've written that she has a cold. Influenza is more serious and contagious—they might not allow her entry if that's listed. Return the release to the customs agent, and he'll accept it," Snow directed.

•

Britina spent four weeks with Mattie, Marion, and their family. For the first five days, she could only remain in bed with mustard plasters and Snow's medicine. The fever broke on the third day, but she was still weak. Her cough lingered, though the other symptoms gradually receded. The sisters kept her isolated in a remote bedroom in the large farmhouse and took precautions whenever they visited. They told Britina that brandy was a natural preventative, so they had increased her dose.

Once she left her bed, the rest of the household welcomed her. She had never encountered a group so jolly and boisterous. There was plenty of food at every meal for the whole family—ten of them—plus several farmhands and their families. The family served home brew in glass tumblers at the evening meal, and everyone partook. Britina enjoyed it, especially since she believed it helped ward off illness.

Each night, with bellies full and several glasses of "preventive medicine" consumed, the evening turned to singing and sometimes dancing—often with a farmhand performing a prisiadka. She delighted in the teasing and laughter. The sisters' rescue and the joy of these generous, vivacious people were a blessing.

After a month, it was time for Britina to move on to her work in Melbourne. The cough would have to resolve on its own. She said goodbye to the family, farmworkers, and their families—everyone hugged her so tightly that she left with sore ribs.

Mattie and Marion took her to the train station.

As Britina was boarding, she hugged each sister again, though it hurt. "I love you both, and I will pray for you daily. You saved my life, and being with you and your extended family has restored my faith in the good in people. Thank you."

Britina waved goodbye out the window as the 4:15 train to Melbourne pulled away. She had sent a telegram to the Sisters of Charity home, where she was to be stationed to complete her service as a novitiate. She didn't know whether someone would meet her at the station or if she'd have to find her own way.

CHAPTER 10

THADDEUS SNOW

Thaddeus Snow sat at his large, oak rolltop desk in the cramped examination office of his medical practice in Sydney. Multiple certificates of education and praise lined his wall—all fake. He had a tough decision to make, and he was exhausted. He thought about how much his life had changed in the years since he'd left Melbourne and felt a surge of pride: *I put together a masterful plan and executed it to a fine degree.*

But there was always a price. He'd had to leave Melbourne behind and disguise himself. His mustache and beard, pure white like his hair and sideburns, needed attention. *It's almost time for another treatment of chlorine and fishbone powder to maintain my white hair.*

His current problem was his success. He needed help, someone not afraid to bend the rules. Next to his medical practice on Thames Street, Snow maintained an apothecary storefront with extensive storage facilities in the rear and on the second floor. The inventory was essential; most of his drug trade was off the record. A second-floor laboratory handled the processing of certain drugs and chemicals, as well as bottling patent medicines of his own creation.

The third leg of his operation pulled him away from his practice more often than he liked. To keep up appearances, he met with patients three days a week; the other days, he visited various institutes, maintaining relationships and fulfilling patient duties.

It's time to go, he thought. *It's the best solution I have.*

He exited through the rear of the surgery to the stable, where he kept his carriages. One of the horses was already harnessed to the enclosed, windowless wagon he'd be taking tonight.

His young aide, Asa, greeted him. "All set for you, Doctor Snow. I harnessed Blackie—he's the best." Asa patted Blackie on the neck, and the horse nibbled affectionately at his shoulder. The aide laughed and slipped Blackie a sugar cube. "I love this horse, Dr. Snow."

"I know you do, Asa, and I think it's mutual, especially if you keep sugar handy."

Blackie was the pride of Snow's stable, an outcrossed breed of a heavy farm mare and a lighter racing horse. She had speed, agility, endurance, and strength—a marvelous creature. All her talents wouldn't be needed for this trip, but a little exercise never hurt.

"Will you need any help?" Asa asked.

Asa lacked full cognitive function, but had specialized talents. Thaddeus had found him during a service call to one of Sydney's children's homes a few years back. After learning Asa's strengths and weaknesses, Thaddeus had become his guardian.

Asa could master repetitive tasks, and once learned, he performed them with unwavering precision. He loved caring for animals and pleasing Snow. Now sixteen, he was taller than Thaddeus and strong, but he still thought and behaved like a much younger child. Thaddeus had trained him to assist in his operations and, more importantly, to stay loyal and silent about everything he did. He had even given Asa his last name—since the boy had never had one of his own.

Asa worshiped Dr. Snow.

"No, Asa. I'll be gone for over a week. Don't forget to feed the guard dogs in the apothecary," Thaddeus said.

"Already done tonight, sir."

"You're a good lad, Asa." He flipped him an extra coin as he climbed onto the driving seat. Taking the reins, he guided the heavy carriage down an alley leading to the main street, several blocks from the surgery, and headed toward the rail station.

•

Snow had once been Matthew Rohwedder in Melbourne. A talented, trained nurse, he made most of his income by assisting in criminal activities. His primary client had been the wealthy crime boss Mrs. Hill of London, though that work eventually extended to tasks for Edie Black (then known as Minnie Rose), who worked for Mrs. Hill, and for James Henderson, a far less trustworthy associate in Hill's circle. When the custom authorities discovered the stolen *Ferret* and arrested Henderson, Snow had orchestrated his escape from jail for a substantial fee, arranged before the trial.

When disembarking the *Ferret*, Edie had entrusted Rohwedder with three trunks of valuables she'd brought from London. One belonged to her, one to Hill, and one to Henderson. Rohwedder had hidden and protected them as promised—for a time. But when Henderson cut him out of a potentially lucrative operation, Rohwedder exacted his revenge. He vanished with all three trunks and reemerged in Sydney under a new name and identity, using the valuables to establish his current operations as a "Doctor of Diseases, Surgeon, and Anatomist."

He let his hair and beard grow and shaped his sideburns into prominent features. For his new name, he selected that of a graduate from the Old College at the University of Edinburgh Medical School—found in ancient university obituaries. He was confident no one would ever check. The man had died young, unremarkably, and without fame, but had held the proper degrees to support a legitimate practice. Snow updated the dates on the former diplomas and had certificates of study and graduation forged. He also created glowing letters of recommendation from prominent figures in medicine and politics, knowing full well no one would verify them.

One of his favorite fabrications was a letter from Louis Pasteur himself, praising "Dr. Snow's" contribution to vaccination studies during university. He had paid a student to write the entire thing—in impeccable French.

•

This time, James Henderson walked out of Melbourne Jail a free man, and without having to scale a prison wall. He made his way to the waiting wagon driven by Snow, tossed his duffel behind the seat, and climbed onto the driver's bench beside him.

"You bought my release. Thank you . . . I think," Henderson said, speaking before Snow could. "I can't get over your change in appearance, Rohwedder." He turned to face him. "Why?"

Snow's face stiffened, his voice cold and precise. "It's Snow. Dr. Snow, Henderson. Thaddeus Snow. Rohwedder is dead. Never use that name again. I bought your freedom because you owe me—and you'll have the chance to make something of that debt. But hear this: one mistake, and I'll have you back behind bars so fast you won't remember what daylight feels like. And don't expect any favors from the warden."

I don't take orders from jerks like Rohwedder, Henderson

thought. *But under the circumstances* . . . "Alright, I understand. Where are we headed?"

"You'll spend a few weeks with me and my operation in Sydney. Then, you'll move back to Melbourne and start managing some business interests. My assistant will help you—he's a bit slow, but he's loyal."

Henderson let that sit for the moment, biding his time. But one question gnawed at him—the fate of the three trunks entrusted to Rohwedder when he'd gone to jail for the *Ferret* steamship theft.

"Those trunks," he said cautiously. "What happened to them?"

Snow snapped. "Henderson, I'll say this once, and I don't want to hear about it again. Your so-called partner in crime and occasional 'wife'—Minnie, or Edie Black, whatever name she's using now—claimed them while you were still on trial. She made damn sure they were out of my hands and out of your reach, conviction or not. I haven't seen her since, and I don't care to."

Snow pulled the wagon up to the jail's rear gates, where deliveries and pickups took place outside the prison walls. The guard knew him and let him through, guiding Blackie to one of the smaller storage sheds. Two men in work clothes opened the shed door. Snow and Henderson climbed down from the wagon's bench and opened the rear doors of the vehicle.

Inside the wagon, Henderson saw wide shelves lining the left side, a narrow aisle down the center, and a long, worktable-shaped structure along the right wall. The two men carried a white cloth bag sewn shut at both ends, sagging in the middle and clearly heavy. One climbed into the wagon, crouched, and pulled the bag down the center aisle. The second followed, and together, they hoisted the sack onto the lower shelf. Neither spoke a word. Snow shut the doors behind them and locked them. Then he and Henderson got back on the wagon's seat and drove off.

They left the jail behind, heading toward the outskirts of Melbourne and into Kew. Snow finally pulled over at a roadside tavern and parked the wagon. Then he waited.

"Are we going in?" Henderson asked, his mouth watering at the thought of a foamy ale.

"Henderson. No. Just be quiet for now, will you?"

"Is that what I think it is in the back?" Henderson asked, voice low.

"It is. You heard about the execution by hanging a few days ago?"

"Everyone on the inside always knows when there's an execution."

"Family did not claim the body. They notified me to take possession."

Henderson felt a tremor ripple through him. *What the hell am I in for? The dead scare me.*

About a half hour later, as they sat in silence, a rickety wagon drawn by a plow horse pulled up beside them. An old man in grimy overalls and a stained felt hat climbed down and shuffled to the back of Snow's wagon.

"Henderson, go help the burial contractor move the body."

CHAPTER 11

PARLIAMENT INTERVIEWS

Her years in London had taught Edie to check the weather first thing every morning. The sky today was black, and ominous thunder rumbled in the distance. Rain was usually light in Melbourne, but this looked like the exception. She grabbed her umbrella and stepped out just as the first heavy drops fell. Cabs seldom passed through her district unless arranged ahead of time—and walking to the nearest cab stop in the next neighborhood would soak her, anyway.

Benji had left earlier for a meeting, having arranged a cab to pick him up. He'd recently had one of those newly invented telephones installed, as service began spreading into additional parts of Melbourne; now, over two thousand were in use. Edie recalled meeting James Trackson, an electrical engineer, on her voyage back to London—the same trip where she'd met Chief Inspector Raymond McElroy. Trackson had given a shipboard lecture about installing the first exchange of one hundred telephones in Australia.

She hadn't yet used the contraption herself and felt a bit intimidated. But she'd watched Benji make a telephone call that very morning, so she tried it. She went back inside and picked up the handset, then placed it to her left ear and turned the crank.

A voice startled her.

"Who's there?" she blurted, leaning closer to the speaker cone.

"Edie, you don't have to scream—it's me, Ruth. I've got a new job as a switchboard operator, three days a week when Elizabeth is in school. It's exciting!"

Lowering her voice, suddenly self-conscious, Edie said, "Hi Ruth, glad it's you. Do you know how I can telephone a cab? It's going to rain buckets out there. Can you help me contact a cab company?"

"I don't know if any have service yet," Ruth said, "but there's a hansom right out front of the exchange. I'll send them over—I sent one earlier for Benji."

"Thanks, Ruth, that would be a great help."

"You working the Mace case? My dad told me some details, and it's all over the papers."

"Yes, I am. I'm heading back to Parliament today. The cab can stop by a stand and I'll grab today's papers. See you soon."

"Edie, you may know this, but just in case—you should be careful what you say or do around the station. There are factions trying to push my father out of his job, and I think it comes from the top."

"Thanks, Ruth. I had some suspicions about your father's situation. I'll be careful and see what I can learn."

•

The cabbie stopped at a newsstand, and Edie opened her umbrella, stepping out into the downpour to grab the day's editions from several papers. She skimmed them as the hansom rolled toward Parliament. Most of the stories were similar— likely pulled from the same enterprising news-gatherer or fabricator selling information to multiple publications. Speculation far outpaced the actual investigation.

Two papers named the electrical engineer and carpenter Thomas Chester as the prime suspect. He was Edie's next interview. Another pointed a finger at the Speaker himself, offering flimsy reasoning that Edie suspected was politically driven.

At Parliament House, Edie secured a small interview room from George Chaloner, who—though clearly not thrilled to see her—remained at least courteous.

Thomas Chester entered and gave Edie a slight bow. He was tall, with outsized muscular arms that seemed to belong to another body. The rest of his frame was skinny, almost gaunt, and his face carried a distinctive yellow tint. His right eyelid was bright red, and he rubbed at it now and then.

Chester stated that on the date the Mace disappeared, he'd worked the entire day in a different section of the building. He tried to stay away from the halls during sessions. He said Mr. Watson, the doorkeeper, had let him out of the building around 10:00 p.m.

"Why so late, Mr. Chester?" Edie asked. His fidgeting conveyed his discomfort in Edie's presence. She would assess that further as the interview went on.

"I get more done after hours when I'm left alone."

"Do other workmen assist you in your work here?"

"Sometimes I need help. I've got a small group I trust that I might call on now and then, but I prefer to do the work myself. That night, Mr. Chaloner insisted on helping—as he does sometimes. He enjoys getting his hands dirty."

"Did you notice anyone else around the building?" Edie asked.

"I didn't notice anyone. I just took a tram and went home."

Edie found herself at a brief loss for further questions, so she dismissed Chester with a polite nod. "We may have to talk again," she said.

"What for?" Chester replied.

Edie didn't answer. *Let him worry about it. He's not comfortable—and I don't want anyone too comfortable until this is solved.*

Edie next met with Mr. Anton Watson.

"Mr. Watson, you are the doorkeeper. Is that correct?"

"That is correct. I lock up all the doors nightly, and anybody coming or going needs me to let them in or out."

"The sergeant at arms tells me you lock up once everyone has left or gone upstairs to their chambers. Is that correct?"

"Ma'am, that would be nearly impossible. That's what my duties call for, but it's not what happens."

Edie leaned in slightly, more alert now; something was about to be revealed.

"What happened the night the Mace went missing, Mr. Watson?"

"I'm not a snitch, Milady. I forgot how many slept in the house that night, but I talked to Henry, the housekeeper—he told me the Speaker didn't sleep here that night. Sir Matthew Drew has a habit of staying for a time in his room, then sometimes leaves—I think to a nicer hotel. I'm thinking just me and Mr. Worthington were the only ones sleeping here that night."

"And who is Mr. Worthington?"

"Heath Worthington. He's the attendant to the MPs who are away from home. He assigns rooms or finds other accommodations if an MP is from a distance."

"Could others have slept here without you knowing?"

"I suspect so, but I have the keys—at least, the official keys."

"Mr. Chester says you let him out around 10:00 p.m. Is that correct?"

"I don't recall for sure, but I believe it was close to that," Watson replied.

"Does he often stay that late?"

"Sometimes stays all night."

After the interviews that day, Edie's head was spinning. Several people had contradicted others—and even their own earlier statements to her. Clearly, what she was gathering wasn't evidence but hearsay and speculation. What she could deduce was that the Parliamentarians—at least some of them—had activities outside parliamentary procedure on the evenings when sessions were held.

She underlined a note, mentioned by two interviewees, that at least two women had been in the sergeant at arms' room with members of Parliament, and the group had later left together, walking towards Lonsdale.

Chaloner was giving false evidence or had suppressed information. He didn't want it known that he entertained after hours.

By now, the day had faded into evening, and the doorkeeper, Watson, let her out of the building.

"Good night, Milady."

The rain had stopped. Streetlamps cast their glow across the wet pavement, and the air held a damp, earthy scent. Edie paused on the first step and turned.

"Mr. Watson, on the night the Mace went missing, I received information that Parliamentarians and the sergeant at arms left the building, walking toward a place called Lonsdale. Can you tell me where that is?"

His face changed—his expression darkened with something like horror. "Milady, you should not go there!"

"Tell me why," she said gently, switching to his first name. "Anton."

"It's where the brothels and ladies of the night reside. Also, opium dens, gambling houses, and drunks. It would be dangerous for a lady."

"Do members of Parliament frequent these establishments?"

"Milady, you put me in a very uneasy position."

"I will keep your name secret. I need to know. What can you tell me?"

He hesitated, lowering his chin toward his chest. "Milady, members of Parliament often drink after sessions. Some invite women to the rooms, but sometimes the partying continues at one of the houses in Little Lon. Often it's Annie Wilson's place, but not always—sometimes the Bellevue Villa or one of the others."

"How many places are there?"

"Well, over twenty, maybe thirty, of varying quality. Some mansions, some shacks—and I understand temporary facilities can appear, then disappear."

"Can you tell me where Annie Wilson's house is?"

"I cannot. I have never been to houses of sin." He lifted his chin, his tone taking on an air of superiority.

"The general area, then, please."

"Ma'am, it's the area directly across from Parliament, across Spring Street, where you're facing now. There's Bourke Street— that one and the streets to the right. Little Bourke, Lonsdale, and Little Lonsdale are the primary brothel areas, but there are other streets with houses as well."

"Thank you, Anton. I truly appreciate your willingness to help me."

He knows the area quite well, I'd say, Edie thought.

CHAPTER 12

LITTLE LON AND THE TRAM RIDE

Edie left the grand Victorian Parliament Building behind, crossed Spring Street, and entered Bourke Street. Twilight quickly faded into darkness. Her footing shifted from a smooth surface to uneven cobblestones. The distinct smell of coal smoke, with a hint of horse manure, stirred memories of her childhood in the London slums.

As she ventured farther, the streets narrowed. Gas lamps flickered, casting shifting shadows on the street and buildings. Turning up Lonsdale Street, she found more people bustling about, and in the distance, she heard laughter and music. The side streets grew narrower and darker. "We hold secrets," they seemed to whisper. The air carried the scent of tobacco pipes and a cloud of sweet, unfamiliar smoke.

She turned again, heading toward a side street that connected to Little Lon Street. Her breathing rate increased. Her heart beat harder. Venturing deeper into the congested area, she heard indistinct sounds from the tenement houses. Heavily curtained windows revealed only vague shadows in motion. She had the unsettling feeling of being watched and walked more quickly, glancing first one way, then another.

Shadowy men in long coats and hats walked close to the

buildings' walls while women, dressed to attract, roamed the streets. More noise drifted from deeper in the block. She rubbed the back of her neck, an intense unease washing over her.

This is senseless. I see no danger. Why do I feel like this? Perhaps the warnings from Watson . . . She was sweating now; her scalp tingled. *This may have been a mistake.*

It became noticeably more crowded as she advanced. Most of the people were men—some elegantly dressed, others in garments of lesser quality. She caught glances her way. Keeping close to the walls next to the boardwalk, she looked around and noticed many narrow alleyways branching off the street between buildings. At the ends of some alleys, shacks or small structures glowed with light; others contained nothing but heaps of rubbish. The houses lining the street were tidy—some fancy, some approaching mansion-like status. *What a peculiar assortment of buildings*, Edie thought, *but not without a certain charm. I'm safer with more people about—I think.*

She jumped back as two men stumbled out of a door in front of her, landing at her feet, pushed by a man with a long ponytail cascading down his back. He was shirtless—Chinese, she guessed from his features—and in prime physical shape. The open doorway reeked of smoke and that sweet scent she'd noticed earlier.

The man with the ponytail locked eyes with her, his gaze intense and penetrating. "You shouldn't be here. Avoid these men; you don't belong," he said, speaking with an accent she didn't recognize.

"I understand," she replied. *If I'm going to investigate crimes, I have to go where crimes occur. That's why I belong here.* Taking a deep breath, she resolved to see the investigation through to the end.

The men lay face down in the wet earthen roadway, hardly

moving and unthreatening. She walked past them. The streets became more populated with men as she moved deeper into the Lon, but no one bothered her. Glancing over her shoulder, she spotted a man in a bowler hat and long coat staring at her from across the street. They made eye contact, but she couldn't discern his features before he twisted away.

Edie continued down the street. She turned into an alley and peeked around the corner. The man was still following her. She looked for a weapon, found a half-filled bottle, and dumped its contents, holding it by the neck. Her heart pounded in her throat; her breathing turned shallow. She stepped back into the street and walked away, hiding the bottle at her side.

He ran across the street. She stood frozen. He grabbed her and shoved her into an alley. She tried to swing the bottle at his head, but dropped it as he wrapped his arms around her. She struggled to get away, but he held tight. Balling her fist, she landed a blow to the side of his masked face. He groaned.

He forced a wet cloth into her mouth and up over her nose. She struggled to breathe as he grabbed the back of her head, pressing it into the cloth. The sharp smell of chemicals over-whelmed her. Her knees buckled, and she fell to the ground.

"Be quiet, and I won't hurt you," he said.

She couldn't scream. She felt numb all over. Grabbing her with both hands, he pulled her up and pressed her against the brick alley wall.

"I could kill you; I could rape you. You're stupid to be here in this part of town—no one would save you. Right now, I'm protecting you from all the evil out there because we have unfin-ished business."

Her head clearing a little, she recognized the voice.

Suddenly, his head jerked backward. He released his grip on Edie, and she slumped to the earthen alley floor. Her attacker collapsed on top of her, unconscious, his skull bleeding—blood running down his face onto her blouse.

A tall, robust woman, perhaps fifty, stood over him. She wore a frilly white dress, a bit too small for her and not exactly flattering, and a feathered hat. In her hand was a statue of Lady Godiva, naked on a horse—or half the statue, now broken, one piece in her hand and the other resting on the man's head.

She pulled the piece back from his skull. "I would have used something less expensive if I'd had time to choose," she said in a distinct German accent. Her face was full, with large cheeks and a prominent chin. Her eyes were bloodshot, but still an attractive shade of gray.

The man groaned. The lady pulled him off Edie and rolled him onto his back. Edie sat up and pulled the mask from his face. She gasped. He had aged—and not well—but the scar from ear to throat was unmistakable.

"Henderson! I know him," Edie said.

"So do I," the lady replied calmly.

"Who are you?" Edie asked.

"You seem all right. Can you stand?"

"Perhaps with a little help."

The lady offered her arm and picked up Edie's hat.

"Come with me. I am Madam Brussel, and you are in one of my alleyways. We mustn't disrupt customer pathways." She took Edie by the hand and half-dragged her through a side door into the building beside the alley.

"I take care of my ladies," Madam Brussel said gently, "and I cannot have violence disrupt business."

They entered a small kitchen, where a youngish man sat at a table eating a bowl of stew. He nodded at Edie, appearing unsurprised to see her escorted in by Madam Brussel. He smiled at her; she didn't smile back. He was good-looking, with large, bushy sideburns and fairly short, golden hair. His teeth were bright white, and his lips full. Edie wondered what his role was here with Madam Brussel.

"Take care of the man in the alley," Madam Brussel said to him. She led Edie into a sitting room filled with lavish decor, the scent of incense, and sweet, lingering perfume. A large crystal chandelier hung from the center of the ceiling. Thick Persian carpets covered the floor and velvet couches lined the walls. Small stands held pitchers of water and flutes of sparkling alcohol. Even the walls seemed wrapped in velvet, patterned with elegant floral designs.

"This is the room where my ladies meet prospective clients. I must always approve—and, of course, collect," she added.

"This is your house of prostitution."

Madam Brussel stiffened slightly and tilted her head. "House of comfort' is the term I prefer. It is one of eight I own in the district. This is how I know your friend from the alley. He never was a respectable client—he spies for Annie Wilson, steals clients, and sells drugs. I have no tolerance for anyone drugging my ladies or our clients. We caught him once and confronted him. Now he fears me, as he should."

Edie thought of her past with Henderson and shuddered. He might have finally met his match in Madam Brussel. She'd dealt with him before and would again if she had to. Still, she wondered what he was doing here—she'd thought he was in jail for a long stretch.

Madam Brussel handed Edie a glass of water. "Drink this. Then I'll have you escorted out of the Lon. Though, if you ever chose a career as one of my ladies, you'd be a favorite."

"No, thank you. I have a career." *I have a new career*, she thought, *and I'm just getting started*. "But I'm flattered." From above, she could hear moans of pleasure and bursts of laughter.

"May I ask you a question?" Edie said.

"Not now, you can't. This is my time to work. If you want to talk, come in the morning. I'm up by eleven. What's your name?"

She had to decide. "Lady Edith Black," she said, hoping the title might help.

The man from the kitchen entered with a gentleman dressed for a night out.

"Maestro, please have a seat," Madam Brussel said. "I'll summon your favorite."

"I'm already happy with what I see," the Maestro said, looking Edie up and down. "Time is short. I have a concert to conduct."

"She's not one of our ladies, I'm afraid. Please, have some champagne. I'll have some oysters brought for you."

Edie studied the young man again. Quiet, clearly a servant to Madam Brussel, but there was something about him. He was young, healthy, and had a decent face. She liked his looks.

Madam Brussel turned to her and gestured toward the young man. "This is my consort, Ralph. Very young, but he pleases me. My husband died years ago—in bed." She smiled.

Edie's head was clearing. She couldn't believe her new path had already led her back to Henderson. She had to find out what he was up to.

"Ralph, I'd like you to escort our guest to the Spring Street stop and see her safely onto a tram to wherever she's going." She turned to Edie. "Do you have tram fare?"

"Yes, but I'd prefer a carriage. I've never been on the tram before."

"Ralph, get her a hansom on Spring, then come back directly. Thank you."

•

The alley was empty when they stepped out. Either Henderson

had left, or someone else had taken care of him.

Edie attempted a conversation with Ralph. *He seems shy*, she thought, *doesn't say much.* She found it odd that a handsome young man would tie himself to an older brothel madam—but stranger things had happened.

"Have you been with Madam Brussel long?" she asked. *Stupid question. I could do better.*

"A while," Ralph replied.

He was a good soldier—did what was asked of him and, apparently, was well taken care of by Madam Brussel.

There were no hansom cabs waiting across from Parliament.

In his longest sentence yet, Ralph said, "The cabs don't come to Parliament as often at this hour. We'll go around to the back of the building. A tram will be along shortly to take you to the town center, where you can get a hansom."

Edie smiled at Ralph and reluctantly agreed. The run-in with Henderson still shook her. She'd thought she was done with him years ago. Best not to mention it to Benji—at least, not yet.

The tram arrived at the boarding platform, and Edie climbed the steps and paid the driver. At that hour, only three other passengers were in the back car, lounging in the permitted smoking area. Edie chose a seat near the operator.

"Ma'am, I'd prefer you sit where I can see you, if you don't mind. Got clobbered once by someone sitting in my blind spot."

"Oh! Of course," Edie said. "Sorry."

"No need to be sorry. It wasn't you," he hesitated, "was it?" He paused, then laughed.

Edie smiled. "Of course not."

"My name's Merrick. I do the Parliament route every day for twelve hours. Usually busy during the day and late at night, but not early night like now."

It's past my bedtime, Edie thought.

"Do you know about the parliamentary Mace theft?" she asked, easing back into her investigator mindset.

"How could I not? It's in all the papers. I think I know more than what the papers are saying, but no one's asked."

Edie's luck in choosing the tram over a hansom pleased her. "What can you tell me? I'm gathering information for the chief inspector."

"Not for the papers? I don't want to end up in the papers."

"I won't release anything you say to the papers, I promise." She leaned closer to overcome the noise of the rails.

Merrick signaled the next stop and began applying the brakes, then uncoupled the tram from the underground cable. The car slowed to let a few passengers board and pay their fare. Edie leaned back and scanned their faces, still wary.

She was relieved that no one stayed too near the driver.

As Merrick recoupled to the cable and the tram resumed motion, she leaned toward him again. "Mr. Merrick," Edie began.

"Name's James."

"Mine is Edie. Please, James, I'm afraid we won't have enough time. Tell me what you know."

He glanced at her, and his voice shifted—his tone and rhythm becoming that of a seasoned storyteller.

"On the reported night of the theft, I was approaching Parliament just like I did tonight—only later. I stopped, but no one boarded. As I was pulling away, I heard the clang of the back gate and glanced around. I saw someone running—more of a drunken scramble than a proper run—toward the trolley. He didn't hail me to stop, but leaped onto the rear platform. He had a large parcel tucked under one arm and only one free hand to grab the boarding pole. When he did, he spun around precariously, and the parcel struck the stanchion. I heard a distinct metallic clang from inside it. I honestly thought he was going to fall headfirst into the street." He glanced at Edie, gauging the effect of his story.

Recognizing the need for encouragement, Edie said, "I admire your recall, and you have my complete attention. Please continue."

He slowed and uncoupled at another stop. The trolley began to fill with people as they approached the city center.

James spoke in a softer voice now, easing off the dramatics. "I stopped the trolley—I never do that, except in designated areas—but I feared for his life. I jumped down and ran back to help him, but he'd regained his balance. He clutched that parcel tight to his chest, paid the fare, and took a seat on the back bench. Never said a word. I went back to my grip deck and kept going."

"Can you describe him—and the parcel he was carrying?"

"That's where it gets really interesting," James said, the story-teller tone creeping back in. "His parcel was about five feet long, wrapped in brown paper. One end was fatter than the rest—tied up tight with rope, so it formed this hooded, round shape. The man wore an enormous hat pulled low and kept his face turned away from me. The package held my attention so completely that I didn't notice any of his facial features."

"James, we're nearing my stop. I need to know—do you know who this person is?"

"I'm sorry, ma'am, I do not."

"It's Edie. Do you know where he got off?"

"I don't always notice, but I think it was the Fitzroy Garden stop near Clarendon Street or the Lennox Street stop. He wasn't in the car after Lennox Street. I've forgotten the exact stop, but I saw him jump. I stopped the trolley again—he wasn't looking where he was going and walked straight into a lamppost. Had to grab it, swung around, and slid to the ground. I ran back, but again, he steadied himself and ran off. I was glad to be done with him. But when the story of the theft came out, I became suspicious of the package he carried—and the sound it made hitting my stanchion."

"Thank you, James." She placed a hand on his arm. "If you ever recognize him boarding the trolley again, please contact Chief Inspector McElroy or leave me a note at police headquarters with a description, a tram stop—anything you notice. And as you travel your route tonight, will you try to identify which station he departed from? I'll ride with you again in a couple of days to see if you can tell me."

"I will, ma'am."

"It's Edie, James."

"It's been a pleasure," James said, tipping his hat, and smiled as Edie exited at Central Station.

Edie thought about the picture puzzles she used to see wealthier children playing with when she was young. She had longed for a chance to play with them, to find the pieces that fit together—but she'd never had the opportunity. Now, she was finally fitting pieces together, and the excitement of it energized her. She was working on a real puzzle, and it thrilled her. She took a hansom cab home, deciding she'd visit McElroy in the morning—or perhaps just telephone him.

She spent an hour updating Benji as they dined on leftovers and shared a nice bottle of Grenache. Benji was upset about her trip to the Little Lon area.

"Benji, you know I can take care of myself." *Although being attacked by Henderson—without help, who knows what would have happened to me?* She decided it was best not to share that part with Benji.

"The clues led me to the Lon. I intend to return during the day to interview the madam I met. Benji, I'm good at this work—this investigating. It's meaningful, and eventually, it will help others. It's something I must do."

"Yes, Edie, I know. I just fear that things could turn dangerous."

"Benji, we've both dealt with danger. I won't let it get out of hand. I have the police force to back me up—and you."

"You have Raymond to back you up. I think few others are truly on your side—or Raymond's, for that matter. I'll always support you, but I can't protect you if I'm not involved with your activities."

CHAPTER 13

THE ASYLUM

"Blast," Britina said, then looked around to see if anyone had seen or heard her. They had, indeed. Laughing hysterically, two of her comrade novitiate sisters sat on the steps of the home that served as their convent and school, watching the spectacle. Sister Britina frowned at them, flaring her nostrils.

Determined to learn how to ride a bicycle despite the jeers from her friends, she stepped over the crossbar and adjusted her skirt. Taking a deep breath, she put all her leg strength into pushing the right pedal. The bicycle rolled forward—but not far. She tumbled sideways into the hedge, scratching her arms and face, already well-adorned with bloody lines from prior attempts.

"Funny, is it? Then show me how you do it."

Sister Sarah took the challenge. She hiked up her skirt, took the bike, and stepped over the crossbar. She happily pedaled in circles. "Sister Britina, the balance will develop with enough speed. You need to pick up a little speed sooner."

She hopped off the bicycle. "Sister Melony, would you stand on the other side? We'll help keep Britina upright until she's got the hang of it."

"Britina, you saw what I did," Sister Sarah said. "When I start, I don't sit in the seat—I stand on the pedals until I'm moving well, then I sit. It's easier to get some speed and easier to balance."

With their help, after a few more tries, Britina had it—not mastered, but she could pedal without falling. She knew that riding a bicycle would be necessary for work assignments.

Mother Superior of New South Wales had no qualms about soliciting donations. Mother Superior in London would be horrified. The novitiate home had received three bicycles from charitable neighbors a few years prior, so the novitiates could travel to provide services.

After arriving at the home from Sydney, Britina had spent several months immersed in chores and prayers, waiting for her assignment. At last, she'd received an invitation to tea at the residence of Mother Superior, just a block away, to receive her instructions. Finally, she was to assume her role of assisting those in need.

Seated in the parlor, Britina accepted tea from a nun who served Mother Superior. She added milk and sugar. Mother Superior's cup and saucer sat on her side table, brought directly from the kitchen. All the sisters and novitiates knew it wasn't tea she had a taste for.

"Your assignment is ready for you," Mother Superior began. "You will replace Sister Mary Rush as the Sisters of Charity representative at the Kew Lunatic Asylum. It's between Princes Street and Yarra Boulevard in Kew, about eight miles from here. Can you ride a bicycle?"

"I can!" Britina said, the scab on her knee throbbing as a reminder.

"Duties begin the day after tomorrow at six in the morning. You will work until six in the evening unless you are called on to stay longer. The work week is six days, assisting doctors and nurses as they check patients, and you will administer care as directed. Also, you will provide spiritual services and support for those in need. You report to Head Nurse Roberta Kramer." Mother Superior took a sip of her drink and waited for Britina to leave.

"May I ask what happened to Sister Mary Rush?"

Mother Superior hesitated. She didn't like questions—just obedience. Still, she paused, then shared a little. "It's quite sad," she said. "She is a good friend of mine. We took our vows together. She worked hard. In recent years, she began telling me—and others—about the terrible visions she had. I won't repeat them to you. Her mind failed her. She is now a patient in the asylum. I'd like you to look in on her daily and, if she's coherent, say a prayer with her. Tell her I pray for her recovery … though I know it won't really happen."

"I am so sorry about your friend—and I promise I'll do my best to bring her comfort," Britina said gently.

Mother Superior escorted Britina out as quickly as she could. She didn't welcome further conversation.

Britina had a purpose, one she'd longed for since she was a child. The kindness of strangers and the healing power of Mattie and Marion's care during the crossing had strengthened her resolve. It was a lesson sent by God—a gift that had saved her life.

The evening before she was to report, she wrote another letter to Edie. She poured out her excitement about entering this new chapter of her life. When she sealed the envelope and placed it with the others that she'd never mailed—because she still hadn't found where Edie had gone—she paused. She prayed that Edie was safe.

The morning she was to report to Kew Asylum, Britina

grabbed some bread and cheese from the pantry, hoping she would find tea at the asylum. She packed her Bible and prayer book, along with her canvas bag of simple medical supplies, and pedaled toward the asylum. She was fairly proficient on the bicycle now, though still a bit wobbly when encountering unfamiliar terrain; the hills leading to the asylum were difficult.

She could see the town's rooftops as she struggled up the incline. The asylum towers, with their mansard roofs, were visible above her for at least three miles before she reached the property. She stopped twice to catch her breath until realizing it was harder to start again on a hill—so she simply pedaled as hard as she could for the rest of the trip.

She rode her bicycle up to the gatehouse entrance at the front of the building and caught her breath. Brushing the sweat from her brow, she studied the architecture and found its oversized brick construction attractive, with the front grounds well-tended.

A man's voice startled her.

"Are you new here?"

"I am," she said, noticing the man walking toward her from the entrance gate. He was a hearty-looking man with an easy gait, dressed in a blue jacket and pants, with an official-looking cap sitting high on his forehead.

"From the Sisters of Charity, I assume? From your habit?" He adjusted his cap as he spoke.

"Yes. I'm not sure where to go or what to do."

"This entrance is for official visits—doctors and administration. That's the administration building." He pointed to the central three-story structure, where a tree-lined drive culminated in an elliptical carriageway. "You, the nurses, other employees, and deliveries enter at various locations at the rear of the building. There's another gatehouse off Princes Street; just follow the road around the property until you see it. Once inside, there are multiple smaller buildings, and you'll see a barn on the right, painted beige. You can store your bicycle in there. Then look for a group of nurses smoking."

"Thank you," Britina said, then began biking around the perimeter of the property. At the rear gatehouse, she gave her name. The gatekeeper directed her to the barn. He informed her it was also the morgue building—where bodies waited for inspection by the coroner. The thought made her queasy, though he added that there were no bodies at the moment.

Two-story wings extended from either side of the front administration building toward the interior of the property. From the activities Britina observed behind the windows and curtains, these appeared to be patients' wings. Between them stood a large, central structure that looked more functional than related to patient care. Multiple courtyards, lined with iron-columned verandas, separated the spaces. A few smaller buildings on the grounds resembled cozy living cottages, and a series of tents nearby caught her attention—people were entering and exiting them. *I'll have to do some investigating when I can,* she thought.

Approaching the back of the building, between one wing and the central structure, Britina found an entrance where several nurses stood smoking. She walked up and introduced herself. Some looked her over mid-conversation but didn't acknowledge her.

"Want a fag?" asked a nurse wearing a name tag that read, 'Betty Robinson.' Betty was more petite than the others. She held her nursing cap in her hand, and her cropped blonde hair looked more snarled, almost chopped, than intentionally styled. Her facial features were small but attractive, and when she smiled—offering Britina the cigarette—her face lit up and her eyes sparkled.

"I don't smoke," Britina said.

"I seldom do, but every morning before work, I have a few drags. It helps."

"Helps what?" Britina asked.

"I'll ask you again tomorrow. Time to go in."

The nondescript door at ground level led to a short flight of stairs descending into a dark, damp basement beneath the asylum. The floor was a mix of packed earth and sections of broken concrete, with built-in drainage troughs. The air reeked of rotting food, soiled laundry, and sewage. Piles of dirty linens lay in heaps, covering the space. Britina gagged, and Nurse Robinson took her by the elbow, hurrying her to the stairs leading to the main floor. She had Britina sit in a chair with her head between her legs for a few minutes.

"It's pretty bad," the nurse—Betty—said. "It used to be cleaned regularly, but now with over a thousand patients, the staff simply can't maintain it. We don't have the facilities for half the people here. Every area has a floor drop where they deposit soiled laundry, and laundry workers pick it up twice daily. Are you alright to move on? We better get to the morning briefing and report in."

Betty led Britina to a small, glass-windowed room where several nurses had gathered. "Head Nurse Kramer, this is Sister Mary Britina from the Sisters of Charity," she said as they walked into the room.

"You're late, Nurse Robinson. Take your seat."

"Yes, ma'am." Betty opened a wooden folding chair and sat down.

Britina stood there, unsure whether she should do the same or leave.

Head Nurse Kramer turned her attention to Britina. "Every

morning, the night nurses and senior attendants report the events of the previous shift and the condition of certain patients to the nurses coming on duty. Take a seat and listen. I'll deal with you after the reports."

Deal with me? Britina thought. *That's rather severe.*

When Head Nurse Kramer had heard all the reports and assigned roles to the day nurses, she dismissed the night nurses to return to their residences. Some lived on the grounds or in the children's cottages, but most returned to the city to their families.

"Nurse Robinson, stay behind. You too," she said, pointing at Britina.

"Yes, ma'am."

"Now, Sister . . . Tina, is it?"

"Brit-Ina," Britina said, emphasizing the pronunciation.

"Sister Brit-Ina," Kramer repeated, matching her emphasis. "Your predecessor was a pain in my derrière. Do you know what a derrière is?"

"Of course," Britina replied. "I wasn't always a novitiate."

"Because of her meddling in my duties and those of my staff—and the doctors—she imagined crazy things. It drove her to hallucinations and, eventually, insanity."

There was a moment of awkward silence.

"And now?" Britina finally asked.

Head Nurse Kramer bent toward her, just inches from her face. "She is now a patient here—and still a pain in my derrière."

Britina hesitated, then, staring back, unflinching, said, "I am here to assist you and your staff, and the doctors if needed, and to provide spiritual support and prayer to those in need. I do not intend to be a pain in your arse. I just need direction, and I will try to help."

Head Nurse Kramer offered a slight smile at Britina's choice of words.

"Your duties are to stay out of the way of my staff and the doctors unless called upon. I don't want to see you unless there is a patient crisis. I'm assigning Nurse Robinson to show you around. Visit the patients and avoid the refractory and criminally insane wards. There are also several rooms for procedures that are off-limits to you. As you visit patients, attend to the needs you're able to. If you run into an emergency, seek the help of a nurse or attendant. We are substantially understaffed because we are substantially overcrowded and underfunded—so do what you can, but don't interfere with ongoing operations. Understood?"

Britina hesitated, surprised at the lack of acceptance of her service. Pinching her lips together, she replied, "I understand."

"I hope your fate is better than that of Sister Mary Rush."

To Britina, it sounded more like a threat than a concern. She looked directly into Kramer's eyes. Her gaze wasn't compassionate; her brow furrowed.

She doesn't want to deal with me at all, Britina thought.

"Mother Superior has asked me to see her daily and to pray with or for her."

"I wish you luck," Head Nurse Kramer said as she rose from her seat, turned, and left the room.

"Pleasant, isn't she?" Nurse Robinson said.

Britina turned to her. "I guess I can understand the situation she's dealing with, but I came to help. She could be pleasant. At least I can work with you."

"Give it time—but try to stay out of her way. This is her kingdom. Even most doctors kowtow to her. The hospital doctors only visit periodically, but they avoid Head Nurse Kramer when they can."

Britina pondered what she was stepping into. She had expected to be welcomed as support and comfort for the patients, but Head Nurse Kramer would likely be just as happy if she disappeared.

"Shall we start with Sister Mary Rush?" Britina said.

"Very well. Second floor, Ladies' Wing, room 10. She's in a secure room, not with the ward beds, in restraints—she accosted a young doctor in a fit of rage a few weeks ago. Staff quickly contained and then confined her."

Britina and Nurse Betty walked past a dozen patients lying in beds in the hall before reaching the stairs to the second floor. Some patients moaned or made other noises; a few clearly needed attention and cleaning.

"Should we help any of these patients?" Britina asked.

"No," Betty said. "Attendants will be along—they tend to these patients. They don't need medical care at the moment. Work is territorial; helping would infringe on attendants' duties."

They hesitated at the entrance to room 10. The door was closed, and Britina heard strange noises coming from inside. She carefully turned the handle and peeked in.

Sister Mary Rush was in leg and hand restraints, flipping left and right in her bed, pulling on her bonds. Each time, she uttered some indistinguishable sound. Her wrists were raw and bloody. She didn't speak words, only sounds that meant nothing to Britina. But when she saw Britina in her habit, she calmed. Her gray, droopy eyes fixed on Britina's face. She raised her hand about three inches—the most she could manage from the restraint tying her to the bed frame.

Britina realized she was seeking her hand. She took it gently, and the movement seemed to indicate she should lean closer. Sister Rush's mouth moved without sound.

She's trying to tell me something. Britina leaned closer to Sister Rush's mouth.

"Would you like to pray, Sister Mary Rush?" Britina asked.

Sister Rush slowly formed the words, "I have met the devil. They kill people here. You will die."

Britina glanced at Betty, who rolled her eyes. "I'll just step outside," Betty said.

"I'm sure we'll all be alright, Sister Rush. Mother Superior wants me to tend to you and pray with you."

Sister Mary Rush motioned with her restrained hand, signaling for Britina to lean closer. She did.

"Would you like to pray now?"

Sister Mary Rush raised her head toward Britina and, with a sudden thrust, bit her earlobe, severing a small section. She chewed and swallowed it, then laughed long and hard.

Britina screamed and grabbed her ear. "My God!" she exclaimed.

She left the room in shock, crying, holding the sleeve of her habit to her injured ear, blood dripping down her face.

Betty put an arm around her shoulder and guided her to a station with bandages. She washed Britina's ears and face as tears rolled down over her hand. Then she mixed a plaster, cleaned the ear again with alcohol, and pressed a quantity of the mixture to the bleeding wound, holding it in place until it hardened. Britina continued to sob.

"I can't believe she did that. She must be crazy." Britina was shaking all over.

"Do you want one on the other ear so they match?" Nurse Betty asked, trying to lighten the mood.

Britina looked at her with watery eyes. "One will do," she said. "What evil causes such madness?"

Betty ignored the question but said, "I'm required to report this."

"Must you? I'm not damaged too much," Britina said, touching the plaster on her ear and frowning. She wiped the last tears away with the back of her hand. She already had concerns about her reception from Head Nurse Kramer—this could damage their relationship even further.

"If I don't, it could cost me my job. I have a husband who doesn't work—I have to," she said. "I'll minimize it and wait until tomorrow. In the meantime, I'll give her a barbiturate shot. It'll calm her and make her more comfortable."

Britina waited as Nurse Betty went to the drug room and returned with a syringe containing a drug unfamiliar to her.

Back in room 10, Britina picked up her prayer book and Bible from the floor and lingered near the door as Sister Mary Rush screamed and fought against Betty. The nurse spoke to her calmly and administered the injection. Soon, Sister Rush eased into a state of calm.

The next morning, Britina took a couple of puffs from the offered fag. She coughed at first, then held her breath and a lungful of smoke. Crossing to the stairs, she headed to the first floor and hurried to the meeting room with Betty.

Dr. Bran Brookfield attended this session, arriving from the Royal Melbourne Hospital.

Betty whispered to Britina, "Doctor Brookfield visits regularly. He's not afraid of Kramer; they have a special relationship. He and Head Nurse Kramer run a program teaching new doctors how to become surgeons, and they're developing new brain treatments for patients. He's very smart."

"Head Nurse Kramer, nursing and attendant staff," Dr. Brookfield began, "I admitted a young lady this morning who was beaten and possibly raped. She has no detectable cognitive function. We've treated the wounds—they will heal. I doubt the brain will, but that's your bailiwick," he said with a faint smile at his choice of words. "Her bodily functions are strong, but they receive no direction from the brain. We don't know who she is, so we've addressed her as Jane Doe. She'll need around-the-clock attention. Watch for any signs of mental activity. I'll visit her when I can."

With that, he turned to Head Nurse Kramer. "I'll visit a male patient of mine and return to cover our other business when your meeting is done."

"Very well," Head Nurse Kramer replied.

She informed Britina that from now on, her duties at the asylum would focus on the women's wards and attending to their needs. "You don't need to join us in this meeting any longer. I am assigning this new patient to you. Check on her several times a day—she's in the infirmary. We'll move her into Sister Mary Rush's room later today."

"Yes, Head Nurse Kramer," Britina said, unconsciously touching the plaster on her earlobe.

"I hope you learned a lesson from your little incident yesterday. Sister Mary Rush is being moved to the female refractory ward. It's mandatory when a patient is violent toward caregivers. They will administer drugs to her, restrain her, and give her mind treatment to cure her spell. You are not to see her again." Head Nurse Kramer didn't expect a reply.

Britina just nodded, stood, and left the room.

Head Nurse Kramer then dismissed the attendees to their duties.

•

As Britina left the meeting room, a tall, broad-shouldered woman dressed in a long skirt, waistcoat, blouse, and tie bumped her shoulder on her way in. She didn't apologize. Britina glanced over her shoulder as she started down the hall. Head Nurse Kramer welcomed the new woman, and Dr. Brookfield, returning from the men's wards, headed toward the room to join them.

Britina heard him greet the new woman. "Good day, Elizabeth."

"You know I hate my first name, Bran," she sneered, drawing out his name in return.

Brookfield frowned at the use of his first name without his title.

"Alright, Sturgis," he said. "I'll never use it again—address me as Doctor Brookfield."

As they took their seats at the large oak table, Brookfield began. "The progress on the brain stimulus shocking system is nearly complete."

"How many more patients will we lose completing it?" Head Nurse Kramer asked.

Brookfield turned to her. "Yes, we lost a few patients in experiments. Those patients were mostly all undocumented, with no family affiliations—most from the pauper wards—so they're not recorded."

"I'm not complaining, Dr. Brookfield—just trying to control appearances and maintain good standing with the Inspector of Lunacy Statutes. They sanctioned and inspected us before for lesser infractions. We cannot tolerate any suspicion."

"Each patient lost generated a substantial amount of money as a specimen for your medical students, Dr. Brookfield. It wasn't a complete failure," Sturgis said.

"It wasn't a failure at all. Every attempt provided clues to the ultimate design and the success of the process. Those souls contributed to the future of breakthrough mental treatments. Eventually, that will make us all wealthy," Brookfield replied.

Head Nurse Kramer turned her attention to Sturgis. "We must be careful not to raise suspicions about our experiments or losses—inside or outside this institution. A natural death or suicide from the pauper patients we can deal with. But we cannot tolerate another investigation. I'm afraid we're being targeted after the recent charges of neglect and abuse. Just do nothing to draw attention."

"The fatalities I dealt with were nameless to the outside world, and we were able to dispose of the remains without reporting any deaths." Looking down at her lap, Sturgis shifted in her seat, crossed her legs, and smoothed her skirt. "The board doesn't even know the identity of many of your patients or how many patients you actually have."

"I've assured the hospitals providing us with surgical students that we have a constant supply of donated cadavers for training—supplemented with workhouse deaths and executed criminals, all of which are legal," Brookfield said. "The fact is, we cover a little more than half our needs in this manner. We've cultivated a lucrative venture, and we need to seek every source possible to maintain our supply. I'll contact our partner, Dr. Snow in Sydney, to see if he can provide any additional sources."

CHAPTER 14

HOUSE CALLS

What a lovely morning, Edie thought, sitting on her front porch with her morning coffee. Tea would come later, but she liked the strong, slightly bitter flavor of black coffee first thing. As she contemplated the day ahead, she reached for her plate of warm crumpets, smeared generously with spiced pear butter. *I'll walk to Queen Victoria Market—or Vic Market, as the locals call it—and shop before heading into the Little Lon district to visit Madam Brussel. I want to know more about her comment that ladies sometimes visit Parliamentarians after hours.*

Edie savored the feeling of waking up each morning with a plan, a small mission. It made the day feel full of purpose. *If I keep at this, I'll improve my techniques. This could be an actual business someday.*

She wished she could have discussed her plans with Benji before she left. But he'd traveled to Adelaide early that morning, off to consult with the major produce importer for the conglomerate that was preparing to buy their London farm operation. Finishing her crumpets and taking the last swallow of coffee, she went back inside to get ready and found Carolyn mopping the kitchen floor.

"Don't step on the floor, milady," she warned. "It's wet and slippery."

"You're supposed to call me Edie. Why will no one call me by my name?" *Perhaps because I've had too many.*

Carolyn giggled. "Yes, milady Edie."

Edie sighed, setting her breakfast tray on a side table in the living room. She crossed the space to the stairs and climbed to her second-floor bedroom. Remembering something, she called down to Carolyn, "The groceries and purchases will arrive this afternoon. Please tip the delivery lad from the kitchen money dish."

"I will!" Carolyn called back.

Edie enjoyed a long and pleasant walk, but when she reached Vic Market, she couldn't remember what she'd seen along the way—her mind had been busy working on the case. None of her interviewees had shared adequate information, and she felt certain they were covering something up. What had really happened the night of the theft? Perhaps it was time to widen the investigation and include others who might know about Parliamentarians' after-hours activities. But who might that be?

The market was massive, but Edie had her favorite vendors. She visited each one, placed her orders, and arranged for them to be packaged and set aside for the delivery boy when he came by. Visiting the stalls always reminded her of her friends from the London stall days. A pang of emptiness settled in her chest—she had no contact with any of them now, no idea how to reach them.

Dutch's judge friend in London had finally learned that Britina had received a work assignment—but according to Mother Superior, it was policy not to reveal assignments once a lady reached novitiate status; they now belonged to God.

Mother Superior needs a kick in the butt.

Edie planned to visit Chief Inspector McElroy the next day and wanted to have something meaningful to report. She boarded the tram and soon disembarked at Lennox Street. Sitting on a bench, she observed where the trolley stopped and considered how the unknown person at the rear—heading in the opposite direction—would have landed. There wasn't a nearby lamppost for them to run into and collapse against.

She caught the next tram—quite convenient, she thought, and even enjoyable when not too crowded—letting go of her previous reluctance to use them. She got off at Fitzroy Gardens. Edie had visited the gardens several times, drawn to the tree-lined paths and the peaceful atmosphere. Still, she had no intention of coming at night; it was rumored the park housed microbats and gray-headed flying foxes ... basically, much larger bats. The thought made her shiver. She was relieved to find that lampposts were indeed at the rear disembarkation point of the tram heading into town. *Another puzzle piece*, she thought.

A few blocks away, small houses for the working class lined the streets. Edie considered it possible the Mace had ended up in one of them. She wondered if there was a way to learn where all the Parliament workers lived.

She disembarked at the Parliament stop and walked to Madam Brussel's bordello. The engraved plaque at the front entrance read 'Bellevue-Villa.' An attractive young woman in a nightgown escorted her to the central sitting room. With the shades up, the room looked a bit more worn than it had under the chandelier and candlelight.

Madam Brussel entered, smoking something that wasn't typical tobacco and wearing a plain cotton nightgown. Edie sat, sinking into the couch cushion.

"Morning isn't my best time," Madam Brussel told her pleasantly.

"It's noon," Edie replied, but smiled.

"Yes," Madam Brussel said. She took a drag, blew the blue smoke into the air, and stubbed out the fag in an ashtray.

"Did you fix the statue of Lady Godiva?" Edie asked.

"I'll get another. I gave it to a young boy to give to his mother down the street. He's sweet. She'll be happy—or shocked."

"Madam Brussel, I am investigating the disappearance of the Mace for the Melbourne Police Department on special assignment." Edie liked that she had come up with the 'special assignment' title.

"I heard about that," Madam Brussel said.

Edie wondered which of the madam's friends had passed along the information.

"On the night of the Mace's disappearance, I have witnesses that observed four people—two women and two men, I believe—heading into this area, somewhat inebriated. The men were involved in Parliamentary activities that day. Do you recall such a group arriving here the evening of the ninth?"

"My dear, I build my business with discretion. I might not tell you if they had—but I will tell you they didn't."

"I don't know what to make of that," Edie said.

Madam Brussel smiled. "Whatever you choose."

"Do you ever send women to visit men at Parliament House?"

"I don't recall any." Madam Brussel smiled again. Her expression suggested she might be telling the truth—or might not.

"In interviews, I've been told that members of Parliament visit your brothel and that of Annie Wilson most often."

"I can't say we haven't entertained MPs, but there are a lot of brothels. I service individuals, and Annie sometimes entertains groups. You might do better talking to her."

"I will do that. I appreciate your help the other night. You mentioned the gentleman who attacked me sold drugs. Is this an occasional thing, or are you aware of it being ongoing?"

"I have no need for his kind! He makes the rounds—every brothel, dance hall, opium den, and church, for all I know. He's doing a foul thing that will lead to terrible outcomes. It's not just him; it's an organized operation of some size, I assume."

"The police don't interfere?"

"There's little enforcement on drugs; most aren't actually illegal. The dealers have a lot of ways to cover their activities. It's rumored he has gang connections. He takes orders, others make discreet deliveries, and he collects the money."

"Do you know where he operates from or lives?"

"I don't and don't care to." She wrinkled her nose in disgust.

"Thank you, Madam Brussel. I'll probably call on you again. Can you tell me about Annie Wilson's brothel and direct me there?"

"Annie Wilson's Boccaccio House brothel is named after the Italian writer and poet of the fourteenth century. She refuses to say why. She doesn't exude literary superiority. Her brothel is clean and neat, like mine, and she tries to make it very elaborate. But you won't find her there now; she spends each weekday in the city proper or socializing elsewhere to build her reputation and discreetly invite new clients to visit her home. I suggest you send her a formal request by messenger, asking for a meeting. That will make her feel important—which she needs—and will probably get you invited to visit."

Edie thanked Madam Brussel and continued on to Parliament House. She had learned more about Henderson, but she couldn't stop wondering who he was working with. Was he part of a gang? She shuddered. The encounter had rattled her more than she cared to admit. She had uncovered little about parliamentary activities, but she sensed there was plenty left unsaid—plenty between the lines.

•

Edie had a flash of inspiration as she reflected on her interviews at Parliament. There was one person who might know more about the movements and habits of MPs and Parliament staff: the chef.

Entering the first floor, Edie made her way to the ornate dining room and then to the stairs leading to the spacious, well-equipped basement kitchen. Some staff members were busy preparing for the evening meal, while others were still cleaning up from midday. Edie spotted the chef, recognizing him by his tall, white, pleated hat, white jacket, and black trousers. When he saw her, he barked a few commands to his staff, then left his station to address her.

"Chef Roland, I'm Lady Black. I am investigating the theft of the Speaker's Mace on special assignment from the chief inspector and I wondered if you could spare a few minutes."

"Lady Black, it is my pleasure. We are very busy, of course—we prepare meals for all of Parliament and every guest they choose to bring—so I mustn't take too much time away." His slightly French accent was softened by his perfect English.

"I understand, Chef. I promise not to take very long," she said as he led her to his office. He held a chair for Edie at his desk, then rounded it and sat down across from her. Removing his toque, he placed it on the desk, surprising Edie as his long hair unspooled down the sides and back of his head.

"Chef Roland, I'm seeking clues that will help me unravel this mysterious disappearance of the Mace and identify the party or parties responsible."

"Yes, well, I must admit I'm not terribly sympathetic. I find it rather barbaric to require a weapon in order to govern. But I'm afraid I have no knowledge that could assist you."

"I was thinking, Chef," she said, leaning forward and meeting his eyes. "You may have information that doesn't seem important to you—but it could be very helpful."

"Please continue your questioning then, Lady Black."

"Thank you. Do you get requests or provide services to members in the quarters when they're in residence? Do you provide late-night food and beverages?"

"Yes, to both. But space for overnight stays is quite limited. The sergeant at arms has a room he uses when Parliament is in session. The Speaker has an adjacent room he sometimes uses. There are five others. I have two staff members who stay late into the evening when Parliament is sitting. Sometimes, the rooms request service, and often, there are small group meetings on issues that continue after the session has adjourned. For those, we usually provide tea service and water—occasionally a small food request."

"Are records kept of all requests and services provided?"

"Of course. Our recordkeeping is very accurate."

"I'm sure it is, Chef. Could we look at the records for the evening of the ninth?"

"I think it would be best for you to speak with my assistant, who was on duty that night. He can provide the records and might have some information you can use."

"Excellent suggestion, Chef."

Chef looked pleased as he gathered his hair and placed his toque on his head to contain it. "Wait here. Michael, who was on duty that evening, will return with the records. I wish you good luck, Lady Black. It's a pleasure to meet you." He bowed slightly and left the office.

Edie wanted to maintain authority during the interview with Michael but also wanted him to feel at ease. Chefs often displayed a sense of superiority over their understudies. She hoped to quell that in this meeting and considered how to foster a sense of cooperation. Taking a chair from the far wall, she turned it to face the one she was sitting in.

When Michael entered, Edie extended her hand for a shake. While not entirely an uncommon gesture for a woman to make, it conveyed equality and confidence. After a moment, he shook her hand; his grip was firm, though his shake lacked force.

"Michael, I am Lady Edith Black. I'm assisting the chief inspector of the Melbourne Police Department with the investigation of the missing Mace. I need your help." She'd chosen her phrasing to elevate Michael's role. He wasn't just there to provide records; he could be useful, of genuine assistance.

Michael stood a little straighter. At Edie's invitation, he sat and placed the record book on his lap.

"Michael, can you tell me about the night of the ninth—who placed orders and what they were?"

"I have the page here," he said, consulting his register. "I stayed in the kitchen with a helper until midnight after the evening meal. Around nine forty-five, I received a note: a group in the sergeant at arms' room requested a bottle of whiskey, two bottles of red wine, and cakes. Not a typical order, but we try to accommodate when we can."

"Do you always have alcohol available?"

"Yes, we keep a fully stocked service bar and wine stores."

"Michael," she leaned toward him, "did you make the delivery yourself?"

"I did. Sometimes, there's a nice tip—though not this time."

"Can you describe what you found and who was in the room?" Edie asked hopefully.

"There were five persons, ma'am. The room was full of smoke, smelled horrible. Two, I believe, were ladies of the evening—one kind of frilly, the other more fashionable. There was an MP I've seen before, though I don't know his name. He's young. And the sergeant at arms. Another man sat off to the side while the other four were laughing and teasing."

Edie felt a strange knot in her stomach. "Can you describe him?"

"A little. He wore all black, with a black bowler hat on the chair beside him. He looked at me—his eyes were penetrating. There was a long scar down the side of his face. He said nothing, but he made me feel like I needed to leave the room quickly."

"Did they appear inebriated?"

"No, not that I could tell. But with my delivery, it wouldn't take long."

Edie thanked Michael and the chef on her way out.

It seems Henderson is part of my case.

She pictured placing another wooden puzzle piece into place and felt proud of her expanded approach to interviewing. *Not bad, Investigator Black*, she thought.

•

Edie took the tram from Parliament back to the city center and walked to the police station to deliver an update to Chief Inspector McElroy. As she headed for the stairs, Frank at the control desk called out to her.

"Lady Black, James Merrick left a message for you or the chief inspector," he said, handing her a folded piece of notepaper.

At last, a break. She'd asked the tram driver to contact the chief inspector at the station if he had any information, and it seemed that he'd come through.

"Thank you, Frank. Is the chief inspector in?"

"No, he's been gone all morning. I hope he's back soon—the chief superintendent is on a rampage. The mayor's on his back about the missing Mace."

Edie scrunched up her face and puckered her lips. "That is

disturbing," she said. "Please tell him I was here and ask him to call tonight."

"I will, Lady Black."

Edie read the note on the steps of the station. It said, "Please ride with me again. I have an identity for you."

She boarded the next tram heading back toward the Parliament Building. Entering the lead car, she asked the operator when Mr. Merrick would begin his shift. Her timing was good—she stayed aboard past Parliament House, and Mr. Merrick boarded at the Treasury Garden stop, taking the seat next to her.

"Nice to see you, Lady Black."

"Edie."

"Edie, the gardens are beautiful, don't you agree? I enjoy an hour, sometime two, walking the paths and savoring the trees and plants before I start my shift. I live about a mile from the park."

"They look beautiful. I haven't visited. I'll make a point when my husband and I have a day together." She felt a pang of loneliness for a moment, then turned to business. "James, what have you learned?"

"Last evening, as I stopped at Parliament House, a gentleman exited through the same gate I'd mentioned before—it was my 10:00 p.m. stop. I recognized his hat and coat; this time, he wasn't carrying a parcel and seemed sober."

"Did you speak to him?" Edie asked.

"I couldn't just stop the tram and ask his name, so I faked a mechanical issue and braked hard. The car only held four passengers, who were now looking concerned. Brake problem, I told them. It was a simple problem with the cable grip, but I'd need help. I turned to the gentleman and asked if he could hold the levers while I adjusted the grip through the slot in the floor."

"Pretty clever, James."

Merrick smiled, puffing up a bit.

"I warned him not to let them move, or I could lose a hand."

"Could that have happened?" Edie asked, concerned.

"Only if I connected the grip, which I wasn't going to do. I fiddled under the floor for a couple of minutes, not really doing anything. Then I stood up and said, 'All is good.' I stuck out my hand and said, 'Thank you, Mr. . . .' Then I paused, and the gentleman did just as I hoped—he gave his name: Chester, Thomas Chester. I thanked him again and returned to my duties. He got off at the Fitzroy Garden station, just as he had before. I waved, he waved back, and walked off toward the park."

"Brilliant, James. This is very helpful."

"I hope you solve this case, but keep riding my car."

"I'll always look for you when I take the tram." She smiled and departed at the City Center.

That makes Thomas Chester a suspect, no question. But I'm still very concerned that the sergeant at arms, Chaloner, misled me—hell, not misled, he lied to me. He's covering up. I need to see Raymond about how to handle him.

Something had to be done to investigate Chester further. Edie could be on the verge of solving the case. She returned to police headquarters, and this time, Raymond was in. When she walked through the door of his office, he looked angry—his forehead wrinkled, eyes squinting.

"What's wrong, Raymond?"

"Not here, Edie. Not now."

"I have a suspect in the Mace theft, and I have a witness to support the suspicion. I think we may be close."

"That's good news." His face softened slightly as he looked up at her. "That would certainly be timely—everyone's breathing down my neck about this. Tell me."

Edie shared the details of her interviews and her conversation with James Merrick—starting with his experience on the night of the ninth, their discussion about tram stops, and then Merrick's clever way of learning Chester's name. She also told Raymond about her concerns with Chaloner and what she'd learned from Michael, the chef's assistant.

"Edie, I need your notes in writing. I'll take the information to a magistrate and request a search warrant. We'll need to know when Chester is home, and then we'll pay him a visit. Do you have an address?"

"I'm sorry, I don't."

"We can assume it's in the neighborhoods around Fitzroy Garden. I'll send Constable Penn to do some checking—he'll get the address. I'll call you at home when we're set to go. As for Chaloner, don't confront him outright. It might be time for me to question him further."

Edie scowled. "I want advice, Raymond, not to be replaced."

"Not replaced, Edie—assisted. I have the authority to bring someone in for questioning or make an arrest."

"I get it. Chaloner doesn't seem directly tied to Chester's actions. If Chester left for the ten o'clock tram and the kitchen deliveries happened around ten, he was probably acting alone."

"Let's wait until we've interviewed Chester, then decide how to handle Chaloner. Alright?"

Edie nodded and left McElroy's office, feeling a little uneasy about his demeanor. He still looked angry—or was it worried? She figured it probably had something to do with the "rampage" Frank had mentioned earlier. *Perhaps we'll fix that problem soon.* She spent an hour writing up her notes at the office she'd rented on Collins Street, then returned to leave them with Frank before catching a hansom home.

McElroy called in the early evening.

"Edie, Constable Penn got an address and found out Chester is home sick. It's late, but I think we should pay him a visit tonight. I've got a warrant. Can you meet us?"

"Yes. Where?"

"We'll head to the tram stop near Fitzroy Garden in a patrol wagon."

"It'll take a little while, but I'll be there." She hesitated. "We're not going to walk through the garden, are we?"

Bats! she thought.

•

They pulled up to a row of terraced houses on Hotham Street. The connected homes stood three stories high, neatly kept, and constructed of brick. Chester's family lived in the second from the left. Like its neighboring residences, theirs featured a balcony with intricate ironwork. A bay window looked out onto a small porch on the first level. As they approached the front door, they heard coughing from inside.

Chester's wife answered. A young boy in pajamas peeked out from behind her leg, watching the visitors with wide eyes. Edie noticed the woman had a swollen black eye and dried blood at her eyebrow and cheekbone.

"Mrs. Chester, I'm Chief Inspector McElroy of the Melbourne Police. We'd like to speak to Mr. Chester. May we come in?"

"You can take the risk for all I care. He's been sick, spewing phlegm for a couple of days now. I think we'll all be sick soon."

She led them to what looked like a child's bedroom.

"The children and I are all sleeping in my bed to stay away from him," she explained.

Edie wondered if she was keeping her distance just to avoid illness—or as an act of self-preservation.

Chester was obstinate. He was incensed that he was suspected of taking the Mace and demanded they leave.

McElroy reached into his jacket pocket.

"I have a search warrant here, Mr. Chester. I suggest you be more cooperative."

Mrs. Chester and her two sons had gone to the kitchen when the questioning began. Realizing he couldn't stop the search, Chester called for his wife to come back and barked at her, explaining what was about to happen.

Edie followed McElroy and Penn toward the bedroom. A thorough search turned up nothing of interest to the case.

Reentering the living room, Edie noticed Chester had abandoned his bedroom confinement, and his wife was facing him directly, speaking close to his face.

"Tell them," she demanded, loud enough for all to hear.

He calmed down and turned to McElroy. "Alright. There are times I take parcels of firewood, scrap metal, and odds and ends from Parliament House. I may have taken a parcel that night, but I don't remember. I always disguise the parcels with paper and tied ends." He coughed.

"Do you drink, Mr. Chester?" McElroy asked.

"I have a low tolerance for alcohol." He glanced at his wife. "Therefore, I seldom do."

Edie watched Chester's wife. She stared at the floor, not wanting to make eye contact.

"When asked by an MP or the sergeant at arms or others at Parliament, I'll occasionally have one or two, just to be polite. I crave a good one now and again, but I know it's best I don't have it."

"On the night of the theft, were you in the sergeant at arms' room, and did you drink?"

"Yes, a little too much. They poured me whiskey when I arrived. But I left when they ordered more to drink and then decided to move the festivities to the Lon. Once the others have a drink or smoke or two, I can usually slip away without them noticing. It was a difficult trip home, but I wouldn't get into trouble just to be polite."

"Was the Mace mentioned during this gathering?"

"I don't remember."

As they headed for the door, Edie turned to Mrs. Chester. "Mind if I ask what happened to your face?"

Mrs. Chester hesitated. "Little Ian here hit me with his rattle real hard." Then she patted him on the head.

McElroy took Edie by the back of the arm and steered her out the door.

Back in the patrol wagon, McElroy said, "We'll take you home, Edie."

"I'm sorry, Raymond. I thought we had a solution to the Mace theft—and I don't believe she got hit with a rattle. It looked like a fist."

"We can't monitor domestic conflict, Edie. Not without charges."

"And we didn't get any additional evidence on the Mace, but I still have a witness—and he could be lying about the parcel."

"Chester will remain under suspicion. If he did it, more evidence will surface. I'll plan a visit to Chaloner—for the two of us."

CHAPTER 15

BRITINA'S SENSE OF FOREBODING

As she settled into a routine during the first few weeks of her expanded patient responsibilities, Britina began suffering from nightmares. There were so many women who needed care. Some patients in the communal wards were sweet and coherent, and Britina enjoyed talking to them. Some weren't insane at all—just abandoned by their families. Others displayed clear signs of a damaged mind. They needed more care. Those who weren't dangerous moved to halls or communal areas to make space for beds in the rooms. Britina wanted to care for all of them, but she followed the rules given to her.

She became obsessed with Jane Doe. There was something peaceful about her. Although Britina knew others considered the woman brain-dead, she couldn't help wondering what it would feel like to be unable to talk or move while remaining fully conscious—her mind trapped within her unresponsive body. More and more, she became convinced that Jane Doe could see her, could hear her. *Sometimes, her eyes move slightly, just briefly.*

With other patients, what troubled Britina most was the look of hopelessness on so many of their faces and the way they moved. The asylum kept violent patients in the separate refractory ward, off-limits to Britina. They held the criminally insane in their own locked section. Betty told her that each cell in that ward was five feet by twelve, with one small window placed so high no patient could see out. Cells meant for one person now held two or even three.

"What happened to Sister Mary Rush?" Britina asked Betty one day during lunch.

Betty put a finger to her lips, hushing Britina. Britina glanced around—no one was within earshot.

Betty leaned forward and whispered, "Sister Britina, you can ask me anything, but be careful around the other nurses and staff. There are different loyalties, different priorities within the ranks. It's best not to ask too many questions of others. As for Sister Rush—she became too protective of some of her patients."

Britina thought of herself, of what she considered her relationship with Jane Doe.

"She clashed with Head Nurse Kramer more than once, objecting to certain treatments and medications. She even confronted a few doctors, including Dr. Brookfield. This place can drive you insane. A lot of disturbing things happen here. I just try not to think about it—I need this job."

"Will you tell me about those things?"

Betty glanced at the other wooden lunch tables. It was late in the break, and the dining area was nearly empty.

"Sister Britina, it's best not to get involved in things outside our duties. But I've had patients who just disappeared—no explanation. The experimental lab in the basement below the kitchen treated other patients who appeared coherent, and these patients were never the same again. My advice is to stick to your assignments, don't ask questions, and don't go wandering into places you're not allowed."

Britina just stared at Nurse Betty, her mouth dry and her throat seizing up. She wanted to get up, walk out of the asylum, and never look back—but she couldn't. God had placed her here to help these people and save lives, and no one else would care for Jane Doe the way she did.

Betty's eyes darted left and right, making sure no new set of ears had appeared nearby. Her chin had a slight tremor. "Britina, listen to me. Head Nurse Kramer has a few nurses who act as her enforcement team—watch out for them. They report to a woman named Sturgis. She's not a nurse; I don't know what she is. But they're all dangerous."

Britina regained her composure. "Betty, what did they do with Sister Mary Rush after they removed her?"

"I don't know for sure. They probably took her to a treatment room until she was sufficiently subdued. The barbiturates I gave her only last several hours. You can keep administering them or take other steps. Treatment for a patient acting like Sister Rush starts with shocking the system. They would have put her in an isolation chamber—it's a wooden box just large enough for one person to stand in. It has a window at face height if standing, and it has restraint devices. When a patient having a fit calms down, they take them out. If they don't calm down, they pour ice-cold water through an opening over the patient's head to shock the system."

"That's inhumane, Betty. Horrible."

"I thought so when I first learned of it. But it seems to work. They try different treatments all the time. That's Kramer and Brookfield's special project. I think it's sometimes better than keeping a patient on drugs constantly."

Britina realized she was rubbing her wrists and wringing her hands. "Betty, I may have become too obsessed with Jane Doe. I think she can hear and see me. Will you come with me to her room?"

Britina didn't wait for a reply. She stood and left, and Betty followed.

They walked into Jane Doe's room. Dr. Brookfield was with the patient. He looked up. "Nurse Robinson, and . . . I'm afraid I've forgotten your name, Sister."

"Sister Mary Britina, sir. But I go by Britina or Sister Britina. I check on Jane Doe several times each day."

He forced a smile. "I'm checking on her medical condition. You've done an excellent job—she's healing well from her wounds, and you've kept her clean, which I can't say for some patients. I'm afraid she's no more responsive than when I first attended her."

Britina interrupted. "I had eye movement yesterday; she seemed to watch me move as I attended her. It didn't last long, but I noticed it."

Britina saw a change in Brookfield's eyes; he wasn't pleased.

"You did, did you? It might be reactive nerves, but she sure isn't healing mentally."

Seeing the glare in his eyes, Britina said nothing more.

Dr. Brookfield finished his examination without another word and then left the room.

Betty didn't notice any changes in Jane Doe.

•

Nurse Kramer had Britina brought to her office by a stocky, unfriendly nurse she hadn't seen before. When prompted, Britina sat.

Head Nurse Kramer put her paperwork aside. "Sister Britina, we have just lost Attendant Childs to an illness," she said, shaking her head with a quiet sorrow. "She has returned to her parents' home in Adelaide for convalescence."

She interlocked her fingers and looked up into Britina's face. "I sent a message to your Mother Superior, and she has agreed that you are to move into Childs's living quarters in the ward until we find a permanent replacement. We always need a floor attendant who can be called on for service day and night. After work today, you can return to the sisters' home and pack your things. Bring them in the morning."

Stunned by the decision and frustrated that Mother Superior hadn't consulted her, Britina stalked out of Head Nurse Kramer's office. Betty joined her when they left that evening. They walked their bikes—Britina was in no hurry to return home and pack.

"Betty, please tell me more about Sister Mary Rush while we have this time away from the asylum."

"You're asking a lot of questions about Sister Mary Rush. Why?"

Britina hesitated. "I don't know. I feel I need to understand what's happening around the asylum—especially now. Maybe just to protect myself. I'm not comfortable with this new arrangement. I want to stay out of trouble."

Betty thought for a moment. "I understand that. Sister Rush was always ornery, but pleasant to me. Day after day, she got worse—shaking, mumbling to herself—until one day, she came out of a room where a patient had passed in the night and came face-to-face with a young doctor, an assistant really. She screamed at him, called him a murderer, and tried hitting him in the face with her fists. She had to be restrained. I'm surprised they didn't take her to the refractory ward right then."

"Can't someone help her? Shouldn't we help her?"

"No. I haven't seen her, nor have I heard anyone mention her name since her move. I'm not allowed in Refractory—Head Nurse Kramer's private nurses administer care there."

Britina sighed. "It doesn't seem caring. We're supposed to

help patients."

"Something damaged Sister Mary Rush's mind. It happens. Minds can snap—she just slipped into lunacy. Our brains can turn on us in minutes. I've seen it happen before. She imagined a lot of things."

"Are you sure she imagined them?" Britina asked.

Nurse Betty said nothing.

•

Britina's duties stretched from day to night. After completing her daytime tasks, she supervised dinner with a group of patients, ensured everyone returned to their beds, and helped settle them for sleep. She made rounds of the patient rooms assigned to her and locked the doors where appropriate, then checked on those in the communal wards, assisting anyone who needed help.

Only after all this would she make her nightly visits to Jane Doe. Sometimes, she bathed her or clipped her nails. She had been so attractive—it was truly sad, the damage done to her. Britina always read a prayer from her prayer book aloud and spoke to her as if they were having a conversation. She felt a responsibility toward Jane Doe that she couldn't quite explain. These late-night visits also helped her avoid going to her own room as much as possible.

Britina had grown used to the patients' noises during the day, but at night, the moaning, wailing, occasional screams, and maniacal laughter echoing through the dim halls and barred windows sent chills through her. Sleep was sporadic. She hoped she would grow used to the more disturbing aspects of her assignment with time.

She realized she hadn't spent a night alone in any part of her remembered life. There had been roommates at the home in Melbourne, shared rooms at the Sisters of Charity home in London, and before that, she'd slept near nineteen or twenty other girls and women in the stall residence. She prayed God would give her the strength to meet the challenge set before her.

Nightly, after her last visit with Jane Doe—and sometimes a walk around the grounds—she reluctantly returned to her room. It was small, about ten feet wide and fourteen feet deep, with a single window fitted with wooden shutters and barred glass, looking out onto a courtyard.

The room held only the basics: a small coal stove for heat, a coal bin, a small table with one chair, and a narrow cot. A stool with a bedpan stood nearby, and a side table next to the bed held a lantern and a water pitcher. There was no closet, only wooden pegs on the wall for hanging clothes and a shelf for personal items. The ceiling was high and painted the same color as the walls.

Britina tried to think of it as a monk's cell, remembering the books she had read about monks in remote colonies, meditating in small, austere spaces to draw nearer to God.

Each night, she knelt and attempted to pray, but her connection to God was growing less fervent. She tried to meditate, to make sense of her circumstances, but found no answers. She realized she was afraid.

CHAPTER 16

ANNIE WILSON VISITS

Madam Annie Wilson tied her horse and carriage to the hitching post in front of the police station. She hadn't made an appointment with Chief Inspector McElroy, but she was sure he would see her.

Without stopping at Frank's desk, Madam Wilson walked straight up the stairs to McElroy's office. Frank didn't stop her—he figured the chief could handle her. He also knew McElroy liked her; she had spunk, and they occasionally attended the same social functions.

"How can I help you today, Madam Wilson?" McElroy smiled, knowing it was pointless to remind her she should make an appointment. She wasn't one to follow conventions.

Madam Wilson cleared her throat. "A young lady—possibly Heather—was dropped at the delivery door of the Royal Melbourne Hospital in the early morning of the tenth, after her disappearance from my home. She was unconscious, but alive. My informer described her as wearing a green dress, ripped and soiled. It sounds like the dress Heather had worn the prior evening."

"And how did this come to your attention?" McElroy asked.

"It doesn't matter, Inspector. There isn't much that happens in the Lon that I can't find out. I tried to get information at the hospital, but they wouldn't give me the time of day. Can I count on you to check this out?"

"Were you able to find out who made the delivery?"

"That I couldn't find out. I'm still working on it."

"Have you told Constable Penn?"

"Penn's a likeable lad, Raymond, but he can't even talk straight when he's around my ladies—they're merciless in the way they tease him. He usually looks like he's about to burst into flames, or tears, at any second."

McElroy smiled. "I understand, but I want him to continue his investigation. He needs the experience. As for the hospital visit, I have an idea. I'd like to introduce you to a dear friend who might help. I'd visit myself, but unfortunately we're short-staffed at the moment . . . especially if the visit leads to further investigation."

They left the building and headed toward the market. As they walked, Raymond listened to the vendors calling out their offerings to the crowd. He loved the energy of the stall market, and today, the scent of honeysuckle mixed with fried meat to create a lively street market bouquet. They turned onto Collins Street, stopping in front of a modest professional storefront. The sign overhead read "Lady Edith Black" with "Discreet Investigations" in smaller print below. Benji had made the sign for her.

Raymond opened the door, setting off the bell overhead. Since his last visit, Edie had added a bookcase to complement the stylish couch and chairs.

Hearing the bell, Edie stepped out from her office. "Raymond, what a pleasure." She came forward, and he kissed her cheek.

"I apologize for not sending a message first, Edie." He turned to his guest. "Madam Annie Wilson, proprietor of Boccaccio House."

Madam Wilson extended her hand. "Call me Annie."

"Madam Wilson," McElroy continued, "Lady Black is an investigator we occasionally hire for special assignments. She might help with Heather's disappearance. Her experience is extensive." *Not all of it legal,* he thought to himself. "If she has the time, it will ease the department's load—and might help you find Heather faster. She can gather information without the protocols we're bound to."

"I just sent you a note by mail this morning requesting a visit," Edie said. "For a discussion," she added quickly, not wanting Madam Wilson to assume it was a request for professional services.

"You're a friend of Raymond's. You're welcome anytime," Madam Wilson said.

Raymond explained the disappearance of the young girl, Heather Stone, and Madam Wilson described the information she had gathered, including her treatment at the hospital. The grace with which she carried herself impressed Edie.

"She is my niece," Madam Wilson offered.

I wasn't aware of that, Raymond thought.

Bringing family into the family business, Edie mused.

"Has she ever disappeared before?" Edie asked.

"She never has. None of my ladies have ever disappeared. Some leave—some get married or move away—but not without my knowledge. We're all very close."

"What can you tell me about the night you last saw her?" Edie asked.

"There was a party that night attended by eight distinguished gentlemen. They had arranged for a group of my ladies to entertain. Everyone gathered in my parlor. I sometimes stay to supervise when it's a group, especially with drinking involved, but I wasn't feeling well and went to bed early. I could still hear a lot of singing, dancing, and hollering before I finally fell asleep.

"The next morning, the girls were already cleaning and straightening up before I got out of bed. I could hear them laughing and chatting, trying to get the place respectable again—like I expect it to be. Heather wasn't among them. No one had seen her since the prior evening." She sighed. "The last gentleman reportedly left around 4:00 a.m.—alone, I was told—claiming he had work before sessions began. I think he'd been sleeping on the floor."

"What type of sessions?" Edie asked.

"I'm not sure, but he could've been from Parliament—it was in session."

"Do you entertain MPs often?" Edie asked.

"They're among my clientele, but if there were MPs that night, they weren't alone."

Our government at work, Edie thought. She made a mental note and probed a little further while Annie seemed open to sharing.

"Can you tell me any of the names of these men?"

Madam Wilson stiffened slightly. "As I told the chief inspector here, I can never share names. I'd be out of business in a heartbeat."

Edie smiled and nodded. "I suspected as much—I had to ask."

Raymond stood. "I need to get back. Madam Wilson, are you comfortable working with Lady Black? And Lady Black, are you on board to work with Madam Wilson?"

Both women agreed.

"I need to keep Petty Constable Penn involved. I'll send him over."

"We'll pick him up in half an hour once we finish here," Edie said. She turned back to Madam Wilson. "No doubt alcohol was plentiful. Were there drugs?"

"There's always alcohol. Most of the time, my ladies water down their drinks to keep control of their escorts, but occasionally, one slips. As for drugs—I don't encourage it, but it happens. Sometimes men show up already under the influence, having visited a den or smokehouse before arriving."

•

Arriving at the hospital, Penn tipped a stable boy to take the horse and carriage, instructing him to tend to the horse's needs while they visited. They made their way to the front entrance, where an attendant held the doors open. They approached the reception desk in the lobby. Madam Wilson took the lead.

"I was here earlier—I spoke with you," she said firmly. "When you were uncooperative, I visited my friend Chief Inspector McElroy. I've returned with one of his constables and an investigator to look into this matter."

Penn stepped forward. "I understand that someone dropped a comatose woman off at your receiving dock some days ago. I need to speak with the attending medical staff about this person." His tone left no room for objection, and he displayed his badge.

The reception nurse glanced at Madam Wilson, then at the badge. "Please take a seat. I'll see if Doctor Brookfield is available."

Edie silently put two and two together: Heather Stone's disappearance and the Mace theft had happened on the same night.

The nurse soon returned with a doctor in tow. "This is Dr. Brookfield," she announced before stepping away, leaving the group to introduce themselves. Brookfield looked harried, but motioned for them to follow him to a small meeting room furnished with only a table and a few chairs.

Once seated, he recounted the circumstances of Jane Doe's

arrival, detailing the care provided and the examination he had conducted.

"Someone severely beat her—mostly around the head and face," he said. "She showed no signs of regaining cognitive function. I believed there was nothing more we could do for her here. Kew could better provide her necessary care."

Madam Wilson moaned, bent forward, and buried her face in her hands. Edie leaned toward the doctor and quietly said, "There's a possibility this 'Jane Doe' is the madam's niece."

"Madam Wilson, please visit and confirm whether this is Heather Stone," Dr. Brookfield said gently. "But be aware—if it is, she will never regain cognitive function. However, they will treat her with respect at Kew. I will inform Head Nurse Kramer to keep you updated on her condition, should anything change."

Madam Wilson suggested that Lady Black should receive all updates. She wasn't sure if the hospital had drawn a connection between her and Boccaccio House, but she preferred to keep that confidential if possible. "Doctor Brookfield, please arrange the visit."

"I will—and I'll try to be there to assist," he replied. "I'll notify Lady Black as soon as I've cleared it with Nurse Kramer."

Edie handed him a card with her contact information.

CHAPTER 17

PENN'S REPORT

Raymond welcomed Edie to his office and offered her a seat, gesturing to the tea service on the table. "Help yourself. I'll be right back."

He returned shortly with Constable Penn.

"Penn, tell Lady Black what you've found out," McElroy said.

"Yes, sir. One of Madam Wilson's ladies, Estelle, sat with me—the other ladies tried to humiliate me into being intimate."

Edie chuckled out loud. "Sorry, Penn."

Penn gave a brief nod and continued. "Estelle said that night was far from normal. A group from Parliament was ready to party, and many of the ladies who weren't with customers wanted to join in. Since Madam Wilson had gone to bed early, there were no limits on the activities.

"After some drinking by the men and teasing by the women, two gentlemen made advances. The women rejected them—'ladies' choice,' one woman said—and the others cheered. One man then stood and suggested a game of dance and song using a 'magical wand of selection' that would match each man and woman with the perfect partner. He sent another man out to fetch the so-called magic stick.

"Meanwhile, another gentleman said he could arrange for

a pipe and some drugs to keep the evening enjoyable. He left, saying he'd be back in twenty minutes—before the magic wand arrived. Two of the women clung to him, teasing him with caresses and kisses, asking to go along, but he left alone."

Edie assumed this was Henderson. She leaned forward, encouraging Penn to continue.

"The second gentleman returned with a long pipe, a pipe lamp, and a packet of drugs. While the women were being careful with their drinking, most partook of the pipe. Not long after, the other man returned with a long object wrapped in cloth. He was sweaty—like he'd been running. He unwrapped a beautiful, jewel-covered golden rod, and seemed to be in a trance until one lady took it away from him. He sat on the couch, catching his breath."

Edie had to stand up and pace to continue listening. *We know where the Mace ended up—at least for a time.*

"The men passed the pipe around, and the ladies organized a game. They sang and danced, passing what they called 'the magic matching wand.' Several of them pretended intimacy with the object to tease the men. When the song ended, the lady holding the wand would point it at the man she chose, then pass the golden wand to the next lady before taking her selected gentleman to private quarters.

"Estelle said it was late in the game when Heather chose her man," Penn continued. "He was both drunk and drugged, and she led him out of the room. No one has seen her since. Her bed remained unused."

"Did you discover who this man was, Penn?" Raymond asked.

"No, sir. Estelle said she didn't know any names. I'm not sure that's the truth. I think Madam Wilson told her not to use names. She admitted to being quite drugged at the time and said she wished she'd never tried the pipe. She's normally careful with alcohol, but after a few hits, she was drugged for the night. Not unconscious, just sluggish and sick, so she sat in the corner, on the floor by the side of a couch, and watched quietly."

"Anything else, Penn?" Raymond prompted.

"Much more, sir."

Edie sipped her now-cold tea and waited. "Continue, Penn."

Penn scratched his nose, coughed lightly, and then said, "Sir, Lady Black, I'm afraid it gets a little delicate from here."

"Continue," Edie said firmly.

Penn took a deep breath and leaned his head back, avoiding Edie's gaze.

"Well, knowing that her bed was unused, and that she intended sex—and payment—I checked the rest of the home. That provided no clues. I then walked the streets and talked to locals where I could. A few opened up to me. Apparently, the party was the talk of the street.

"I found a pair of brothers, bar owners who'd observed several couples that could match the description of our missing lady and friend—but none of the women had worn a green dress like Heather Stone's. Later, though, a couple stopped by the brothers' establishment, and the woman had on a green dress. The man with her asked for beers. He could hardly stand, and she was saying she needed to go back home, but he had a tight grip on her arm. One of the brothers refused to serve them, and the man grabbed him by the collar and threatened him. The barman gave them two beers, then asked them to leave, which they did."

Penn opened his notebook and read aloud.

"'We followed the couple for a distance—she was obviously nervous. He was clinging tightly to her. She tried to calm him by caressing his hair and arms. Then she tried to pull her arm free, and he exploded, grabbing her by the neck and pulling her to him. He kissed her but missed her mouth, which made him madder. Swearing, almost growling, he ripped the front of her dress and pushed her into the alley. She fell hard. We couldn't see them, but it wasn't hard to assume what was happening. Trying to stay hidden, we crept forward. Dreadful noises were coming from both of them, but we didn't dare approach. We went to find a constable to help.'"

Penn looked up at McElroy, cleared his throat again, and said, "They returned without help—there were no police officers available. They then went to the alley. They said it was horrible. The assault had left the woman severely beaten and unconscious, with her dress and undergarments torn and her face and head bloody. The brothers got their wagon and took her to the Royal Melbourne Hospital. They left her on the dock, pulled the bell rope, and left. They said they couldn't get involved any further, and there was nothing more they could do for her."

Penn closed his notebook.

"Sir," he said, "I found these things in the alley." He handed over a gold pendant and a broken chain.

"Excellent work, Penn! See if you can hire a couple of men to rake and clean out that alley. See if anything else turns up. Have the trash hauled to a proper site."

"Yes, sir."

Edie spoke up. "Raymond—Penn—the magic wand is obviously, at least to me, the missing Mace. The question is—who removed it and under whose direction? I think this takes us back to the part Chaloner played and what he isn't telling us. It's all connected."

"Yes," McElroy agreed. "But where is the Mace now?"

CHAPTER 18

BRITINA

More and more, Britina thought about leaving the asylum and abandoning her novitiate status. She wished she had Edie to counsel her—if only she knew how to find her.

Returning to her cell-like room, she shut and locked the door, then stoked the coal fire. As she did most nights, she added a small shovel of coal from the pail. She'd been outside and felt a chill, though the night was pleasant. *I'll have to replenish my coal tomorrow,* she thought.

She had spent some time exploring the asylum and its grounds. On bright moonlit nights like this one, she wandered farther, crossing into sections separated by brick walls—partitions designed to divide the patients by classification and keep them apart. The grounds were extensive, spread over twenty-five acres, though buildings and courtyards occupied much of the space.

After pouring a glass of water and taking her nightly pill, she jotted a few notes in her notebook. Then she slipped under the covers, pulling up the extra blanket she had brought from the sisters' home in Melbourne. The room always felt cold to her, regardless of the outside temperature or the fire.

When she was first assigned to overnight duties, sleep had been difficult. The unsettling sounds of disturbed patients kept her awake. After a couple of weeks, Nurse Betty had commented on her haggard appearance. When Britina explained, Betty had handed her a small envelope of pills.

"These are safe," she'd said. "Take one before bed and another if you wake in the night. You'll feel calm and sleep soundly."

"Thank you, Betty. I'm not accustomed to taking pills, but if it will help, I'll try it."

"They will help. Just let me know when you need more."

She took them nightly now and sometimes an extra in the night.

She saw Betty less often now, their duties and schedules having diverged. Still, they made a point of meeting a few mornings a week for tea before the staff breakfast.

Britina made her nightly rounds of several wards, checking on certain patients and locking doors where required. She still stopped by Jane Doe's room to say a prayer for her soul and returned later in the evening for a final check.

One evening, she heard violent screaming coming from the pauper wing—a sure sign of some kind of crisis. She ran toward the sound and found a door ajar. Entering quietly, she saw a patient with her back to the door, holding two nurses at bay with a stick.

"Distract her!" one nurse called to Britina.

Britina raised both arms and shouted, "Over here!"

The patient turned and charged toward her. In that moment, the huskier nurse stepped behind the patient, wrapping her arms around her and clasping her hands together. But the patient broke free and kept coming. Unsure of what else to do, Britina simply stepped aside and stuck out her foot. The patient tripped and fell flat on her front, the stick sliding out of reach.

The second nurse quickly straddled the woman's back and pulled her arms behind her.

"Karla, give her a shot," she said.

Nurse Karla retrieved a kit from a leather bag on the bed, prepared a syringe, and administered the injection. The patient, wailing and sobbing, slowly calmed, though she remained conscious.

Karla and Britina helped the patient to her feet while the other nurse—her name tag read 'Verna'—picked up a heavy canvas garment from the bed.

A straitjacket, Britina realized.

Verna and Karla coaxed the patient's arms into the overly long sleeves and slid the jacket into place. With the woman's arms crossed tightly over her chest, Karla secured the straps across her back.

As both nurses held the woman upright, Britina asked, "What happened?"

"She became violent when we tried to give her the medicine Head Nurse Kramer ordered," Verna said. "She also saw the jacket," she added. "Kramer instructed us to place her in a straitjacket to prepare for morning treatment."

The patient, now nearly unconscious, hung her head and drooled, a low moan escaping the back of her throat.

"We need to take her to a padded room in the paupers' refractory ward. Will you help us?"

"Certainly," Britina replied, though she wished she hadn't. She wanted to get away.

Karla gathered their things, placing the patient's belongings into a cloth bag and handing it all to Britina. "If you'll carry these, we'll each take a side. Her name is Eunice Wiley. She has tendencies toward visions and violence."

Britina thought of Sister Mary Rush. She feared her knees

might buckle, but she followed the nurses, walking behind them and their subdued patient through the connected corridors.

"What will happen to her?" Britina asked.

"She'll spend the rest of the night in the straitjacket in a padded cell so she won't hurt herself—or anyone else," Verna replied. "They will assess her condition in the morning. She's scheduled for brain treatment by Nurse Kramer and Dr. Brookfield."

"What type of treatment is that?" Britina asked.

"I don't understand it," Karla said. "It's something Dr. Brookfield is pioneering. He's making a big name for himself in treating mental disorders."

"I think he thinks he's a god," Verna muttered.

Karla shot her a sharp look.

"Sorry," Verna said quickly.

Nurse Karla led them into a dimly lit hall and unlocked a door using a key from her ring. The room inside was very narrow, with walls padded by mattress-like material. There was a small hole in the door, presumably for observation. Verna locked the door behind the patient, and they left.

Though Britina had recovered somewhat from the shock of the encounter, her insides were still trembling—an unfamiliar and unsettling feeling.

"She'll be fine there until morning. The dark will help to calm her. Thank you for the help. What's your name?" Nurse Karla asked.

"I'm Sister Mary Britina. I replaced Sister Mary Rush, but they have now appointed me an attendant. It's not what I expected."

"You're in Bess Childs's old quarters."

"That's right. Nurse Kramer assigned me to duties and gave me the room when Attendant Childs became ill and went to her parents."

Verna and Karla exchanged a look.

"What's wrong?" Britina asked.

"I hope it's not haunted—your room," Karla said. "I don't want to frighten you, but Bess didn't get ill and leave. Bess killed herself in that very room. She didn't have any family left. Following her mother's institutionalization, she took a job here as an attendant. Her mother also killed herself."

Britina gasped. The trembling she'd felt inside overtook her entire body—her head, arms, and legs spasmed uncontrollably. Then everything went black, and she collapsed.

The nurses quickly sat her up, gently slapping her face to rouse her. Karla fetched water and urged her to drink.

"What happened? What am I doing here?"

"You had a spell, then fainted. I think you'd better get to bed; we'll walk you back to your room."

"I'm scared. Don't take me there."

"I don't think you have a choice," Karla said.

•

It was already very late, and she needed sleep, though she didn't know if she could manage it. She took two pills and lay back on her cot. Even with the medication, her sleep was restless. After tossing and turning, she took a third pill.

What's that noise? She started shaking again. Clutching the blanket to her neck, she sat up and stared into the darkness. She had forgotten to stoke the fire—the coal had burned out—and the room was bitterly cold, far colder than it should have been this time of year. Her heart pounded in her chest and ears. She was breathing in short, rapid bursts.

Why am I so afraid? She stared into the dark, willing herself to calm. And then she saw it—a darker shadow moving across the room. It paused at the end of her bed. A wave of icy cold washed over her. The shadow seemed to reach for her.

She wanted to scream, but the room spun around her—and then everything went black.

She woke in the pre-dawn light. As she replayed the night's episode, she tried to justify her fear—and her vision. The events of the previous evening, especially learning about Bess Childs, had unsettled her deeply. She convinced herself that her imagination had overwhelmed her common sense.

I will calm down, do my work, and I will be alright.

She washed her face in the basin. It was still early. *I'm awake and have time—I'll take a bath.* She undressed, laid her gown neatly on the bed, put on her robe, and gathered her bath supplies, her head still foggy but beginning to clear.

Then she remembered—she hadn't visited Jane Doe the night before. Guilt hit her hard. She had never missed a single night. *I'll go now*, she resolved.

She returned her bath supplies to the shelf, dressed in her regular clothes, and chose not to wear her habit. Grabbing her prayer book, she walked to the door. And stopped.

Her heart raced, pounding in her ears. The door remained unlocked—and not fully latched.

Could I have left it that way? She always latched and locked the door before bed.

She sank to her knees, crying. *I'm going insane*, she thought, weeping hard, terrified it might be true.

CHAPTER 19

JANE DOE

Britina took another pill, hoping it would calm her without putting her to sleep. She waited, regained her composure, gathered her things, and headed to Jane Doe's room.

When she entered, she walked over to the bed. A pillow was on the floor—that seemed strange. She picked it up. Jane Doe's head faced the opposite wall, and Britina eased it back onto the pillow, shivering; the woman's flesh was ice cold. When she glanced down, Jane Doe's eyes were wide open, staring, lifeless.

Britina felt like she might pass out again, but fought it. She needed to get help.

A pinpoint of blood dotted Jane Doe's neck. Britina touched it—a needle mark. She wiped the blood on her sleeve. Looking around, she saw a hypodermic needle and plunger on the floor, broken in two. She picked up the pieces. As she moved to leave, the door opened and Nurse Kramer entered.

Britina looked at her hands holding the pillow and the hypodermic parts. She dropped them, let out a low moan, and ran past Nurse Kramer, pushing her aside. She went to her room, grabbed a few things, left the building, went to the one housing her bicycle, and pedaled out the gate, down the hill toward the

Sisters' home.

I'm never going back. Mother Superior will help.

I'm sure I didn't hurt Jane Doe. I didn't go to her last night. I'm sure I didn't.

Head Nurse Kramer sent for Doctor Brookfield at the Royal Melbourne Hospital. He arrived late that morning and declared Jane Doe deceased. In her chart, he noted that death resulted from injuries sustained in the attack that had led to her confinement at the Kew facility. It would be up to the coroner to add further details.

Attendants wrapped the body and took it to the wooden barn that served as the facility's morgue, for the coroner's inspection and later burial preparations. Since Coroner Marshall Wallace was away for several days, they moved the body to the cold cellar beneath the kitchen and laid it out on a wooden table.

•

Immediately upon receiving a hand-delivered message from Dr. Brookfield, Edie left her office, hailed a hansom, and headed to Boccaccio House.

She and Madam Wilson sat alone in the latter's private sitting room. When Edie told her about Jane Doe's death, Madam Wilson's face quivered. She bit her lip, trying to hold back emotion, then burst into tears.

"I know it's Heather, I just know it," she sobbed.

Edie put her arms around her and held her until the crying eased.

Madam Wilson then summoned all her ladies to the living room. When told, they all burst into tears, which made Edie cry too.

Edie explained they wouldn't be able to visit until after the coroner had inspected the body and issued a death certificate.

Then she and Madam Wilson would go to identify the remains. At this, the group cried again. The house was closed until after the visit to Kew.

•

Coroner Marshall Wallace cut his trip short and arrived three days after Jane Doe's death. He met with Head Nurse Kramer and Dr. Brookfield, then inspected the body, took fluid samples, and noted his findings.

After the inspection, Dr. Brookfield, Nurse Kramer, and Coroner Wallace met in Kramer's office.

"An attendant discovered the patient deceased, I understand. There is some evidence that Jane Doe received a drug injection, followed by smothering—perhaps a mercy killing?" the coroner speculated.

"The attendant was a novice nun from the Sisters of Mercy. Goes by Sister Mary Britina. She had developed an obsession with Jane Doe," said Head Nurse Kramer.

"Any other evidence?" the coroner asked.

Kramer handed him the pillow and the hypodermic needle and plunger found in the room and recounted her encounter with Britina.

•

Britina didn't provide any details but left a note with Mother Superior's attendant, saying she was back, would be in her room, and needed to speak to Mother Superior. She added that she wasn't returning to the asylum. That night, she lay in her own bed at the sisters' convent home; however, sleep eluded her. Neither of her roommates was there, and she didn't want to be alone.

In the morning, Britina made herself tea and sat in the simple parlor of her room. A note arrived mid-morning, instructing her to present herself at Mother Superior's residence at 4:00 p.m.

Britina intended to ask for her help. She washed, donned her habit, and walked to the residence. Her breath caught in her throat when the woman she recognized as Head Nurse Kramer's enforcer—the one who had brushed past her as she entered Nurse Kramer's meeting room—greeted her. *Sturgis, I think.* She asked Britina to make herself comfortable in the den.

"Mother Superior will be with you shortly."

What is she doing here? Britina thought. Her insides shook, then her chin. Grabbing the back of a chair to steady herself, she took a deep breath.

The den was vacant. Britina looked around and spotted the sidebar. It might displease Mother Superior, but she just didn't care right now. She went to it and poured herself a sherry, her hands trembling. She took a seat.

"Well, Sister Mary Britina, a little early in the day, isn't it?"

"But perhaps late in my life."

"I'll join you," Mother Superior said, pouring her own.

Britina took another sip and held her glass out for more. Her nerves were raw, close to overwhelming her; the alcohol did her good.

Mother Superior needs to help me.

"I received a message from Nurse Kramer earlier this morning asking that I keep you confined. She said she suspected you were upset by the loss of a patient you had cared for. Is that correct?"

"It is, but it's more than that. There is something frightening about that place, and I am terrified. My patient—as she referred to her—did not die a natural death."

"That's what Nurse Kramer said—that the death is suspicious."

She stared, unblinking, into Britina's face.

"I'm frightened, Mother Superior."

"As Sisters of Mercy, we must face what confronts us and our actions. We must believe God will protect us."

"I'm not sure I believe that any longer," Britina said, taking a sip of her sherry. Her hand shook so violently that some spilled down her habit sleeve.

"We all question our beliefs. It's natural."

"I don't know what to do, Mother Superior. I need help. Please."

"Nurse Kramer has suspended you. Under the circumstances, I am revoking your novice status, at least until further notice. You are to return to the asylum under the supervision of Miss Sturgis, whom you met at the door. You are to be confined to your room there until the investigation is complete. I suggest you rest, pray, and truly talk to God. I was told they will bury the woman at the Kew cemetery once the coroner completes his report. You may attend and say a prayer for her—under the supervision of Miss Sturgis. I suggest you say one for your-self as well."

"Why do I have to be confined? Am I a suspect in her death? I cared for her." Her heart was racing harder than it ever had, and her voice broke into a shrill edge of panic.

"You are the only suspect, my dear. You should pray for redemption."

Britina didn't know what to say or do. Obviously, Mother Superior would not be of help. She had little choice; she felt trapped, already in custody. *This can't be happening. How do I make people understand I didn't harm her?*

I didn't, did I?

•

Back at the asylum, Britina paced her room constantly. The only person she saw was Sturgis. *My jailer,* she thought. She knew sleep would be impossible. It was getting late when she heard a gentle knock, followed by a pill envelope sliding under her door.

The note read: "I'm sure you are being framed. You need to demand legal help."

"Betty, help me," she whispered. But there was no answer—her friend was gone.

Britina took two pills and slept fitfully until dawn.

CHAPTER 20

THE FUNERAL

When Edie and Madam Wilson arrived at the asylum to identify the body, they entered through the main gate, following a tree-lined drive to the elliptical carriageway at the front of the administration building. An attendant took their horse and carriage, assuring them that when they were ready to depart, he would fetch them for their return trip. Madam Wilson tipped him with a quiet nod.

They climbed the steps to the main entrance. Miss Sturgis opened the door. She didn't greet them but simply said, "I'll escort you to Head Nurse Kramer's office." She turned and led the way.

Nurse Kramer invited them to sit at the conference table. "I understand that our Jane Doe may have been your niece, Madam Wilson."

"Perhaps," Madam Wilson replied. "I need to see her, to be sure."

Head Nurse Kramer showed no signs of remorse or compassion.

Finally, Madam Wilson asked, "May I see her now?"

"Yes, her body is in our morgue building, Madam Wilson. She will be prepared for burial after your identification. The coroner's inspection is complete, and he determined an attendant murdered Jane Doe; that attendant is now in custody pending further action. There will be an inquest."

Edie gasped in disbelief as Madam Wilson slumped from her chair in a faint. Head Nurse Kramer revived her with smelling salts but offered no comfort.

Madam Wilson took Edie's hand as they walked to the morgue building. Head Nurse Kramer walked in front of them. Standing at the inspection table, Nurse Kramer removed the cloth from Jane Doe's face and upper body. The face showed scars, but the wounds had healed.

Madam Wilson spoke with a quiver in her voice. "That is my niece, Heather Stone." She knelt, folded her hands, and said a silent prayer, her eyes moist. Edie grieved for her.

Madam Wilson gave Edie a ride back to the city center. As she stepped down from the carriage, Edie gently placed a hand on Madam Wilson's arm. From there, she took a cab home, feeling guilty and lonely—she had spent so little time with Benji.

Benji had returned from Adelaide and was sitting on the couch with a stack of papers on his lap. He glanced up as Edie opened the door.

"Have you read the papers?" he asked before she even removed her hat and scarf.

"I haven't had time." *A 'hello, darling' wouldn't have been too much to ask.*

"Your Mace case is in the headlines of every one of them. Each has a different theory. One claims two local thieves, former ironworkers, had it but tossed it in the river when confronted. Another has Parliament's electrician running off with it. And the topper is it ended up at an orgy in the Little Lon district with members of Parliament. What do you think? Oh, and what about these body parts *The Age* is reporting on?"

"Benji, I think we don't have enough evidence to narrow the Mace investigation, so we investigate all leads. I've made my recommendations. Can we forget it for tonight and just have a quiet dinner—and maybe a little cuddling?"

Benji smiled. "I'll cook," he said, jumping to his feet. He set the papers aside, wrapped his arms around Edie, and hugged her. She hugged him back, then pushed him towards the kitchen.

"I hope I'm doing the right thing for us by undertaking this investigation business," she murmured.

"Rough day?" Benji asked.

"Yes," she said, looking up into his eyes.

"You'll do fine, Edie. You always do. Just trust yourself."

Dinner was a welcome roast of chicken, potatoes, and gravy, with plenty of greens dressed in oil and vinegar—it was perfect. So was the evening. Benji's embrace comforted Edie.

In the morning, Edie updated all her notes, observations, and thoughts on the Mace case, citing each of the rumors and offering her opinion. She sent the report by messenger to Chief Inspector McElroy, including a note on the previous day's activities with Madam Wilson and the discovery of Jane Doe's identity.

•

On the day of the burial, Miss Sturgis remained on the road overlooking the asylum's cemetery and the Yarra River, but allowed Britina to walk down the hill and stand by the shaded evergreen trees, where she could look across the lawns to the burial plot. Britina wore her habit; she still considered herself a novitiate. She stared at the chocolate-colored dirt piled beside the grave that would hold the remains of Jane Doe, now known as Heather Stone. *Just a week ago, Heather responded by squeezing my hand . . . or at least I think she did.*

The Yarra River flowed over shore rocks near the burial plot, and a breeze whispered gently through the pines. Britina crossed herself, closed her eyes, and said a silent prayer as the attendants lowered the casket into the ground. Heather Stone was not being buried as a pauper; she would have a marked grave. However, because they'd identified her as a prostitute, her grave lay outside the designated religious areas.

At the direction of the burial contractor, the patients chosen for the job began shoveling dirt over Heather's casket. A small group of attendees had gathered. Britina opened her eyes and observed them.

•

Edie caught movement out of the corner of her eye and glanced toward the woods, near the road. A woman stood there, watching the grave, dressed in a brown habit. Neither spoke; their eyes locked, and they both started running. Their arms intertwined as they fell to the earth, wrapping around each other and rolling in the grass.

Madam Wilson turned to McElroy as the others watched the commotion. Miss Sturgis began running down the hill.

"Did Lady Black just attack a nun?" Madam Wilson asked.

"It appears that way," McElroy replied. "But the nun doesn't seem to mind."

"Britina, I've been trying to locate you for years," Edie huffed as they rolled down the embankment.

"I've prayed to find you. I wrote you a hundred letters." Britina said. She hesitated. "I didn't kill her," she added, just as Sturgis caught up to them and pulled Britina to her feet by the collar of her habit. McElroy ran across the lawns, and Madam Wilson followed.

CHAPTER 21

CORONER'S INQUEST

Edie's elation at reconnecting with Britina faded when Sturgis arrived and hauled Britina to her feet, announcing she was taking Britina back into custody.

"Custody for what?" Edie demanded.

"Murder," Sturgis said, looking from Edie to McElroy. "Miss Myers is suspected of taking the life of the patient just buried."

"It's Sister Mary Britina," Britina interrupted.

Miss Sturgis shot a sharp look at Britina, then continued, now addressing both Edie and McElroy. "Miss Myers is a suspect—the only suspect—in her death."

Edie watched in shock as Sturgis pushed Britina back toward the asylum. Britina glanced over her shoulder, her face tight with tension, and Edie mouthed, "I will help you." She turned to McElroy. "I can't let this happen."

"If the coroner has called an inquest, you can't prevent it, Edie. Let's see where that leads."

•

Dr. Brookfield was worried. The suspicious death of a patient at the hands of an asylum attendant—a nun, no less—could lead to a full investigation into the asylum's activities. This would not serve him well. He summoned Head Nurse Kramer and Miss Sturgis to a meeting.

"Things are escalating dangerously," Dr. Brookfield said. "We need to take more precautions."

"What do you propose?" Kramer asked.

"The inquest into the person known as Sister Britina will draw too much attention to the asylum and our activities. I think we need to control this situation rather than remain under observation."

"I would agree, Dr. Brookfield," Head Nurse Kramer said, careful to address her lover by his title, as was best on professional occasions. "Do you have a plan?"

"I'll start with the facts as we know them." Brookfield turned to Kramer. "You found Sister Britina in the room of the deceased Heather Stone, alone, early in the morning. She was holding a pillow in her hand, and she dropped a hypodermic on the floor behind her. When you surprised her, she ran away, shoving you into the wall. Later, you found missing medications in her room.

"All this is incriminating, yet not convincing enough to have her convicted and locked away. A trial may reveal more than we desire. I suggest we find more evidence showing that our young sister is criminally insane. We need evidence and three medical opinions declaring her unfit for jail and in need of treatment.

"Our colleague, Dr. Snow, will be here for the surgery training in a day or two. I will have him conclude it was an act of euthanasia caused by a mental ailment. You, as head of medical care, can do the same," he said, looking at Head Nurse Kramer. "I will present the medical findings to the magistrate and claim that I've reached the same conclusion. I will request an order for admission and treatment as criminally insane, avoid a trial, and eliminate police interference. She will be under our control."

Nurse Kramer nodded. "I think that's wise, Dr. Brookfield."

"Leave the evidence to me," Miss Sturgis said. She knew her job.

•

The notice read: *Coroner Marshall Wallace conducted an investigation into the death of Heather Stone at Kew Asylum and determined that there was sufficient evidence of poisoning and suffocation to label her death suspicious. A full examination of the evidence will be presented at an inquest.* The date, time, and location were provided.

The courtroom was open to the public, allowing anyone to attend and listen to the proceedings.

Edie entered with Chief Inspector McElroy, accompanied by Madam Wilson, who had requested they arrive together.

The room was functional—"sober" was the word that came to Edie's mind. The walls were plain, adorned only with a coat of arms and the emblem of Queen Victoria. A frail-looking man had already seated himself at the testimony table. The rest of the room contained long benches, like church pews. The coroner roped off the first row for key participants—those called to testify, the accused, and officials, including Chief Inspector McElroy. They filed in together.

Next, he called for a jury of twelve local citizens chosen from the community. As their names were called, each stood from the benches and made their way to a seat to the right side of the large testimony table beside the coroner's bench. They were sworn in one at a time, each placing a hand on a Bible.

The coroner stood tall at his bench and surveyed the room, which held a large, interested crowd, including reporters from various newspapers. He wore a dark frock coat buttoned neatly over a crisp white shirt, displaying authority, but his field trousers and dusty leather boots conveyed a different side of his position—he had clearly come straight from another investigation.

His beard, speckled with gray, framed a small mouth. Standing rigidly, he placed glasses on his nose and read from his official statement.

"I have inspected the body of Heather Stone, examined the evidence associated with her death, and taken testimony from involved parties. Heather Stone was a patient at the Kew Asylum. She was admitted . . ." He glanced at his notes and stated the date. "She was the victim of a vicious beating from which she never regained consciousness. That crime is not the subject of this inquest. She was admitted to the Kew Institute as Jane Doe and attended to until her death. Her identity was not known until after her passing."

He then turned to the jury. "As a jury, your obligation is to listen to testimony to determine the cause of death and, if possible, identify any criminal activity involved. I have conducted a thorough investigation of the body prior to burial and have determined two things. She received an injection in the neck, possibly a lethal dose. Also, she showed physical signs of suffocation: primarily, a slight bluish discoloration of the skin, which can occur when the body is deprived of oxygen, and petechial hemorrhages—tiny red and purple spots in the eyes, face, and neck that are also signs of oxygen deprivation."

The coroner began calling witnesses, one at a time, and questioning them.

He first called Head Nurse Kramer to testify.

"It was very early in the morning," Nurse Kramer said. "I was up early to prepare for my daily meeting with the nurses and attendants. As I passed Jane Doe's room, I heard noises. I opened the door. Sister Britina was inside, standing over the bed and talking to the patient—or the corpse, at that point. A whining noise or a moan escaped her when she saw me. She seemed to snap to alertness, as if coming out of a trance.

Looking at herself with a pillow in one hand and a hypodermic in the other, I think she realized what she had done."

"Please, Nurse Kramer, you are not to provide supposition or conclusions, just report the facts. The jury will disregard Nurse Kramer's conclusion," the coroner said. Turning back to Nurse Kramer, he asked, "Did you or she say anything at that moment?"

"No. I was in shock. I couldn't ask anything. She dropped the pillow and a needle part, grabbed her prayer book, pushed me aside, and ran from the room. We found later that she went to her room, gathered some belongings, and fled the asylum."

"Was any other evidence found in the room?"

"The syringe plunger was behind where Britina Myers was standing."

"Did you find the syringe?"

"No, I think it was still in her hand."

"Conjecture, Nurse Kramer."

"Sorry. We didn't find it then. However, an assistant of mine later found a syringe that we assume matches the plunger in the coal bin in Britina Myers's room, along with an empty vial of morphine."

Britina snapped to attention. A murmur spread through the attendees, growing loud with collective reaction.

Britina sprang to her feet, bent at the waist by the length of the restraints on her wrists. "This is not true! I found both parts of the hypodermic in the room!"

"Please, Miss Myers," the coroner said. "The purpose of this inquest is to uncover facts and determine the cause of death. Formal charges have not been brought against you. However, if any are brought later, anything you say now can be used against you. I advise you to remain silent."

Coroner Wallace pointed to the center of the table. "Are these the items you are referring to?" he asked Head Nurse Kramer.

"They are, sir."

"They were not discovered in the earlier inspection of Miss Myers's room?"

"No, sir. We didn't think to inspect the coal bin."

"Was there any other evidence to confirm that morphine was the medication administered?"

"No, sir. But an inventory of the medicine supplies following the incident revealed that a supply of morphine was missing."

"Do you take medication inventory regularly?"

"Every day, sir."

"Has Sister Britina been trustworthy? I believe she was an attendant—is that correct?"

"She was an attendant. Prior to that, she was a patient assistant. We had an opening, and I felt the role suited her. She seemed to grow too attached to a couple of patients, one being Jane Doe—Heather Stone."

"I believe you told me that there was one more piece of incriminating evidence found in Sister Britina's room. Is that correct?"

"Yes. When we searched her room, we found an envelope of stolen pills on her side table. They were chloral hydrate."

Britina looked down the row at Nurse Betty, her eyes pleading. Nurse Betty looked back—then turned away.

The coroner turned his attention to Dr. Brookfield.

"State your name for the jury, please."

"Dr. Bran Brookfield."

"Are you the resident doctor at the Kew Asylum?" the coroner asked.

"I am not. I am the head of medicine at the Royal Melbourne Hospital and a consulting research doctor for Kew. There is a team of medical professionals that oversees the care and treatment of patients."

"What do your duties entail, Dr. Brookfield?"

"I conduct psychiatric research and develop new treatment methods. I also train junior doctors who lack experience."

"You committed Jane Doe to Kew. Is that correct?"

"Yes. After she was left on the Royal Melbourne Hospital loading dock, I assessed her condition. I determined she had no hope of ever regaining consciousness and sent her to Kew, where the staff was better equipped to care for her."

"Are you familiar with Britina Myers, also known as Sister Mary Britina?"

"I am."

"Are you familiar with the medication found in her possession?"

"I wasn't aware she was taking any medication, but I examined the findings. The drug was chloral hydrate—a sedative and hypnotic."

"Will you describe its uses and its potential side effects?"

"It is used to induce calm and sleep, often before surgery. While effective, it can disrupt normal sleep patterns and lead to phenomena like sleepwalking, talking, and performing complex tasks while asleep. It can also occasionally depress the respiratory system, causing blackouts and fainting."

"Thank you, Doctor. Let me shift the direction of the questioning. In your opinion, did Sister Britina have a healthy attitude toward the patients at Kew?"

"I have not observed Sister Britina do anything but provide care for patients. But I believe what you're really asking is whether she had an obsessive attachment to Jane Doe—and I believe she did. Heather Stone, as we now know her, had no needs that Sister Britina could fulfill. The doctors and nurses gave her the required treatment. Yet I observed—and also heard from Nurse Kramer—that Sister Britina would visit the patient several times a day. She would talk to her, she claimed to have observed eye movement or hand-squeezing, and even asked me to accompany her to the patient's room. On both occasions, I showed that there was no change in Heather Stone's condition."

"As coroner, it is my job to assess all possibilities surrounding a suspicious death. Dr. Brookfield, is it possible that Sister Britina was sleepwalking under the influence of chloral hydrate and committed an act of euthanasia, taking the life of Heather Stone?"

The doctor nodded and placed a hand on his chin, thinking for a moment. "It is possible, and the description of the encounter by Nurse Kramer seems consistent with that possibility."

Tears ran down Edie's face as she looked at Britina.

Britina clasped her hands tightly, shut her eyes, and bowed her head—she was praying.

"I have one last question for you, Nurse Kramer," the coroner said, turning to her. "Would it have been possible for Sister Britina to get morphine and a syringe from the medical supplies kept at the facility?"

"The supply is in the same locked room where the chloral hydrate is stored."

The coroner collected statements from the nurses present. Karla reported on the fainting incident. Betty did not volunteer that she had provided the pills. Madam Wilson, bristling at the implication that Heather Stone had been a prostitute, firmly replied, "No. She was a respected comfort worker."

This set off a fit of laughter and whispering among the attendees. The coroner shouted, threatening to clear the room if order wasn't restored.

After two hours of testimony, the coroner requested the jury retire to consider their verdict. "You are to decide on the cause of death and whether there is any criminal activity involved.

You may recommend filing charges, if you determine them appropriate."

The jury withdrew to a private room next to the courtroom. Few people left, all waiting to see what they would decide.

Britina, though accompanied by Miss Sturgis, was not in formal custody—at least not yet. Edie stood, walked to the far end of the bench where they sat, and asked to sit with Britina. The nurse relinquished her seat, and Edie and Britina embraced.

"Britina, it doesn't look good for you right now. If you tell me again you didn't do this, I will find a way to help."

"Edie, I hope you know I could never kill anyone. I felt my duty was to care for this lost soul."

"Not even as an act of mercy?"

"Edie!"

"I know, I had to ask—forgive me."

Britina hoped she was telling the truth.

McElroy approached the coroner. "Marshall, can I have a word?"

"I was expecting you would ask, Raymond. Let's take chairs in the corner away from the crowd."

"It seemed like you drew the conclusions for the jury. I have little doubt they'll call for charging the sister with murder."

"It is possible she committed murder. In my interviews, I realized that the doctor and Nurse Kramer had already reached that conclusion. If I had simply let them testify to their beliefs, the jury would certainly come back recommending she be tried for murder. I tried to introduce other possibilities—leave the door open for lesser charges than a hanging offense."

McElroy paused, assessing the coroner's approach. "Marshall, if what we both expect occurs, you would typically recommend that the police investigate further?"

"That's right."

"Will you expand on that and recommend the police take custody of the accused here today?"

"I don't have that authority, Raymond. You need an arrest warrant."

"I don't think she's safe returning to that asylum. If someone planted the evidence in her room, who did it—and why? Someone may want to silence her."

"There is no evidence supporting that or suggesting others were involved. I can't act on speculation. Besides, it would look very suspicious if something happened to her after this public hearing. I'll emphasize that the police must conduct their own investigation and that full cooperation from Kew is required. It will be up to you to monitor her. If you don't get full cooperation, then I can take steps."

McElroy nodded. "What if we kept her in our jail for safety during the investigation?"

"That would imply I suspect others are involved. There's no evidence of that. I don't have the authority—I've done what I can. Get an arrest warrant."

CHAPTER 22

THADDEUS SNOW

It was evening, and Thaddeus Snow had work to do. Henderson had significantly grown the Melbourne drug business, and it was time to return there to deliver drugs. Besides, Thaddeus had other matters to attend to at the asylum.

Leaving the surgery and descending the stairs onto the stable grounds behind the buildings, he made his way to the back door of his apothecary. It was dark, with no moon to light his way, but he had done this a thousand times. A faint glimmer of light shone through a scratch in the blacked-out paint of the upper windows. Asa would probably still be working. Thaddeus had taken the boy under his wing, provided him with food and shelter, and, once trust was established, taught him the meticulous processes of product refinement. What a stroke of luck finding him had been.

He climbed the steps to a landing and called to the dogs so they'd know it was him. Two large, powerful bullmastiffs greeted him when he unlocked the door. He patted each dog and, as they expected, gave them a piece of dried beef.

Crates and bundles of herbs lined the side walls of the apothecary's storage room. The air was thick with the scents of lavender and peppermint, which overpowered the other herbs used in preparing treatments for patients and Snow's patent elixir. A locked door separated the storeroom from the front apothecary. He would fill the day's orders before leaving.

At the center of the room, an open staircase led to the second floor and his laboratory—off-limits to the apothecary staff. He climbed the stairs. Though the space was mostly dark, a dim light glowed, so he didn't bother lighting a candle or lamp.

Asa, wearing a cloth mask and glasses, was bent over one of four wooden tables that ran down the center of the room. A faint oil lamp burned beside him. He was so focused on his work that he didn't notice Snow until he reached the floor level. Asa gave a quick nod, then returned to his task.

Cabinets and shelves filled with glass jars and containers lined the walls. Behind the fourth table stood a large cabinet with glass doors, filled with jars, pills, and vials—each labeled. A safe nearby held poison extracts reserved for a select few clients.

A large shelving unit stored an inventory of Snow's Universal Elixir, which claimed to cure all ailments and promote good health. It was a mixture of distilled alcohol and measured amounts of chamomile, lavender, echinacea, peppermint, valerian, dandelion, and morphine. Snow adjusted the recipe to balance taste and aroma, using just enough herbs to blend with the alcohol. He kept the formula secret, filing formulas for all products in notebooks locked in a cabinet on the back wall.

Several oak barrels lined the benches at the back. On one table, two large, porcelain mortar and pestle sets sat side by side. Asa stood at one, grinding a block of opium into fine powder.

After the poppy harvest season and initial processing in China, Snow received large shipments of opium blocks. He refined these into various products to supply demand throughout the year.

The third table housed an elaborate array of distillation

equipment: alcohol burners connected to retorts, with glass condensers to cool and condense vapor into liquid. Filtration barrels stood nearby, separating liquid extract from solid impurities. The fourth table was Thaddeus's workspace for final preparation. A collection of wooden barrels sat beneath it, each fitted with taps for easy dispensing.

He distributed his patent medicines to apothecaries across Australia, but his most profitable product was laudanum, which he supplied in bulk to commercial clients, including opium dens. He worked with several criminal organizations, but his largest shipments went to Britain, where the demand was insatiable. It was this product they were working on tonight.

Asa continued grinding a second block of opium into the second mortar to keep the quantities measured.

"When you finish that block, Asa, we'll get started." The earthy, slightly sweet, and musty smell of the ground opium permeated the room. Thaddeus donned his own mask.

He poured the contents of the two mortars into separate retorts, then carefully measured and added a precise amount of rectified spirit alcohol to each. The alcohol acted as a solvent, extracting the active alkaloids from the opium. Asa and Thaddeus each took a retort and placed it on a shelf; then they retrieved two others that had been processed the previous night. Overnight, the clear alcohol and light brown opium had blended slightly in color.

Thaddeus lit two alcohol burners and placed one retort on each burner frame to begin the distillation process. He attached glass condensers and tubing to the retorts, positioning collection containers beneath the discharge tubes to catch the alcohol and extracted alkaloids.

"Asa, monitor these retorts. This will take a while. I'll prepare my ingredients for tonight's batch. You can take the oak keg from the filtering equipment from last night's work and bottle the product so we can take it with us tomorrow. Pack for four nights and bring your shovels, wraps, and supplies."

"Yes, sir," Asa replied. He enjoyed accompanying the doctor. Dr. Snow taught him things and trusted him. *He made me into somebody. What I do is important*, Asa thought.

They were making laudanum to be drunk at opium dens, sold at drug outlets, and prepared for shipment. Thaddeus had developed his own formula, involving several delicate steps. He added saffron, which gave the brown liquid a bright orange tint and a distinct herbal odor and taste. He also incorporated cinnamon and clove in carefully measured amounts. The mixture eventually took on a dark yet luminescent red-orange color with a delicate, inviting scent and flavor. Winning the business of dens and distributors had been easy with Snow's carefully refined formula.

As he worked, Snow pondered the upcoming trip. A year earlier, he and Dr. Brookfield had formalized a partnership, anticipating enormous profits once their curative brain inventions gained acceptance. Snow had invested a significant sum. In the meantime, he'd agreed to partner in the school Brookfield was running to train new surgeons. Medical schools from several countries had signed on, and the returns were profitable—but the operation remained secret from the public because of its reliance on human dissection.

The inventions hadn't yet yielded returns, and Snow was growing impatient. The school was lucrative, but it demanded too much of his time. Worse, there simply weren't enough corpses. Brookfield had assured him the asylum would provide sufficient "material," but now he was pressuring Snow to deliver more bodies. A confrontation was overdue—one Snow planned to initiate after the upcoming training.

CHAPTER 23

COMMITTED

The coroner read the jury's findings to himself, then aloud. "'In the inquest into Heather Stone's death, the jury determined she died from a morphine overdose and suffocation caused by a pillow obstructing her airways. We judge this to have been an attempted act of mercy. We recommend bringing charges of euthanasia against Sister Mary Britina, a.k.a. Britina Myers.'"

Coroner Marshall Wallace looked up, toward Britina. "Miss Myers, you have heard the findings of the inquest jury. No charges have been filed against you yet. You will have a chance to defend yourself at trial. You will need representation."

Britina showed no emotion. She folded her hands on the table in front of her, her mind in prayer. Wallace turned to Chief Inspector McElroy.

"The jury has made a recommendation of criminal charges related to the death of Heather Stone against Britina Myers. In my capacity as coroner, I now refer further investigation and legal action to the City of Melbourne Police Department, here represented by Chief Inspector McElroy. It is the responsibility of the Kew Asylum and its representatives present to fully cooperate with the police investigation that will now begin.

Kew Asylum will hold the accused until a warrant is issued."

Coroner Wallace next looked at Nurse Kramer. "I trust you will care for and protect the accused until Chief McElroy has completed his investigation and takes custody."

Chief McElroy stepped aside as the first row filed out of the court. Edie walked on one side of Britina and Miss Sturgis on the other, her hand resting on Britina's arm. As Nurse Betty exited the bench, she turned toward McElroy, who stood and watched.

"May I speak with you?" she asked.

"Of course."

"In private."

They stepped out of the courtroom and around the side of the building.

"The nurses have access to the medical storage room and drug cabinets. Attendants do not. Sister Britina didn't have access. Nurse Kramer could have mentioned that. I gave Britina the pills—she couldn't sleep. Britina was shaken by the former attendant's suicide in her room. It upset her, and Nurse Kramer had lied to her. Nurse Karla and Nurse Verna told her—that's why she passed out, as they testified. My fear of being fired kept me from speaking up sooner, as I really need my job. But if I have to, I will."

The chief inspector nodded, studying her face. He looked around to make sure they were alone. "You've just confessed to a crime, but I appreciate you came to me. I'll keep it confidential for now." He hesitated. "Do you think Sister Britina could have killed Heather Stone?"

Nurse Betty shook her head, meeting his eyes. "I do not. It's not in her nature."

"Even if she was under the influence of a hypnotic drug and she was not fully aware?"

Nurse Betty hesitated. "At the asylum, we have frequent unexplained deaths—deaths that seldom get investigated, mostly among the paupers or refractory patients. We're expected to accept that this one, or that one, died in the night. I know that experimental treatments, which regular nurses cannot take part in, killed some patients. Others I don't know about. But I know patients disappear, and I know Britina could not have killed Heather Stone under any circumstances."

They paused as several spectators from the inquest rounded the corner and lit fags. Nurse Betty and McElroy moved farther along the wall. From there, they could hear the river.

McElroy tilted his head and looked directly at her. "Betty, does the coroner inspect these unexplained deaths?"

"Some. But usually, cemetery workers take patients with no family from the paupers' wings and bury them in unmarked graves. Nobody informs the coroner."

"What did you mean by 'regular nurses'?"

Betty's expression hardened. "We're not part of Nurse Kramer's inner circle. Those nurses assist with the experiments—and they rule their little kingdom. Kramer and Brookfield fired the few nurses who challenged them."

McElroy found her account of the asylum's operations deeply disturbing. His frown lines deepened. He considered whether to speak with the coroner, but decided he needed more information first.

"Nurse Betty, keep your eyes and ears open—and stay in touch with me. I want to know more about anything that might affect Sister Britina or point to illegal activities."

•

Edie tried to speak with Britina on the lawn after the proceedings, but Miss Sturgis took Britina by the arm and led her firmly to a waiting carriage. They departed for the asylum without a word. Through the carriage window, Edie glimpsed Britina's bowed head, clearly deep in prayer. *Doesn't seem to do much good*, Edie thought. *I need to get her side of the charges. We've exchanged maybe a dozen words. Maybe Raymond can help me get in to talk to her.*

•

The carriage entered the asylum grounds through the front gate, pulling up to the main entrance. Miss Sturgis would never consider entering through the cellar.

Sturgis escorted Britina back to her former room and let her walk in ahead of her. But Miss Sturgis did not follow—she shut the door behind Britina.

Britina turned to face the door. Her mouth fell open, and she stepped back, raising a hand to her lips. They had removed the door latch and replaced it with a solid metal plate. A slide bolt clicked into place from the outside—then a second.

She broke out in a sweat. Her breathing quickened. She stumbled to the bed and slumped down, dazed and trembling. Dizziness filled her head, and she fell back against the stone wall.

•

After Britina and Sturgis left, Edie looked around for Raymond. She spotted him coming around the side of the building with a woman in a nurse's uniform. She wasn't the only one who noticed; Head Nurse Kramer stood with a small group on the lawn, quietly observing.

McElroy introduced the woman as 'Nurse Betty Robinson' to Lady Black. He didn't offer further explanation.

Edie didn't wait for a better opportunity. "Raymond, I need to be involved in this investigation," she said, her voice urgent and pleading.

Betty excused herself and rejoined the other nurses, signaling for a cab to return to the asylum.

"I believe you're a close friend, Edie, and that's reason enough not to be involved," McElroy replied. "I can't allow it. Lawyers could challenge any evidence you found in court. It could work against Britina."

Edie protested, but the Mother Superior of the Sisters of Mercy interrupted them.

"Excuse me," she said. "Chief Inspector, I feel you should know that I've decided, under the circumstances, to revoke Britina Myers's novitiate status permanently. I do not want any publicity to include her religious name or mention of our order." Without waiting for a response, she turned and walked away.

Edie murmured, "Britina will be devastated."

She excused herself and wandered toward the lawn, spotting the nurses about to board a cab. She jogged toward the carriage.

"Excuse me, Nurse Betty, may I speak with you? I'll get a cab and ride with you to the asylum."

"You were here with the chief inspector," Betty said cautiously.

"Yes. I'm an investigator—I work with the chief inspector on cases." Edie held out her hand. "Lady Edith Black." She handed over a card.

Betty nodded and excused herself from her colleagues, telling them she'd see them back at work. Then, not realizing she shouldn't, Betty repeated everything she'd told McElroy.

"I promise to keep it confidential, Betty. I could use your help—both investigating the asylum's operations and helping clear Britina. We need to find out who really killed Heather Stone. If the asylum engages in illegal activities, those activities may be a threat to Britina and certainly need exposing."

Edie felt the sting of frustration. She didn't have access to

Britina, who now seemed trapped in the hands of those who might want her silenced to protect themselves. She had to get the facts. "Who at the asylum could help us and is trustworthy?" she asked Betty.

"Lady Black, I don't believe there's anyone there you can trust," Betty replied. "The few honest, hardworking staff are too afraid of Head Nurse Kramer and her squadron of enforcers to speak out. Britina knows she has no one to help her in that place—except me. And I can't do much."

"Call me Edie," she said. "Britina and I grew up together. Other than blood, we're sisters. I can't get in to talk to her—but maybe you can."

"I really doubt it. They won't give me access, and they'll watch me," Betty said, shaking her head.

"I don't know what we'll do yet," Edie admitted, "but I need an ally—someone to help me get to the truth. Will you be that ally?"

"I'll try," Nurse Betty said. "The chief inspector had me promise to keep him informed. I don't want to be charged with stealing drugs."

"Please keep this between us for now," Edie said. "I'll try to protect you if I can. If there's any evidence of illegal burials— that could help."

Edie feared for Britina. She felt trapped, helpless, and increasingly uneasy in her ability to do anything meaningful. She needed answers—but how was she going to get them?

CHAPTER 24

EDIE'S DILEMMA

The day after the inquest, McElroy paid a surprise visit to Edie's office. The bell over the door chimed as he entered. Edie rose to greet whoever had arrived but wasn't quick enough—McElroy was already stepping into her office.

"Stay seated, Edie," he said, taking the guest chair across from her desk without waiting for an invitation. "As I said at the coroner's court, I can't endorse your involvement in the investigation into Britina's guilt or innocence. You left with Nurse Betty. I suspect that wasn't just a courtesy. You could put Sergeant Kernot's investigation in jeopardy; I've put him in charge."

"That toad," Edie snapped. "He nearly knocked me down the stairs a few weeks ago and didn't even apologize. I think it was on purpose."

"Probably was," McElroy admitted. "It's a request of Chief Superintendent Cartwright. At least with one of the superintendent's men investigating, it might keep him off my case. Right now, he's threatening me daily if I don't resolve the Mace theft. That's in your hands—he doesn't know that, of course, but I need a resolution. He's ready for me to fail so he can get rid of me."

"Raymond, I'm sorry. I have made some progress. I

summarized everything in my memo to you—recommendations, too."

"Yes, sorry, I haven't had time to read it yet. Why don't you tell me?"

"All right," Edie said. "There are three theories about what happened to the Mace. One comes from Mr. Merrick, the tram driver. He claims to have seen Thomas Chester, the electrician, acting suspiciously the night the Mace went missing. We both visited Chester, and that's where that lead sits. It's possible Chester took it, but we have no proof.

"The second theory comes from a less-than-reputable reporter. He says two well-known crooks—mill or iron workers now in jail—took the Mace from an unnamed MP and transported it to the Maribyrnong River sugar refinery, where it was to be melted down. But somehow, it ended up in the river. No one's left at the refinery, and the crooks are inaccessible. Even if it's true, they're not likely to talk.

"My theory, the third one, is that someone transported it to Madam Wilson's brothel, where it became part of a night-long orgy. What happened to it after that is still a mystery, but that's the lead that deserves far more attention. I know the sergeant at arms is withholding details—he's outright lied to me. I can't haul him in, but you could. And given what we've uncovered about Heather Stone, I suspect that her assault may have been connected to the orgy. If so, investigating further might not just solve the Mace case—it might help find the assailant and help Britina, too.

"I recommended in the note," she added firmly, "that you apply pressure to Sergeant at Arms Chaloner and compel Madam Wilson's girls to talk. Get names, follow up. The next move is up to you."

Glaring, she leaned forward across her desk, her voice sharp.

She wasn't sure if she was truly angry with McElroy or simply reacting to the growing frustrations around Britina's situation.

McElroy sat silently, mouth ajar, his face flushed.

"Well?" Edie asked.

"I get your message," he said at last. "I'll get back to you—and I will keep you informed on the investigation into Britina's circumstances."

"Betty said there have been many patients that have gone missing over the years," Edie added. "Many undocumented. That's illegal. Burying them without records is illegal. If that's what's going on, Britina could be a threat—and that means she could be in danger."

"I'm working on taking custody as quickly as possible," McElroy replied. He couldn't help but wonder how he'd ended up being the one lectured instead of doing the lecturing. "The court wants to study the transcript of the inquest before issuing an arrest warrant."

Neither spoke further. McElroy stood, gave Edie a brief nod, and left her office with a clouded expression.

Once back at his own office, he called for Penn and closed his door behind him.

•

Constable Penn stood at attention in front of McElroy's desk. McElroy didn't invite him to sit.

"Penn, you did decent work. I've just reread your report. I have one complaint—you don't have a description of the man from the alley. Did you ask the two witnesses?"

"I did—I think I did."

"Your report says the man grabbed one of them and pulled his face to his. He should be able to describe it."

"Yes, sir. I think I forgot."

"Penn, always get descriptions."

"Yes, sir."

McElroy still felt the sting of his encounter with Edie. He also knew that if something didn't break soon, he could be out of a job and walking the streets. He wanted to push Penn harder, but it wasn't the petty constable's fault.

"Witnesses often remember additional details after a few days. Go back, dig a little deeper, and get a description."

"Yes, sir."

"Did the alley get cleaned out and searched?"

"I had two men clean it out and wheelbarrow the rubbish into a dumping area. I hired a couple of urchins to sort through it—handful by handful. They were glad to earn a few shillings. It's slow work, but I expect it will be finished by tomorrow. I'll check on them after I re-interview the brothers."

·

Edie didn't care if Raymond disapproved. She needed to take action—police procedures were simply too slow. She'd arranged to meet Nurse Betty after her shift at 7:00 p.m. the next day, asking her to monitor Britina and watch for anything suspicious at the asylum, related to the investigation or otherwise. Having Kernot involved might at least keep Britina safe, she hoped. She had the beginnings of a plan, and with Benji headed back to Adelaide, she had a little more time.

Early the next morning, Edie packed a wicker basket with supplies she anticipated needing. She waited on the porch for the cab she had arranged, which took her to her office. There, she stored the basket to be picked up later.

She walked to Dutch Hammil's office and asked him to take a walk with her. A light breeze stirred the market, making the tents flap like birds' wings. The scents of fresh food and flowers mingled in the air. As they strolled the stall market, Edie explained the dire situation she was now in. "Dutch, with the way the inquest went, they'll prosecute her for murder by euthanasia. She could hang."

"If they deem it a mercy killing, she might avoid the gallows—but the court could commit her to an asylum for the criminally insane. That might not be any better."

She stopped walking and turned to face him. "Oh, Dutch. . . ." Her voice broke. She cleared her throat. "That can't happen. Britina needs the best representation if she goes to trial. I have the money. I can pay."

"Edie, I manage your financial affairs—I know you can. The very best for a murder trial would be Barrister Quill. I'll speak with him, but he won't want to take the case unless there's substantial evidence pointing to acquittal. He won't argue just for a reduced sentence. And I'm sorry, Edie, but from what I've read, the evidence looks very convincing."

"I know she didn't do it."

"How do you know that?"

"She told me."

"That's not evidence, Edie—and you know it."

"I know Britina's heart. She could not have done it."

"A mercy killing could come from the heart, too—but it's still murder."

Edie hung her head. It was up to her now. She needed answers—and she had to get them herself.

•

Edie's next stop was Walter's carriage rental, where she'd done business for a couple of years.

"Walter, I need a specific type of carriage for a couple of days. It should be a single-horse carriage with a small, two-person enclosed cabin and a box seat up front for the driver. I've seen them occasionally—I don't want to be visible inside."

"Edie, you're describing a Brougham carriage," Walter replied with a knowing smile. "They built it to Lord Brougham of London's specifications. A favorite of Sherlock Holmes, if I recall. I have one."

"Oh, wonderful. Do the windows have shades or blinds?"

"The side windows do. The front window doesn't."

"That'll work." Edie selected a small, sturdy mare with a calm disposition named Elouise. She paid for two full days and nights in advance.

Placing a cloth bag of food she'd bought during her market walk with Dutch inside the passenger compartment, she drove the carriage to her office, retrieved the wicker basket, and stored it inside. She scribbled a note to Bart explaining she'd be away for a night or two and dropped it back at the market with a delivery lad, to be included in Bart's evening grocery order.

Later, Edie rang the bell at the front door of Bordello Boccaccio. A young woman in a nightgown answered—not yet fully into the evening's work. Early in the life of a prostitute, Edie thought. Or a comfort worker, she corrected with a small smile.

Annie Wilson was waiting in the kitchen, a tea service set on a small dining table. "The girls are still cleaning the other rooms," she said. "I thought this would serve for now. Tea?"

Edie nodded and accepted a cup, adding a cube of sugar but no milk.

They had already been through distasteful business together, so Edie chose a more familiar tone. "Annie, I understand the need to protect your clients' identities. But I need to solve the Mace incident—and I know the answer lies here in your house. I'm not police. I can keep what I learn confidential, but I need to bring justice to where it belongs."

She paused, then added with conviction, "It starts with the beating. The answer to who assaulted Heather lies in identifying one man who was here that night. We need more information from Estelle, and she needs your permission to speak openly. I think she may help."

"Edie, the police have already talked to Estelle. She told them what she could."

"She may know things without realizing they're important—bits and pieces that could help identify or eliminate suspects. I know she recalls more names than she is willing to provide, because you've told her to keep them secret."

Annie considered, then nodded slowly. "I trust you, Edie. Protecting my innocent clients is mandatory, but if you believe one of the men here assaulted Heather, I'll allow Estelle to be questioned again. She's away at the moment, but I'll arrange a meeting when she returns."

Edie was disappointed Estelle wasn't available now and wouldn't be for a while. "Thank you. I'll ask Penn or the chief inspector to follow up once she's back."

•

She still had time before meeting Nurse Betty, so she drove to the Parliament House and marched straight to the sergeant at arms' office. He wasn't there, so she directed one of the staff to find him. She took a seat in his office.

Chaloner wasn't in the mood to deal with Lady Black again. "What do you want now?" he said as he entered his office.

Edie found that offensive and felt an urge to knock him off his pedestal. She took a deep breath and tried to instill her voice with a tone of authority. "Mr. Chaloner, I should be here with the chief inspector, arresting you for providing false information, withholding evidence, and, frankly, lying to me. You know that's a crime in a criminal investigation, don't you? I've decided to give you an opportunity."

He remained stone-faced, but Edie noticed a protective shift in his eyes. "Would you care to explain yourself?" he said.

"I would." She needed to project confidence, even though she was fishing for confirmation. "Mr. Chaloner, on the night of the Mace theft, you entertained MPs, members of your staff, prostitutes, and a drug dealer named Henderson in your room. I'm not sure if the Speaker was there—you may add that to my information, if you will."

Chaloner blinked rapidly. "He was not." His demeanor shifted; his expression became chagrined. He had just admitted to lying.

That confirms a couple of things, Edie thought. "Shall I continue?"

Chaloner hesitated, his defenses crumbling.

"You and some of your group moved from your rooms to Little Lon and the bordello owned by Annie Wilson. And before you make any assumptions, she is not my source. In fact, she was silent on the matter when questioned. I understand she wasn't present during the orgy that followed."

Chaloner gulped audibly, then tried to cover it by clearing his throat. "Where are you headed with this, Miss Black?"

Edie noted the use of "Miss" instead of "Lady" or "Madam." He was trying to regain ground.

"One person in that room took one of Madam Wilson's girls—her niece, in fact—and beat her into a coma. She never recovered. Before her death, which was assisted, possibly to cover up the assault and attempted rape, she named no one. Mr. Chaloner, by your actions and your cover-up, you are currently a suspect."

"What!" he said, his face twitching with several nervous tics. His complexion had gone ashen. Edie noticed his hands trembling as he held one over the other. "You can't believe—"

"I most certainly can. Unless you can give me a reason not to. As of now, you're my primary suspect."

Chaloner hesitated, trying to collect himself. He met her gaze.

"Lady Black, I resent the implication, and I'm tired of your interference in my work. If you have evidence, use it. If not, leave me alone." He sounded more frightened than angry.

"Resent all you want. You sent someone for the Mace. I have testimony."

That hit the mark—she could see it.

"I must serve the MPs," he said. "I was being pressured by colleagues and others, so yes—I sent Donavon. Donavon knew where I kept the keys. His instructions were to return the Mace before morning. He was a bit inebriated when he left, but still competent. I think he passed out when he returned with the Mace. It became . . . something else. The women treated it like a magic wand. They passed it around, singing and dancing. When the song ended, whoever held the Mace chose one of the nearby men and disappeared with him to a chamber."

His hands were visibly shaking. Sweat beaded on his brow. "It was a mistake, but doesn't make me guilty of beating . . ."

Edie interrupted. She couldn't resist. "When were you chosen, Mr. Chaloner?"

Chaloner hung his head, then looked up and met her eyes. His gaze was filled with fear. "I never was. I was on the floor and passed out. When I woke up, there was no one there."

"What happened to the Mace?" Edie asked.

"I don't know. It wasn't there when I came to. Donavon was gone, too—everyone was. I assumed he had returned it."

"Mr. Chaloner, who withheld the information that the Mace

was missing for four days?"

"I did."

"Thank you for your honesty," Edie said in a barbed tone. "I need to know everything you know about everyone at that orgy. Hold nothing back because if you're innocent of the assault, as you claim, then someone else from your group is responsible. Finding and proving who did it is the only way to prove your innocence. Finding the Mace would be a bonus. Now, tell me about that evening and those who were there. I'll know if you're lying."

Edie took notes for over half an hour, gently coaxing more details when the flow stalled. She had opened the spigot—names and details poured out. She was sure they were accurate; no one could make up this much this quickly.

Edie was now running late for her meeting with Nurse Betty. She wished she had time to share what she'd learned with Raymond, but that would have to wait. She stuffed her notebook into her bag. Reclaiming her horse and carriage from the Parliament stable manager, she hurried toward the asylum, feeling competent and solid in her role as an investigator. She had a list of suspects that would lead her to the assailant—and to the Mace. The puzzle picture was becoming clearer. Now she needed to exonerate Britina.

•

Betty flagged Edie down near the top of the hill leading to the asylum. She waited by the roadside with her bicycle. "Let's park in the cemetery until dark. I'll fill you in on what I've learned. I'll meet you there." She mounted her bicycle and coasted downhill.

Edie turned the carriage around and drove to the foot of the hill near the Yarra River Asylum cemetery. She parked on a grassy rise near a stand of pine trees. Betty was already there.

The nurse glanced at the fresh mound of dirt where Heather Stone was buried. A twinge of unease flickered through her. It hadn't had time to settle, and nothing had yet grown over it. It looked raw—haunting. Betty shivered, then broke the silence. "Here's your parcel." She handed over a paper-wrapped package.

Edie couldn't share what she'd learned—at least not yet. That would have to wait until after the asylum, when she could get to Raymond.

"Britina," Betty began, "is being treated as a criminal patient but held in her old room—not in the cells. She's locked in and only escorted outside by Miss Sturgis for one hour a day. I don't think they had time to fit a proper lock, so two slide bolts hold her door locked. It's accessible, but if you plan to see her, be careful. The unbolted locks are very visible.

"Head Nurse Kramer knows she's being watched by the police, so she's careful. The lead investigator, Kernot, has interviewed Britina twice. He interviewed me, too—seems like a clod."

"He is!" Edie interjected.

"I think they might be done with their investigation. I saw Kernot sitting in Kramer's office, going over a stack of papers. Dr. Brookfield joined them. Kernot was nodding a lot, laughed a little, but also talked. I couldn't stay long, but he and his team left soon after. Now that they're gone, I fear Kramer could be a threat to Britina."

Edie decided that sharing her notes couldn't wait any longer. "Betty, I'm going to give you my notebook and ask you to deliver it to Chief Inspector McElroy's office after you get me into position." She added a paragraph to the end of her last entry and handed the notebook to Betty.

"I'll do it, but what should I say if they ask why you aren't delivering it?"

"McElroy won't be there that late. Constable Lyle will be

on the desk. Tell him it's from me and for the chief inspector's eyes only."

Betty took two folded papers from her uniform and spread them out on the cemetery grass where Britina had stood during the burial. Edie watched.

"This is a rough layout of the property. We'll enter through the rear gate here. We'll have to get the attendant—Rodney is his name—to let us in. His cottage is right next to the gate, but I've already spoken with him. I told him I needed to store my rich uncle's carriage and mare while he visits from Sydney." She shrugged and smiled. "It was the best I could come up with. Doesn't matter. He does favors for us nurses, and we tip him.

"When we're in, I'll drive to the barn over here, on the far side of the central storage and kitchen building. I'll park the carriage and take care of your horse."

"Her name's Elouise," Edie said. A flicker of concern crossed her face. "If Rodney catches me, what will he do?"

"Turn you in. He knows the nurses, but not you."

Edie frowned and dropped her gaze to the ground, disappointed. A friend inside would've been helpful.

Betty noticed. She jabbed her finger at the map. "Pay attention—you need this information."

Edie smiled at the scolding and refocused.

"This extensive building is the central wing. It divides the men's and women's sections and their courtyards. The back has loading bays—this is where deliveries come in. It's visible from the attendants' cottages, so be careful back here. The building is tall, with heavy steel lintels at the roof peak and block and tackle to haul goods up into second-floor storage.

"Over here are two barns for storage—one is where your carriage will go. The property spans over twenty-five acres, so don't wander. Some walled-off sections are to confine patients.

To reach the women's wards and rooms, you need to go the full length of the storage area, then the kitchens and dining rooms, before reaching the wings. You'll have to be extremely careful here—don't get spotted."

Edie nodded, overwhelmed.

"Britina's room is down this corridor." Betty pointed to the second map, which detailed the interior. "I'll come for you and the carriage tomorrow."

"Thank you, Betty. First, I want to get evidence of patient abuse. Where are the experimental treatments done?"

"Oh—I forgot! When treatment happens, they take patients below the storage area and kitchen. There's a door in the kitchen that leads down. There's also a rope platform lift that connects all three levels for moving supplies. Staff lower patients and beds there. A second door leads to the upper floor. A large cellar was dug out below—it used to be a root cellar when the patients did more farming."

"They bring patients through the kitchen for treatment? That's surprising," Edie said.

"I think it was the only space available. Part of it's still used for storing fresh vegetables from vendors. But I've heard an extensive section is walled off for research and education. The kitchen stairs lead straight into the research facility. It's kept locked, though."

Edie took the maps, folded them neatly, and tucked them into her bag.

"We better be off," Betty said.

Edie crawled into the small storage space beneath the passenger seat in the enclosed carriage. Betty covered her with blankets, then placed Edie's market bag, the wicker basket, and the parcel she'd brought on top. As a final touch, she wedged her bicycle tightly against the front wall of the compartment.

"You okay in there?" she asked.

"I can't move, but I'll be fine—just don't forget I'm here."

Betty climbed onto the exterior driver's seat and guided the carriage up the hill and around the perimeter of the asylum to the rear entrance. She pulled up before the closed timber gates, which were set into a massive stone gateway. Reaching for the pull cord, she rang the bell for Rodney.

CHAPTER 25

ASYLUM ARRIVALS

Several times a year, Thaddeus Snow had to close his medical and surgical practice for a few days to attend to matters in Melbourne. These trips included training assemblies for junior doctors in collaboration with Dr. Bran Brookfield. He tried to schedule patients around these absences. He wasn't concerned about losing patients—his practice was primarily a means to an end, though at the moment, it was a distraction from other pursuits. Still, it provided important credentials he needed to protect.

The medical training sessions with Brookfield were lucrative. The profession desperately needed trained surgeons, and there were no formal schools for anatomy in Australia. Hospitals across the country, as well as some foreign institutions enrolled in the program, assured that the Brookfield and Snow operation had established legal channels to provide enough cadavers for students to learn surgery through dissection, the required method.

The current production run of laudanum had consumed a week of nights, and both he and Asa needed a rest before leaving for Melbourne. He went over Asa's assignments with him to make sure he understood what he was about to do. An apothecary clerk would feed and walk the dogs while he and Asa were away.

After a late morning, Thaddeus went shopping for supplies and a recent novel; he hadn't had the leisure of reading in far too long. He took a long walk to Sydney City and, after tea, visited the bookseller Angus & Robertson. Speaking with the proprietor—an acquaintance from the Australian Club—he chose what he deemed an appropriate title. The proprietor had just imported copies of a new Robert Louis Stevenson book titled *The Strange Case of Dr. Jekyll and Mr. Hyde*. From the description, he felt it would be a most fitting diversion for the train trip to Melbourne.

He met Asa in the stables behind the surgery the next morning. They went over a checklist that included everything from feedbags and oats for the horses to the quantity of laudanum packed in wooden crates, along with the opium they had processed and stored earlier in the month. He also made sure Asa had gathered all the tools needed.

"Asa, you did a good job. When we get to the train station, we'll load the carriage and the horses into the freight car assigned"—he looked at the reservation—"freight car three. Once loaded, keep the wagon locked, and in the evening, lock yourself inside. You've packed food and water for yourself, haven't you?"

"Yes, sir. And I will feed and water the horses at the stated times."

"Good lad." Thaddeus handed Asa a bag of sweets for the trip.

"Oh, thank you, sir." Asa bounced in place, covering a slight smile with his hand. "I can't wait."

"A little at a time, Asa. I don't have bellyache medicine with me."

They drove the horses and wagon to the Sydney terminal early. It was already bustling with activity. The smell of burning wood and coal permeated the air, carrying with it bits of ash and soot. It mingled with the odor of hot oil and grease used to lubricate the magnificent machines. To Thaddeus, it was inspiring—all that power.

Multiple steam locomotives were arriving, leaving, and waiting on tracks. At their assigned location, their locomotive released a large hiss of steam that rose in a white cloud toward the roof of the station. On the trains preparing to leave, the driving pistons were building pressure, ready to move the mass of steel and cargo.

Thaddeus and Asa coaxed the horses into the railcar. Asa settled the horses in stalls, and chains and clamps secured the wagon to floor rings to prevent it from moving during the passage.

"Remember, Asa, lock the door from inside when you get in for the night. Let no one near the wagon."

"Yes, sir." Asa nodded, clutching his bag of sweets.

"We will spend the night at Albury because of the break of gauge. We will change trains to accommodate the rails. Porters will move the wagon and horses. You stay locked in the wagon. I will switch sleeping cars. I will bring you food when we are once again moving."

Thaddeus left him and wandered off to enjoy the excitement of the hustling crowd and lively activities. The terminal buzzed with a diverse mix of people, all scurrying in different directions; now and then, two would bump into each other, distracted by thoughts elsewhere. Departing trains blew their whistles before pulling away from the station, then slowly built momentum, chugging steadily along the rails. Porters bustled through the terminal, moving loads of luggage and cargo, making sure each piece reached its proper train, storage room, or freight car.

This was Thaddeus's favorite place. He paused at vendor

kiosks, picking up the day's papers, two cigars, and some dried mango fruit. As he stepped aside to avoid a young couple locked in a tight embrace—a reunion after some absence, he assumed— he smiled to himself.

Thaddeus boarded his first-class compartment directly from the platform, helped by a conductor. The man handed his bags to him with a polite, "Have a pleasant trip, sir," then secured the door behind him.

The accommodations were most inviting. Rich wood paneling and plush upholstery adorned the room. Thaddeus ran his fingers along the intricately carved moldings, then placed his suitcase on the seats and set his medical bag on the small, polished wood table in the corner.

He began reading his book as the train pulled away from the station, but soon found himself drawn to the passing rural landscape as they moved farther from the city. After a while, he turned his attention to preparing for the upcoming training assembly, going over his notes with quiet focus.

•

Upon arrival at Melbourne Central Station, Thaddeus and Asa unloaded the wagon and horses with help from two rail porters assigned to freight. Thaddeus then drove to a warehouse he had purchased on Flinders Lane, near the station.

"Asa, unlock the doors and brace them back against the outer walls."

Asa jumped down from the driver's bench, unlocked the two large wooden doors, and swung them open. Thaddeus drove the wagon into the dark warehouse. Asa ran ahead and lit the lanterns, then closed and secured the doors behind them.

They began unloading the boxes of laudanum, stacking them neatly onto sections of the wooden shelves lining the walls, organized by date of manufacture. One section of shelving bore slips with customer names—these shelves were for pre-orders that Henderson would deliver. Henderson had already arranged the corresponding products and quantities, and had sold and distributed a significant amount of the previous deliveries. Only he and Thaddeus had the keys to the cabinets securing opium and morphine.

They made their way to the small office, where Thaddeus placed a dated inventory sheet into the existing folder. He made a mental note: the product was moving faster than it was being produced. With shipments also going to England, he realized he would need to double production—but he wasn't sure how.

It was late afternoon before they finished unloading and organizing the inventory. Thaddeus reviewed records he required Henderson to keep; all was in order. They left the warehouse and headed for a favorite pub for an early dinner. It would be a long night. Asa cherished these opportunities to be with Dr. Snow, just one on one, like father and son.

In the early evening, they traveled to the asylum. Rodney, the rear entrance gatekeeper and caretaker, knew them well. They passed through the gate and drove to the far side of the central building, pulling into the open barn area.

•

Edie lay still under the blanket until Betty safely parked the carriage in the small barn attached to the central wing of the asylum, then removed her bicycle.

"Edie, stay where you are for a while. Are you more comfortable without the bicycle?"

"Not really comfortable; I'm a little too nervous, but I'm all right. Thank you for helping me."

"There's a large wooden wagon next to your carriage; you can only get out the left door. I'm going to check it out."

Betty found she couldn't see into the wagon, and the doors were locked. There were two large stallions, each in their own stall, so she put Eloise in the center stall, separating her from the beasts on either side.

"I'd stay, but I couldn't explain why to my husband—he's not very understanding."

"It's better if I do this alone. And it's important that you get my notebook to police headquarters."

"You might have company, but no one's here now. Just . . . be careful."

Edie had her head uncovered and looked at Betty. "It's all right. You've done so much already. I'll be careful." She cleared her throat. "I'll be fine. If I'm successful, I'll have proof of patient abuse—and something from Britina that might help clear her name. When you pick me up, we'll take everything to police headquarters."

Betty reached out and gently touched Edie's shoulder under the blanket. "I'll be worrying about you the whole time."

When Betty had pedaled off, Edie checked the door locks, then lay quiet for half an hour in case the gate attendant checked on Betty's cart and horse. When no one appeared, she climbed out of her blanket cocoon and lit a candle from her basket. She peeked at the massive wagon next to her, then turned to tend her own cart. The curtains on the side windows needed sealing, and she used a little soft wax from the candle as an adhesive to ensure they were closed well enough to keep anyone from peering in. She applied additional wax to the four corners of a towel and used it to cover the front window. Only then could she settle in until the later hours, when the world outside would quiet down. She unpacked a small picnic from the food she'd bought at the market.

I wish this was a real picnic with Benji.

Edie heard people entering the barn. She could make out the murmur of conversation, but couldn't hear the words. She quickly blew out her candle.

•

A small Brougham carriage and a horse in one stall surprised Thaddeus. While Asa rearranged tools and added items to the wagon, Thaddeus inspected the carriage. He found the doors locked and couldn't see inside. He could break in, but that would be awkward if it belonged to Brookfield, Kramer, or someone else with permission to use the barn.

"Asa, you stay here. I'll get the laboratory set up and Dr. Brookfield will arrive soon. I'll meet with him and then return. Do you have everything in place?

"I'm set to go. I'll have everything ready."

"Good lad!"

"You know when to show up later after our training?"

"Yes, sir."

Edie recognized the deeper voice—it sounded like Rohwedder. *What in the hell is he doing here?*

Snow left the barn and walked to the back of the large central building. Someone had opened the doors just enough for a person to enter or exit. He trekked through the storage area to the internal dock, where delivery wagons backed up for unloading. He took the steps next to the rope elevator used for heavy deliveries and transporting goods to the dock and the level above.

He continued through the kitchen and dining areas into the central core of the asylum until he encountered Dr. Brookfield in the corridor. They greeted each other and entered Head Nurse Kramer's office without knocking. Head Nurse Kramer, Miss Sturgis, and two nurses from the trusted team—Nurse Ashley and Nurse Ralphine—sat waiting.

Dr. Brookfield began. "We will conduct our training for five young medical students that I have selected. All are from prominent hospitals; one is from America. I've collected the required tuition." He placed an envelope on Nurse Kramer's desk.

Thaddeus spoke. "Asa is making preparations."

"He'll make sure he's not seen?" Brookfield said.

"Of course. He's very careful," Thaddeus replied, looking irritated. *This isn't our first time.*

"Excellent," Brookfield said. "The students arrived yesterday and are touring the Royal Melbourne Hospital today. When they arrive here this evening, I have some preliminaries to go over with them. The demonstrations will begin at 1:00 a.m."

CHAPTER 26

WITNESSES

When Chief Inspector McElroy arrived at his office the next morning, Constable Frank greeted him from behind his counter. "Notebook left for you in the night, sir. A nurse named Betty dropped it off with Constable Lyle and said it was from Edie. I deduced it was from Lady Black—said it was for your eyes only. Oh, and Constable Penn came in early; he's waiting for you in your office."

Penn was standing at attention when he entered.

"Constable Penn, have you been standing the whole time you've been waiting?"

"Yes, sir. I didn't think it proper to sit in your office without being asked."

"Why didn't you wait at your desk?"

"Sir, I've had others questioning me about what you're up to and what I'm doing for you. I don't think that's proper, and today, I didn't want to face that. They can often tell when I'm lying."

McElroy pictured Penn turning beet-red in a matter of seconds, like he was now. He wondered how someone like him had gotten into police work. "Tell me why you're here, Penn."

"Sir, I have a description of the man from the witnesses." He handed McElroy a written note. "But there's more. One brother recalled seeing a second man as they left to find a constable. He glanced over his shoulder and saw a man walking alone toward the alley, carrying a large parcel. As he looked back again, he saw that man drop the parcel, grab the man in the alley, and toss him into the street. He then checked on the lady as the alley man stumbled off. The second man left the alley, looked around, picked up his parcel, and walked off quickly."

"Do you have a description of the second man?" McElroy asked.

"There on the sheet, Chief Inspector—though it's vague."

"Thank you, Penn."

"There's a little more, Chief Inspector."

Penn held out his hand and opened his fist. In it sat a large emerald. "This was found in the trash near the alley. I think one urchin had his eye on keeping it. He had it in his pocket when I arrived yesterday, but the first urchin mentioned it right away when I got there."

"We can assume it belongs to the Mace. I'll ask Lady Black to check with her contacts. Penn, you haven't mentioned to the other constables that Lady Black is investigating for me, have you?"

"No, sir."

"Penn, see if the artist we use can create a likeness from the description."

"Yes, sir."

"Lady Black had a notebook delivered this morning. I need to read it now. Not sure why she didn't bring it herself—unless she didn't want to be seen here anymore. I'll get back to you, Penn. We may have some fieldwork to do later today."

·

McElroy opened the notebook and read. Edie mentioned trying

to interview Estelle, but having to postpone. In detailing her last conversation with Chaloner, Edie had compiled a list of twelve men who attended the orgy. She also noted Chaloner's admission that he ordered Donavon to bring the Mace from Parliament. *Good progress,* McElroy thought.

Then he read she suspected Chaloner was covering up details to protect himself. 'I claimed he was our primary suspect in the assault,' she had written. Not standard police procedure, but she wasn't the police.

The last paragraph struck a different tone. She wrote she had to help Britina somehow—'because friends don't abandon friends.' McElroy wasn't sure what she was planning, but it certainly didn't involve taking his orders.

Chief Inspector McElroy called Penn back into his office.

"Penn, Edie has taken extensive notes from her interview with Chaloner. She thinks he's been covering up, but she got a list of attendees at the orgy, some just descriptions. Chaloner is fabricating a story to avoid any implication of guilt."

He paused and looked at a page in Edie's notebook, then continued.

"He admits to being there and says the gathering began in his office after sessions on the ninth. Chaloner sent his aide—what is his name?" He glanced at the notebook. "Donavon! He sent Donavon to fetch the Mace, disguise it, bring it to the orgy, then return it to Parliament before morning. That alone is an admission of guilt in its disappearance, but it doesn't implicate him in the attack. Chaloner claims he passed out on the floor at the brothel and didn't wake until morning. When he did, he says he was alone—the Mace, Donavon, and the others were all gone.

"You mentioned one prostitute, Estelle, spent the night on the floor in the same room and was the only witness." McElroy paused, then looked at Penn. "Lady Black also suggested we speak with Estelle again, thoroughly this time. Get a detailed account of the last people to leave. Try to match up pairs from the selection game. If the attacker wasn't Chaloner, then it's likely another man who wasn't paired with a prostitute. If Estelle can recall enough detail, we can narrow down who might have ended up with Heather Stone."

"Are we going together, sir?" Penn asked, looking visibly nervous at the thought of returning to the bordello.

"Yes, Penn. And I think we should also re-interview your two witnesses—try to pin down the timeline. What were their names again?"

"Otis and Fritz Schneider, sir. They're brothers. They own the Shady Lane, a small, somewhat seedy pub in an alley near the site of the beating."

•

There were no police carriages left in the stable, so McElroy and Penn hailed a hansom cab to take them to Bordello Boccaccio. The driver gave them a knowing smile. "I know the way," he said.

Madam Wilson hesitated when she realized it wasn't Edie requesting to interview Estelle. McElroy assured her he would keep the names of innocent parties confidential, and if they couldn't speak with Estelle now, they would get an order to bring her to headquarters for questioning. Wilson relented. They gathered in the room where the orgy had taken place—Madam Wilson insisted on being present.

McElroy and Penn found Estelle fuzzy at first, but after a few cups of tea, her memory cleared.

"Estelle, you've been very helpful. Thank you. A few more details might help us find who attacked Heather," McElroy said. "Can you tell us who the men teamed up with?"

Estelle looked at Madam Wilson and received a nod.

"I miss Heather. She was very kind to me." Estelle closed her eyes to think and didn't respond for several minutes.

Penn and McElroy waited. McElroy thought she might have fallen asleep.

Finally, she said, "I had to go over it in my mind." Then she began.

"I recall his name now—it was MP Clark. A young, thin, good-looking chap. He was first. Everyone clapped for him. He went upstairs with Megan—she's young, pretty, and, well, you know, well-formed."

Penn instantly turned red.

Estelle continued. "A man not originally with the group when it arrived was second. He teamed up with Brill. I didn't get his name—he showed up at the bordello after the party had started and asked if he could join in. Two other men were joiners too, stumbled onto the orgy, but I didn't recognize them either."

This will make identification more difficult, McElroy thought.

Penn and McElroy waited for her to continue. After hesitating, she did. Madam Wilson sat motionless, listening.

"The third chosen was the second MP, named Arthur. Middle-aged. Rebecca picked him—one of our more senior ladies. She's cautious, prefers someone familiar and safe. Arthur had visited before."

Estelle went through a few more names. Penn noted her comments carefully.

Her recollection slowed. McElroy poured more tea into her cup.

"What about the drug dealer, Henderson?" he asked.

"He's a strange one," Estelle said. "I've seen him here a few times. Not bad-looking. He didn't partake of the drugs—just went and got them. Had a couple of beers. Heather Stone chose him early, but he turned her down. He just sat in the corner and watched."

McElroy wrinkled his forehead, puzzled, and made a note in his notebook. *Edie has had previous business with Henderson—wonder how he became involved.*

"Did he stay the whole night?" McElroy asked.

"I don't know when he left—it might have been while I was asleep—but I think once the room emptied, except for me, he left."

"Estelle, it's important we talk about Mr. Chaloner and Donavon. Do you know who they are?"

"Oh yes. Sometimes, we receive invitations to small gatherings at Parliament. I've met both several times."

"Good," McElroy said. "Can you tell us anything about them that night?"

"A little. It was Donavon who went to get the magic wand. Chaloner sent him."

"What happened when he returned?"

"Well, the drugging had already started a little before the wand arrived. The ladies are careful not to overindulge in drinks and usually avoid the drugs, but the men were smoking and drinking heavily. Some ladies partook." She glanced at Madam Wilson. "I wish I hadn't. The ladies laid down the rules for the selection game, picked a record, and placed it on the gramophone, but they couldn't get it to work at first.

"When Donavon came back, he brought a new man with him, an electrician from Parliament. I hadn't met him before, but I think his name was Tom—or Thomas. I don't know his last name, but I spoke to him a bit. He was interested in me, but I discouraged him. I told him I had the clap—that always works. He got the gramophone working. Once it was going, all the ladies started singing and dancing, having fun. It was kind of like musical chairs—when the music stopped, the one holding the magic wand got to choose her partner for the night."

"Her sex partner?" Penn asked.

"You're cute," Estelle said with a little smile.

"What happened to Tom or Thomas after you rejected him?" McElroy asked.

"The last I remember, he took two hits on the pipe and crossed the room. I don't recall seeing him again. It was still early—I think he just left."

"What about Donavon?" Penn asked, still blushing, trying to refocus.

"He started smoking and dancing. Looked like he was having a good time."

"He didn't pass out?" McElroy asked.

"He was a little drunk, but he didn't pass out while I was watching. He was full of energy and enjoying himself."

"Did he get chosen?"

"I think he did. I think it was Rachel—she's a real spunky one. Everyone likes her."

We need to get to Chaloner, McElroy thought. *We're not going to be able to pair everyone up.* He glanced at Madam Wilson, who nodded, her hands folded in her lap.

"What about Chaloner? What happened to him?" McElroy asked.

"He's usually pretty contained when we've met at Parliament rooms, but that night, he was fuddled."

"Alcohol or opium?"

"Both. He wasn't in good shape. I think he wet himself at one point. Some were laughing at him, but he might've just spilled a drink. He didn't seem to notice." Estelle chuckled at the memory, then coughed and took out a handkerchief to wipe her mouth.

McElroy felt they were close to something valuable. He was

eager to get back to Chaloner. "Did he get chosen?"

"Sort of. He was really out of it. Heather went through the motions of choosing him. She helped him out of the room, out the side door, and escorted him home to his Parliament residence—or at least that was the plan. We do that sometimes when our regulars need help."

"He didn't spend the night passed out on the floor?"

"No. When I woke up, it was MP Clark asleep on the floor."

"You're sure?" Penn asked.

Estelle gave him a sharp look. "I wouldn't tell you unless I was sure."

"Sorry," Penn said.

McElroy smiled to himself. Penn was learning.

•

McElroy and Penn regrouped outside the bordello after thanking Estelle and Madam Wilson.

"Nice job, Penn. The pieces are coming together. Let's find your bar owner witnesses."

Penn led the way, quietly enjoying the compliment. McElroy and Penn found Fritz and Otis cleaning the porch that served as the entrance to their converted cottage, now the Shady Lane Pub. It was a small but busy watering hole in a dark alley near the scene of the beating. As the men approached, the two brothers were bickering about something and took little notice until Penn and McElroy were standing on the porch steps.

"Sorry," Otis said, "didn't see you coming. It's not a good start to the evening unless we can fight over something."

"You fight over everything," Fritz said to his brother. "I have a great idea, and you just start finding every way you can to put it down."

"Gentlemen," Penn said, "this is my boss, Chief Inspector McElroy. He wants to question you about the night someone attacked the lady in the alley."

Otis hesitated, but spoke first. "The lady didn't act like she wanted to be here with the man. He had his hand tight on her upper arm. He was squeezing it hard—I could see she was in pain."

"She looked a little frightened but didn't show she needed help. Perhaps scared to say so," Fritz added.

"I refused to serve him; he'd had enough already. Told him it was past closing time. He grabbed my collar and pulled me forward, without letting go of the lady," Otis recounted. "I gave them two beers and sent them away. He was strong," Otis said, rubbing his neck.

McElroy asked, "Did his skin have a yellow tinge?"

"I saw his face close up—enormous nose—but no, it was bright red. Even his eyes looked red. I didn't notice any yellow."

"You're color-blind!" Fritz interjected.

"I see yellow," his brother retorted.

"You don't see red."

"You told me his face and eyes were red."

"Gentlemen," McElroy said, "will you go back to before you noticed the attack and recount your actions?"

They thought for a moment. Fritz began, "I had forgotten this, but earlier in the evening, I wandered out to Little Bourke Street to have a smoke and see whether there might be any customers coming. Off to my right, I saw a figure coming our way, carrying a long parcel resting on his shoulder. He was quite a way off then."

"Which direction was that, Fritz?"

"He was coming from the far end of Bourke Street—coming from Spring Street. He was a little unsteady, but made good progress. Someone had wrapped the parcel in white cloth, it seemed."

"Was there anyone with this person?" McElroy asked.

"There was a man close behind him, but I don't know if they were together."

"Could you see the alley from where you were?"

"A ways away, yes, but nothing was happening then. It was much later when I saw the same person break up the encounter. Or I guess it was the same person—because of the parcel."

"You could see the end of the alley and the man at a distance when you were standing on Little Bourke Street?"

"That's correct."

"When you saw the man the second time, was he heading in the opposite direction? And was he more stable?"

"Yes, sir, now that you mention it. Thinking back, they were going in opposite directions. And it wasn't the same man—the second was steadier and taller."

"Fritz, did you take more than one trip to Little Bourke Street that night?"

"He took several," his brother answered. "He's always out there smoking—nasty things."

McElroy and Penn thanked the brothers, who returned to their bickering as the officers walked away.

"What did you learn, Penn?"

"A few more details and a description, sir."

"Right. I'm assuming Heather Stone completed her rescue mission and delivered Mr. Chaloner back to his rooms in Parliament, then was returning home when she encountered her assailant—whom she must have known from the orgy. But it didn't sound like she was willingly in his company. We must confirm that Chaloner was back at Parliament when the assault happened. That would help clear him—at least of the assault.

I think there is more than one parcel-carrying man: Donavan delivering the Mace, and someone else walking off with it—the latter encountering the assault."

CHAPTER 27

DETENTION

Britina, sleeping fitfully, was suddenly wide awake. Had she heard a noise in her room? The other times, she'd been half asleep, but tonight, she was more alert. She stayed still, listening. It was pitch-black and freezing cold. She felt a breeze—but that couldn't be right; there was no place for a breeze to come from. She turned her head. Was there another blacker-than-black form in the room? She didn't feel threatened this time. And then it was gone. And the breeze was gone, too. Somehow, she slept for another hour until Sturgis, who had brought her breakfast, ordered her awake.

Britina was astonished. It wasn't slop—it was a proper breakfast: eggs, bread, and bacon. She ate quickly, realizing how much she'd missed proper food. Sturgis sat on the side of the bed, and Britina began talking, telling her about her strange experience the night before. Sturgis listened, gently encouraging her to keep eating and build her strength back up.

Britina didn't understand why she was talking so much—to Sturgis, of all people. But Sturgis asked questions, and Britina kept talking.

Sturgis knew why. She had mixed a small amount of ground dried betel nut and Datura stramonium seeds into the eggs.

The mixture would provide comfort, a sense of euphoria, and a feeling of trust.

•

That morning, a delivery arrived for Judge Bradley, who was to preside over Britina Myers's case. The police investigation was expected to yield formal charges and a trial. The document delivered claimed that additional evidence was being delivered to Chief Inspector McElroy. A copy of the enclosed medical certification of mental incapacity, resulting in Heather Stone's euthanasia, would be enclosed.

The document stated that, based on evidence and medical observation, the Kew Asylum recommended formal commitment of Britina Myers to the criminally insane ward for counseling, treatment, and rehabilitation. It was the determination of three medical professionals that Britina Myers suffered from acute depression and had been insane at the time of committing euthanasia. The form was signed by Dr. Bran Brookfield, Head of Research and Treatment; Dr. Thaddeus Snow, Medical Doctor and Anatomist, Sydney; and Head Nurse Roberta Kramer, Kew Asylum.

The judge was not pleased. If enacted, the order would usurp the legal right of the accused to a trial. His experience with commitment orders was limited; he'd need to read some case law.

He read further: 'Miss Myers experiences ongoing hallucinations and is plagued by nightly spirit visits. She tries to reject treatments that have proven effective in such cases. We conclude that, if not isolated and treated, she will again commit harmful crimes against other patients or inmates if incarcerated. We recommend isolation, medication, and periodic brain stimulation to return this young lady to sanity.'

The judge scratched his chin. *Her condition sounds perilous. I'll need to confirm these accusations and recommendations.*

•

The same paperwork and forms went to Chief Inspector McElroy. Dr. Bran Brookfield delivered them personally.

"Chief Inspector, upon further inspection of Britina Myers's possessions, inside her prayer book we found locks of hair that appeared to match Heather Stone's. Her Bible had a bookmark inserted at a page where Britina had circled a passage many times: 'The righteous cry, and the Lord heareth, and delivereth them out of all their troubles.'"

•

McElroy called Kernot into his office.

"Sergeant Kernot, I've read your report. In fact, I've read it several times. You have a lot of names, dates, and facts—but nothing I can draw as evidence regarding the guilt or innocence of Sister Britina, or Britina Myers, and not much at all on the patient Heather Stone. Can you give me any evidence, or at least some speculation, based on your investigations?"

Kernot flexed his fingers into a fist, then unflexed them. He looked away from McElroy. He had no desire to help McElroy succeed—certainly not in this investigation or within the department. "It's what I could find out. These are fine, upstanding medical professionals and I would trust what they have to say."

"They have now said, as of today, that Britina Myers was insane and committed an act of euthanasia and should be committed to the criminally insane ward instead of trial. Did they say that to you?"

"No."

"Do you believe it?"

"If they said it, then I do." He cleared his throat.

"Kernot, your job is to gather proof. You're not investigating—you're kowtowing to those you consider important. You're off the investigation. I would like to dismiss you from your duties. I'll be issuing a sanction for ignoring the rule of law. Cartwright will ignore it, but I don't care."

Now Kernot looked McElroy in the face, astonished. "How dare you! Superintendent Cartwright will deal with this."

"Of that, I have no doubt." McElroy glared into Kernot's eyes. "I want you out of my office. Now."

•

Britina awoke feeling disoriented. She was sure someone had drugged her. As she shook her head to clear her thoughts, a haunting scream pierced the air. She clapped her hands over her ears.

Only then did she realize she was no longer in her room.

She listened—there were cries and moaning. Without rising from the cot, she looked around. Dim light filtered in through a barred window in the door of her small, confining space. A cold, damp chill settled over her, and she pulled the thin cover up to her neck. Even with the chill, her skin turned clammy. Her blanket from the Sisters' home hadn't made the trip with her.

The walls were made of large stones. The door was solid metal. An outburst echoed from another patient down the hall; another scream followed, then hysterical laughter from yet another.

What has happened? I'm supposed to have a trial, but I'm housed like a prisoner.

She stood barefoot on the cold, damp floor and wrapped the sheet around herself, but it did nothing to stop the shiver that ran through her. There was little light—only a barred window high on the outer wall let in a trace of moonlight. It was so far above her, she knew she'd never see out.

She went to the door and found it locked. *I had to try.* When she pressed her face to the bars, the air that reached her from the hall reeked of unwashed bodies and bodily fluids mixed with a heavy layer of disinfectant. She gagged. Another scream rang out, followed by the slam of a metal door.

A voice yelled, "Silence it or face the consequences!"

Someone will come by. I'll ask to see Nurse Betty—she'll help. I wish I could contact Edie.

CHAPTER 28

INVESTIGATIONS AND PURSUITS

Edie tried to stay motionless, fearful that any sound might alert whoever Snow or Rohwedder had left behind in the barn. As her legs cramped, she tried to distract herself by counting backward from one hundred by threes. She also needed water. Hours passed. It had to be getting late.

Finally, she heard a voice: "Dr. Snow, I'm over here with the horses." Heavy footsteps crunched through the dirt, pebbles, and straw. The horses whinnied and kicked at their stalls. They knew it was time.

"Asa, it's time for you to get started. Hitch up the horses and be as quick as possible, but be careful not to be discovered. When you return, the back gate will be open. Bring the wagon to the dock at the back and take it inside quickly through the receiving doors. I'll unbolt them from inside so you'll have access. The guard and his wife will be sleeping in their cottage— their meal tonight had a little extra ingredient. No one will be in the halls on the storage level.

"You've been here before; remember—after parking the wagon, take the rope lift at the elevated dock and keep moving forward until you see the white door of the research lab in the kitchen. Knock, and the nurses will operate the lift to bring everything down to the laboratory. We need everything in place before anyone arrives. As before, stay back here in the barn until it's time to make your return trip."

"Yes, sir," Asa said.

"Make haste." She heard the footsteps retreating.

Edie listened as Asa hitched up the horses to the wagon parked beside her. One horse bumped her carriage as he was getting them into position, causing her to fall sideways. She held her breath, but Asa continued his work, unaware. When he was done, he spoke to the horses.

"Be calm; it's time we do our jobs."

He led them out of the barn.

Edie breathed a sigh of relief and took a large drink from her goatskin. *I have to stay alert for when he returns*, she thought. *If Rohwedder—or Dr. Snow, whatever his name is—has unlocked the receiving doors, I have a way in while Asa is away doing whatever he's doing.*

She knew she had to allow time for both Asa and Snow to distance themselves. When everything was quiet, she opened the bundle Betty had given her. Inside was one of Betty's old uniforms, complete with a hat and shoes. She quickly changed. *I don't know if this will do any good if I'm caught, but it's worth a try.* The shoes were a little tight, and so was the uniform.

Hearing no sounds, she took her wicker basket and left the carriage, locking the door behind her. She reminded herself of her goal: to find evidence that could clear Britina—evidence of illegal or suspicious activity at the asylum—and, if possible, speak with Britina directly. *No one has given her a chance to defend herself—to tell her side of the incident.*

•

Nurse Betty woke hours earlier than usual; she couldn't sleep any longer. It was still pre-dawn, and her restlessness woke her husband, who turned and suggested she sleep in the living room.

"Go back to sleep. I'll move to the couch."

Betty was sure he'd sleep straight through until morning. Quietly leaving the bed, she carefully gathered her clothes and went to the kitchen. She dressed and left a note saying she'd be back after work that evening.

She felt sick with worry—Edie was alone in the asylum. *What if she gets caught? I have to help.* She had known for a long time that improper things happened at the asylum, but she'd chosen to ignore them for her own benefit. *And now I've left Edie on her own, in danger. I don't care if this costs me my job.*

She would have to be careful biking in the dark, but she couldn't avoid it.

She hoped Edie would be back safely from her venture, asleep in the carriage. Then she would drive the carriage to the cemetery and return in time to wait for the morning meeting. Edie would be safe—and if she'd been successful, she would have evidence to help free Britina.

•

Britina heard a noise . . . someone was opening the cell door. She sat up on her straw mattress, shivering, her heart heavy with fear and questions. What had God brought to her now? No one had visited. No one had given her food or water or emptied her waste pail.

When the door creaked open, a nauseating odor drifted in and mingled with the staleness of her own. A large, burly nurse entered, carrying a stool. She said nothing; she just surveyed the cell before stepping aside to let someone else in. Though she wore a mask to filter the stench, Britina recognized her instantly—Head Nurse Kramer.

"Miss Myers, this is your new home. You are under our care, so we might cure your madness and return you to society." Britina could tell Kramer was smiling under the mask by the curve of her eyes . . . but it was not a kind smile. "If you cooperate fully, we'll provide meals, water, and keep your cell clean. If you resist, you'll remain in solitude—until you comply, or . . . you die."

"Why am I here? I was to be tried—my case argued before a judge and jury."

"There was too much evidence against you to make that worthwhile. The court declared you criminally insane. Frankly, it may have saved your life. A guilty verdict with intent would have resulted in hanging. You might consider yourself fortunate."

"And is this my new life? Solitary confinement?" She shuddered as the weight of her words settled in her chest.

"With cooperation and treatment, your life here could allow more freedom. But first, we must get you sane. I have a few questions."

"Do I get food and water?"

"After the questions, Miss Myers."

"Can I see Nurse Betty, please?"

"Nurse Robinson is to be fired. She was seen slipping an envelope under your door. We found the pills when we moved you."

"Why won't you call me Sister Britina? May I see Mother Superior?"

"Mother Superior has made her stance clear. She has expelled you from your novice status. She no longer wishes to involve herself with you."

Britina shook more violently, her body nearly convulsing. She held her breath, desperate to remain composed. Slowly, she calmed.

"I've answered your questions. Now it's my turn," Kramer said, indifferent to Britina's distress—perhaps even pleased by it. "Do you have relatives or anyone close we should contact?"

"Contact for what?"

"Answer the question," Kramer snarled.

Britina recognized the threat beneath her words. She needed time—needed to think. "I have no family, not that I know of. I have friends." Her voice trembled, but she wanted them to know someone cared about her.

"Do you have a medical doctor?"

"I saw Dr. Thaddeus Snow when I arrived in Sydney."

Kramer chuckled beneath her mask and scribbled in her notebook.

"Any known diseases?"

Offended, Britina snapped, "I do not."

"Have you ever been pregnant?"

Rage flared in Britina. "I don't see how these invasive questions justify this illegal confinement. I want to speak to a legal authority, a lawyer or the chief inspector."

"Miss Britina, I am your legal guardian now, appointed by the court. That gives me every right. You'll only survive and heal if you follow my commands. Now, can I assume from your outburst that you've been pregnant or delivered a child?"

Britina stood. "Neither," she cried, her face inches from Kramer's.

Kramer rose from her stool and shoved Britina backward. Her knees buckled against the bed frame, and she fell hard into a seated position.

"I see you're not yet ready to begin your rehabilitation. No food or water for another day. I'll return tomorrow." She turned to the nurse-guard. "Ralphine, give her the medications I ordered. If she resists . . . fit her with a straitjacket for the night."

Britina didn't resist. She had seen what happened when you did. The rest of the day passed in a haze, her mind dulled by forced sedation, floating somewhere between sleep and sorrow.

•

The time wore on, and soon, it was nearly time for the early-morning doctor training session. In preparation, Nurse Kramer, Dr. Brookfield, Thaddeus Snow, and Miss Sturgis gathered in Kramer's office, sipping brandy from fine crystal glasses—kept under lock and key for special occasions. They held these training sessions in the early hours, when only a skeleton staff remained in the asylum and the kitchen was empty. They wanted no interruptions.

"Dr. Brookfield," Kramer began, "I'm pleased to report that Britina Myers is a perfect specimen for a future session. It will take time, and we'll need to build a solid case outlining her descent into complete madness and, ultimately, suicide. She'll make an excellent subject for our students. An interesting note, Dr. Snow—she listed you as her only doctor in Australia."

Snow's eyes widened. "I'll have to visit her, see if I recognize her."

Sturgis chimed in. "Before we moved her to the criminal wing, I administered a compound that strips away resistance and compels honest responses. I questioned her about what she knew of our activities here. She was surprisingly forthcoming. Apparently, she's been collecting information on patients and procedures ever since her encounter with Sister Mary Rush—hearsay, not facts—but enough to raise alarms if ever shared with the wrong people. The sooner she's no longer fully conscious, the better."

"She's being kept sedated," Kramer confirmed. "Nurse Ralphine has strict instructions. We'll resume feeding her tomorrow, but she'll remain drugged."

Dr. Brookfield, who had been reviewing a financial report while they spoke, looked up. "There's high demand for trained surgeons. We're doing well financially. Each student must complete a full anatomical dissection under Thaddeus's guidance before earning a degree. That means we need more cadavers than we've been able to harvest from Kew or from you, Dr. Snow. We need more bodies from here, especially women. Each cadaver brings in a fortune."

"I think Britina Myers needs an accident of some sort," Kramer said calmly. "Something to speed up her participation. We must do it in a way that avoids suspicion of us or the institution."

•

Edie waited at the far edge of the receiving dock, her eyes fixed on the caretaker's cottage across the dirt road that led to the receiving doors. It was late, but not everyone kept normal hours. If he glanced out his front windows, he'd have a clear view of the receiving area. The cottage, thankfully, was dark. Snow had mentioned something to Asa about the caretaker, but she couldn't hear exactly what. She lingered a few moments longer, hoping she'd heard correctly that Snow and Asa had drugged the caretaker at dinner. Butterflies churned in her stomach. It was time.

She moved purposefully toward the doors. They were large enough for a delivery wagon to pull into the covered space for unloading. Hung on overhead rollers, the doors opened left and right, leaving the block-and-tackle lift at the front wall unobstructed. Though they fit tightly, each had a metal handle for pulling. Edie gripped the bracket on the left door, turned her back to it, and leaned against the length of the panel, using her full weight. Slowly, the door creaked along the rail. At about two feet wide, she stopped. She didn't want to be seen. Peering into the darkness, she checked to make sure she was alone.

Setting her wicker basket on the dirt floor, she stepped through the gap and pulled the door shut behind her, plunging herself into pitch-blackness. Feeling around, she searched for her basket. She took out a candle and matches. With a flick of the match and the soft glow of the flame, the space came into view.

The center was open, large enough for two big commercial wagons. To either side were wooden pallets and dunnage racks. In the front left corner were a raised wooden platform and a rope lift designed to bring heavy goods up to the cement floor just a few feet above, or even farther, through an opening in the ceiling leading to upper storage.

She needed to hurry in case Asa returned. Spotting a set of steps, she carried the basket up to the elevated cement floor. There, rows of boxes, bales, and barrels lined the space. Workbenches stood against the walls, some fitted with sinks. A tall woodstove towered over a few stacks of firewood, and beside it sat what looked like a boiler with a fire door at its base.

A creak reverberated throughout the room as the doors at the far end opened, and her heart sank. She'd waited too long. Asa was back. She blew out the candle and dove under a nearby workbench, rolling a bin in front of her for cover.

Asa worked efficiently. Using the rope lift, he raised a wheelbarrow to the cement floor. A white sheet covered whatever was inside. Edie stayed motionless, heart pounding, and watched him pass. When he disappeared down the hallway she had just walked, she crept forward to another hiding spot, then another, always staying low.

She watched as Asa pushed the wheelbarrow through a set of double doors. Then—finally—he returned, empty-handed, and exited.

•

As Edie ventured forward, she passed windows with wire mesh embedded in the glass. There were half-walled work areas on both sides of the space—some with windows, others without. She pushed through a set of double doors and entered the kitchen. The space was massive, and the lingering smell of yesterday's meals hung in the air. The institution had installed electric lighting here, and a small lamp burned low on the far wall.

She froze as the sound of a rope lift startled her. Flattening herself against the wall, she held her breath. Two large, robust nurses passed within ten feet of her, their backs turned, chatting and swearing as they exited the kitchen. One turned toward where Edie hid and spat a wad of chewing tobacco into an empty pail. Fighting the urge to gag, Edie exhaled slowly, trying to calm her racing heart. She scanned the room.

She had seen kitchens before, but nothing of this magnitude—not even Parliament's kitchen compared. Huge boiling pots, large ovens fed by wood furnaces, and a massive central range with multiple functions stretched before her. Several smaller ovens lined both long sides, clearly designed for use by many at once. Off to one side were half-walled work areas. One was outfitted with mixers and an oven with a roller ramp, holding a line of bun pans. Bags of flour were stacked to one side. *A bakery*, Edie thought.

Another area held crates of vegetables, sinks, tables, and preparation tools she didn't recognize. At the far end, near the exit doors, was what looked like a plating and finishing station. A thousand or more meals, three times a day, she marveled. *I'm surprised they aren't working around the clock.* The thought sparked a flare of panic—baking often started in the early hours. Someone might arrive at any moment. *I better move on. I can't get caught.*

Asa had left the wheelbarrow leaning against the wall near the rope lift that accessed the upper and lower levels. Betty's map had shown two doors. If one led to the experimental room and she could gather proof of patient mistreatment, it might be enough to discredit Brookfield and Kramer—and get Britina out of the asylum and into police custody.

She paused. *If I open the door and get caught, I have no excuse. No going back now.*

She searched for the door to the lower level. Lighting another candle from her basket, she opened the first door—it led upward. She tried the second door. Unlocked. She slipped inside. Though there was an electric light switch, she relied on her candle. After quietly shutting the door behind her, she noticed a key hanging beside the light. She took it, locked the door from the inside, and slipped the key into her pocket.

She descended into the lower chamber.

No one was there.

The space had been dug deep into the earth. The rock walls were cold, and the air was much chillier than in the kitchen. Betty had called it cold storage—and it was. The concrete floor looked like newer construction.

Edie held her candle aloft, scanning the room. Strange contraptions filled the space. One metal chair caught her eye. It featured a recessed headrest and straps to secure someone at the head, arms, waist, and legs. The chair hinged at the middle, head, and lower torso, and crank wheels allowed for repositioning at each section. Electrode connectors clamped onto the surface, with cables running to an enormous machine against the back wall. Other wires from the machine extended to the lights. A boiler fed another machine fitted with wheels and belts—cords ran from it as well. She remembered hearing about dynamos. That must be what it was.

She moved on. A row of deep copper tubs lined one wall, some still holding water. A smaller, dynamo-like device sat nearby, though nothing connected it to any tub.

There wasn't time to investigate everything. She walked to the far end of the room, where a wall of metal doors was built into the rock; all had the appearance of a furnace door.

Edie chose a cast-iron door at random from the twelve before her. It revealed nothing—just a wave of cold that swept over her skin like a faint breeze. The compartment stretched deep into the stone, but was empty. She tried another. The same.

Above the series of doors was a single, wider door. She dragged a chair over and climbed up. The door was hinged at the bottom, so she carefully opened it—and nearly lost her footing. Catching herself just in time, she looked inside . . . and froze.

Bile rose in her throat.

This compartment wasn't as deep, and inside, arranged side by side, was a row of human skulls. There were empty spaces for more. The last skull appeared recent—someone hadn't bleached or cleaned it completely, and remnants of tissue and strands of hair still clung to the bone. A wave of nausea swept through her, and she thought she might faint. As she tried to process what this room was for, the door handle at the top of the stairs rattled violently.

"Why is the door locked? I ordered it opened earlier!" a voice screeched.

The sound of a key entering the lock followed. Edie's heart stopped. She was trapped.

Silently, she pushed the chair back into place, grabbed her basket, and frantically searched for a hiding place.

Footsteps clattered down the stairs—at least six, maybe eight people. She looked around for the darkest corner. Then the lights snapped on, illuminating the stairs and the far wall.

The group entered: Kramer, Brookfield, Sturgis, the mysterious Dr. Snow, and five young men dressed in white. They moved directly toward the large mechanical device Edie had seen when she first entered.

There was storage beneath the stairs—and it remained unlit. *Can I get behind those shelves?* She had to try. There was nowhere else to hide. She glanced back. *Damn—I left the skull door open.*

While the group gathered around the machine, Edie hugged the stone wall and inched slowly toward the stairs. Anyone turning around would see her. She held her breath.

Suddenly, the machine roared to life with a loud mechanical clatter and a whirring hum. Light from an overhead string of bulbs flooded the center of the room. Gasps and murmurs of amazement rippled through the group as the electrical system came alive.

"The first bit of magic, gentlemen," Dr. Brookfield announced proudly, "our little dynamo delivers electricity for both lighting and patient treatment. We'll show you shortly. We pipe steam from the laundry boilers here; it builds pressure in this tank and then we release it in a regulated stream to power the dynamos. The result: electric current. A marvel of innovation."

Edie reached the shelving under the stairs. It stood a few inches away from the uneven stone wall. She squeezed behind the last set of shelves, flattening herself against the cold stone. She couldn't see the group from this angle, but had a partial view of the rest of the room.

Brookfield turned to the young men. "You will address me as Dr. Brookfield. I am a licensed physician and surgeon. You have the privilege of learning skills few in our profession possess. Some treatments I've developed will soon be studied worldwide. You will be at the forefront of a new medical era—treating mental illness with technology."

He gestured toward Dr. Snow. "And thanks to Dr. Snow's expertise, you will gain the skills to surgically treat internal organs with precision. Nurse Kramer, will you alert your team to bring the patient?"

She crossed the room and pulled a rope; Edie heard a bell ring in the kitchen above. Nurse Kramer turned, glanced at the metal doors, took a pole leaning against the wall, and pushed the skull door shut. "Never stays closed," she whispered.

A section of the ceiling in front of the wall of metal doors descended. Edie now noticed ropes and pulleys in motion and heavy blocks rising from the floor. The ceiling piece lowered to floor level. Standing on the platform were the two nurses she had seen earlier, positioned at each end of a patient's bed. The patient wore a straitjacket and a covering over her mouth, but her frightened eyes revealed her terror. They rolled her to the metal chair. One nurse pulled a lever, triggering a loud clanking noise; the platform began rising back into the ceiling.

Brookfield prepared a syringe and injected the patient in the neck. "Chloral hydrate, gentlemen. We need the patient sedated, but the brain active enough to benefit from treatment."

As the sedation took effect, the two nurses lifted the patient onto the metal table, removed the straitjacket, and secured straps across her arms, legs, midsection, and finally, one across her forehead, pulling it tight. "To prevent injury during convulsions," Brookfield explained.

While speaking, Brookfield applied metal electrodes coated with conductive gel to either side of her shaved scalp, then added a third to her midsection. "The intention is to create a seizure that will reset the patient's brain. We've done extensive experiments with electrode placement and power levels and believe we've cured multiple cases of depression, mania, and psychosis."

"Has it worked on every patient?" one student asked.

Dr. Brookfield looked at the student, paused, and then spoke. "No. Like much of medicine, a lot depends on the patient. We have failed a few times, and we've lost a few with weak constitutions. But we lose fewer than we did in the beginning." He turned his back on the group, dismissing further questions.

One nurse rolled a small stand with a device on it to the metal chair. Kramer took a pair of cords from the machine and attached them to one of the smaller dynamos. Donning heavy gloves, she pulled a steam cable from the boiler to the dynamo.

"Ready, Doctor."

Brookfield connected the electrodes to the machine on the stand. "This wheel and gauge," he explained, "control the dynamo's power to deliver a measured current dose through a transformer in my electrotherapy box. This controls pulsing frequency, which can enhance results." He smiled. *This little baby will make me rich.*

When he finished, he signaled Kramer to activate the switch at the dynamo.

Edie couldn't see the activity clearly. She cautiously inched behind the shelving, section by section, until she reached the underside of the stairs. There was just enough of a gap between the stair runners and riser to catch a glimpse.

Brookfield stood at the stand, threw a switch, and began turning a dial. At first, nothing happened, but slowly, he increased the current. The machine cracked, clicked, and buzzed. A faint smell of burning hair filled the air. The patient stiffened; her body arched, muscles contracting. Her limbs jerked, the body shook—then stopped. After a brief pause, it repeated. Three times in total.

Brookfield then switched the machine off. The patient's body went slack. "The patient suffers from melancholia. We will now treat her with medications and monitor her condition over the next few weeks to gauge the effect of the electroconvulsive treatment just applied. We will adjust the treatment time and current as needed to cure her."

"Why would this work?" a student asked.

Pleased to display his knowledge, Dr. Brookfield responded. "The brain is all electrical activity," he said. "When wires get crossed, bad things happen. We try to get the current flowing in the right directions so patients can get better." He smiled, self-satisfied.

As the nurses prepared the patient for transport back to her room or ward, Brookfield moved on.

He walked over to the metal tubs. "These are our hydrotherapy baths. In another session, we will demonstrate them. For now, I will explain their use."

Edie inched her way up to the second row of shelving to get a better view.

"We first fill the baths with cold water and ice to achieve a temperature slightly above freezing. The patient is undressed and placed in the ice bath. Depending on their condition, restraints may be required."

"How long are they left in there?" one student asked, sounding shocked.

Dr. Brookfield's eyes narrowed in irritation. "The goal is to reduce the patient's body temperature and induce a state of shock. The duration can range from a few minutes to several hours. A nurse constantly monitors the patient's vital signs and behavior during treatment. When the treatment is complete, we remove the patient from the tub and gradually warm them with blankets. The process induces calm and is effective in treating agitation and delusions. Use of the baths diminishes violent or erratic behavior."

While Brookfield focused on the tubs, Sturgis rolled a table to the metal doors across the room.

Brookfield continued. "Gentlemen, the education of medical professionals like yourselves has flaws. To become surgeons, you must each conduct an anatomical dissection of a human being—recording your notes and becoming certified in your comprehension and competency with each organ, its diseases, and treatment. This is required to test your understanding and skills.

"Yet, there are not enough cadavers donated to research to train the number of surgeons needed. We cultivate sources to provide the specimens necessary to train the best surgeons of tomorrow. The hospital you represent, which pays your tuition, does not have the resources to train you adequately.

"I now introduce you to one of the finest anatomical surgeons in Australia—Dr. Thaddeus Snow. He received his medical degree from Edinburgh, as I did, and pursued a second degree in anatomical dissection. He also studied apothecary medicine to expand his expertise."

Thaddeus stepped into the center of the room, standing beneath the lights.

Could I possibly be mistaken about Rohwedder? Edie wondered. *His voice is so much the same, and from here, he looks to have the same body shape. If I could see his eyes, I would be certain.*

She moved again, carefully avoiding anything on the shelves that might give her away.

"Gentlemen," Thaddeus began, "I will instruct tonight, and you will take careful note of procedures, my cuts, and the details I provide. You will each perform your own anatomical procedure over the next few months, and I will assess your skill."

Sturgis opened one of the metal doors. The two nurses joined her. She placed a white oilcloth on the table. With effort, the nurses pulled a sheet bearing a cadaver onto the table. They covered the naked body and rolled the table to the center of the room, placing it under the lights.

Glad I didn't get to that door, Edie thought.

"Each of you, retrieve a wooden stool from storage under the stairs and form a semi-circle around the table so you can see, hear, and take notes."

God, I'm about to be exposed. What do I do? I don't want to be the next cadaver.

Four students chatted as they marched to the storage area, grabbing tall stools and joking among themselves. None looked at Edie. The fifth followed, not part of the group. He stopped face-to-face with Edie and looked her directly in the eyes. Her heart pounded. She put a finger to her lips and mouthed, *Please.*

He nodded, took a stool, and rejoined the others.

Edie saw the man she believed to be Rohwedder step forward, now completely disguised beneath a striking head of white hair and a white beard. He wore a white lab coat and donned silk gloves.

With a commanding presence, he scanned the students. "Tonight, we delve into the intricate wonders of human anatomy. Students! Completing this course will grant you status unmeasurable in any hospital in the world."

As Thaddeus spoke, the hushed students fixed their eyes on the long metal table and the figure beneath the white cloth.

With a stern expression, his voice echoing off the cold stone walls, Snow continued, "The superb condition of the corpse's flesh and organs is due to embalming fluid using formaldehyde instead of traditional arsenic-based solutions—a new process aided by the reduced temperatures of our cadaver caves." He gestured toward the metal doors. "Our cadaver storage is located deep underground, drilled into solid stone. It preserves specimens for some time, though eventually nature will claim them."

With a dramatic flourish—equal parts excitement and trepidation—he declared, "Welcome to the realm of forbidden knowledge."

Snow was like an actor; he had rehearsed this performance many times—alone, in front of mirrors, and even on the train.

Stepping to the table with a gloved hand, he drew back the covering, revealing the pale, lifeless features of a woman. The students leaned forward, eyes wide with anticipation and morbid curiosity.

All eyes stared at the cadaver, naked on the table. Once a beautiful young woman.

Repugnance and fear overcame Edie. She recognized the cadaver—Heather Stone. She gripped a shelf to remain upright and placed a hand over her mouth. Blood drained from her head; she was lightheaded, near fainting.

I can't believe this is happening. Could it be? I saw her buried! Wait . . . I saw the casket buried—it was closed.

"Observe, my pupils, the delicate balance between beauty and decay," Dr. Snow continued, his voice laced with a mix of reverence and scientific fervor. "This woman, who shall go nameless, has bequeathed us her mortal shell as a gift—an opportunity to unravel the mysteries that lie beneath the surface."

Quite dramatic! Edie thought. *If I'm right and that is Rohwedder, he's gained some new skills.* Dizziness again swept through her, and she bowed her head until it cleared. She was close to vomiting; she fought back a gag, breathing deep through her nose.

Snow picked up a scalpel, its blade gleaming in the bright light. Slowly, he made a precise incision along Heather's chest, exposing the intricacies of her internal organs. The students leaned in, holding their breath in awe and discomfort. They jotted notes between observations.

"As we begin our exploration, remember that every incision tells a story; every cut leads us closer to the truth," Dr. Snow said, his words a blend of scientific precision and poetic fascination. "Pay attention to the delicate network of veins, the once-pulsing heart that animated this vessel, and the interplay of muscles that enabled her movement."

One by one, Dr. Snow pointed out various anatomical structures, explaining their functions and significance. The students watched intently—some taking notes, others simply absorbing the spectacle, minds caught between fascination and revulsion. Snow removed flesh and organs as he severed them surgically from the cadaver, placing them in pails brought by the nurses.

As the dissection progressed, the basement filled with a distinct scent—a pungent blend of embalming chemicals and decay. It mingled with the students' nervous energy as they wrestled with the tension between their thirst for knowledge and the unsettling reality of their surroundings.

Edie watched Snow's hands move with skilled precision, revealing layer after layer of the intricate human form. His voice wove a tapestry of knowledge, blending scientific theory with philosophical musings. "All that we discover are the inner workings of human creation. What brings it to life? We are challenging the very essence of human existence. We are transcending the boundaries of limitation, peering into the raw mechanics of life itself."

Hours passed. The basement's shadowy corners seemed to absorb the students' apprehension, leaving only the insatiable pursuit of knowledge. The scene unfolded like an eerie ballet of academia and transgression, where legality and morality blurred, lost in the pursuit of enlightenment.

In that dim, subterranean chamber of the asylum, Dr. Snow's theatrical performance and the forbidden secrets they witnessed changed Snow's students, forever marking their minds. As they set aside the last remnants of the dissected corpse, they exhaled a collective breath.

There was a knock at the lab door.

"That will be Asa. Will someone let him in? It's time to clean up for tonight."

The solo student Edie had locked eyes with earlier stepped forward. "I'll put the stools away," he said. No one argued. Reaching the storage area, he whispered to Edie, "Do you need help?"

When he returned with the second stool, Edie said, "I will need to get out of this room when everyone is gone. Can I trust you?"

He looked slightly hurt. "I'll try to assist."

Asa carried the pails upstairs to the kitchen and placed them in his wheelbarrow. He returned for the limbs, gathering them carefully. Finally, he rolled the carcass up in the cloth and hoisted it over his shoulder, carrying it up the stairs—leaving what remained of the head behind. Without delay, he rushed out to the wagon with the wheelbarrow.

The two nurses took the skull, cap missing, but with some hair attached and bits of flesh dangling. One unscrewed the cover of a large wooden barrel; the other pulled on thick rubber gloves and placed the head in a cloth bag, which she lowered through the barrel's opening and released.

•

Edie's body ached from standing still for hours, and she desperately needed water. Around her, the activity continued as Dr. Brookfield and Dr. Snow bid farewell to the students, confirming the next session in two weeks when the hydrotherapy baths would be demonstrated. Dr. Brookfield and Dr. Snow would guide the student who prepared the best report on tonight's procedure through his first dissection. A nurse led the young men upstairs to the front entrance, where a growler carriage waited to take them to their rooms at the Royal Melbourne Hospital.

Eventually, complete darkness surrounded Edie. She felt around for her basket and, upon finding it, located her goatskin and took a long, welcome swallow of water. Feeling safely alone, she lit a candle, hoping it would not only light the space but also help diminish the lingering odor.

I hope no one's working in the kitchen yet. And what about that young man? I don't know if he'll help.

She found the key she had used earlier. Apparently, no one had noticed its absence—and someone had left the door unlocked, anyway. Cautiously, she climbed the stairs and tried the door: locked. She inserted her key, turned it, and heard the satisfying shift of the deadbolt. But when she pushed, the door opened just a fraction before hitting something solid. It was barred. Through the narrow crack, she could see a metal bar laid across the door, likely secured by a secondary lock on its housing.

Damn. Now what do I do? How do I get out of here?

There's the lift to the kitchen—but I hear people working in there.

Could there be another way up? Maybe to the storage floor above the kitchen?

She began her search.

•

Betty made her way slowly toward the asylum. Dawn was still hours away. She concentrated on avoiding the ditches in the dark road, but even with care, she hit a couple of ruts that twisted her handlebars, forcing her to regain balance. She fell once—thankfully slowly—suffering nothing more than a soiled uniform.

As the darkness lifted, she approached the cemetery at the bottom of the hill. Looking across the graveyard toward the Yarra River, she spotted a large, boxy wagon. It was much bigger than a typical hearse—and unlike a hearse, it had no windows. The sight chilled her.

That's the wagon I saw in the barn next to Edie's carriage. It looks like one of those prison transports. I think they're called Black Marias. What is it doing here—at this time of morning?

Betty quietly walked her bicycle through the cemetery gate and laid it down next to the tree where she and Edie had met earlier. She removed her white hat and placed it on the ground, along with the white cardigan she'd worn for visibility during the ride.

She crept toward the river, moving in a low crouch along the tree line, weaving between trunks as she went. When she got as close as she dared, she lay on her stomach, peering beneath the hanging limbs for a better view. *I'll worry about the uniform later.*

The back doors of the wagon were open. A man crouched beside a tarp spread on the ground. Betty watched as he stood, reached into the cart, and removed a human leg—a woman's leg, she thought with horror. Her skin tightened, and the sour sting of bile crept up her throat.

The man placed a second leg beside the first, then carefully rolled the limbs in the cloth, tying a string at both ends and securing the bundle tightly. He carried it to the riverbank and pushed it into the current.

Betty could hardly breathe.

The man returned to the wagon, retrieved a pair of arms, and repeated the process. Betty turned her face to the ground, struggling to contain both her emotions and her stomach.

He rolled the cart back toward the main cemetery and stopped near a freshly dug hole, barely visible in the dim light, near the paupers' graves. Scooting low, Betty left the woods and hurried toward the riverbank. Shrubs along the bank could conceal her. She tripped and fell, heart pounding, but stayed quiet, hoping the man hadn't heard her. He was busy doing something she had to see.

Lying prone behind the bushes, she peeked through the branches toward the source of the digging sounds. A shovel stuck out of a dirt pile beside a grave-shaped hole in front of the wagon. The man returned to the cart—now fully in Betty's view—picked up two pails, and carried them to the hole. Donning gloves, he spread a powder into the bottom.

He then rolled the cart closer, bent down, and reached in. Betty's breath caught in her throat.

He lifted a limbless, headless torso, split down the middle, and dropped it into the grave. Then, he poured a large amount of powder from one pail over the body.

Betty's insides turned. She breathed deeply, fighting the urge to flee. Her chest tingled; her stomach cramped. She covered her mouth and turned her gaze back just in time to see the man lift an armful of intestines and organs and toss them into the hole. He sprinkled the last of the powder over the remains, retrieved another pail, and rinsed the inside of the cart, dumping the rinse water into the grave.

Then he spread an oilcloth over the contents and shoveled dirt back in.

Betty couldn't hold back any longer. She retched loudly.

Knowing she'd exposed herself to discovery, she sprang to her feet and bolted across the open grass toward the knoll where she'd left her bike. Behind her, she heard footfalls close. Too close.

The man dove and grabbed her leg. She felt the slick, slimy fluid on his gloves—fluid that had once been a human being.

Oh God, not Edie.

She screamed.

He was on top of her in an instant, his slippery hand clamped over her mouth. The foul stench of death filled her nose, and she retched again, choking on the vomit.

She couldn't breathe. Her vision dimmed. She passed out.

•

When Betty awoke, she was bound and gagged in the dark. She could feel the cart moving beneath her, jostling as it climbed uphill. Toward the asylum, she guessed. If it passed through the gate, maybe—just maybe—she could make enough noise to get someone's attention. Maybe someone would help.

•

Asa's hands shook as he drove the wagon back to the asylum, passing through the gate without being questioned.

Dr. Snow is going to be angry. I should have buried her, too. All my tools are still there. I'll have to go back.

He hid the intruder far from anything related to Dr. Snow or their work—somewhere she wouldn't be found. Dr. Snow would know what to do with her.

He'll still be angry. I'll be punished.

•

Nurse Kramer sat with Dr. Brookfield and Miss Sturgis in her office, the door locked.

"The training went well. Our clients will be pleased?" Nurse Kramer said.

"I think they will. And training their future surgeons will

serve them well in the long run. We'll change medical education in this country.

"Miss Sturgis, your work in ridding the institution of those who will never recover and have no relatives supporting them not only helps the institution, but also the medical profession. While illegal, it is a service to mankind."

"Thank you, Doctor."

"We just have to be careful, selective, and not too greedy," Nurse Kramer said.

"Of course," Miss Sturgis replied.

Kramer took a cloth bag out of her desk drawer, dumped a pile of gold coins onto the table, counted and stacked them, and then slid the stack across to Sturgis. "For Jane Doe," she said. "Unfortunately, her identity was discovered."

"It still worked out," Sturgis said.

"It would be preferable if our subjects appeared to die of natural causes or by their own hand—but yes, this worked out. We dealt with the remains, disposing of them separately, as before, to hinder traceability. The skulls are the most traceable and harder to dispose of, so we'll keep them separate and hidden for the time being. Our next session is in two weeks, but it's too early for Myers. We'll need one of the undocumented pauper patients this time. We'll have to plan carefully for Myers," Kramer said.

"Very well," Sturgis said. "I'm always ready to help," she added, grabbing the stack of coins and placing them in her bag.

•

Edie examined every inch of the treatment room's walls. There was a square wooden access door where the pipes from the steam system entered the space, but it was tight and too hot to crawl into, anyway. With hesitation, she opened the metal doors to the vaults to explore what they concealed—maybe there was access to the outside at the rear. She thought she could feel a faint movement of air through them. If there was access, it would likely be on the top level.

She chose a vault near the top, close to the adjoining wall. She could feel cold air exiting. Lighting a fresh candle, she set her wicker basket on the floor, slid a student stool into place, and climbed into the crypt headfirst, lying on her stomach, pushing the candle in front of her until she was fully inside the narrow tunnel. Inch by inch, she wormed forward; the cramped space didn't allow for much use of her legs or arms, but her elbows helped.

Why would there be a way out—or in? Only dead people reside here. But there is a small flow of air from the far end.

As she moved deeper, the stone turned to dirt. Then—nothing. A dead end. No back entrance. Her pulse quickened.

Can I back out the same way? I need to get out of here. A sudden and incapacitating fear overcame her. She began hyperventilating. *I can't let this happen.* Holding her breath, she forced deep inhales and slow releases of air until she was back in control.

She tried to back up, but could hardly move. It felt like a Chinese finger trap—the more she tried, the tighter the space seemed. Panic again clouded her thinking.

I'll die here. They'll dissect me next.

The thin air reminded her of being trapped in the pigsty box back in England. Yelling wouldn't help. She closed her eyes and waited—for what? She didn't know. But she was sure she wasn't meant to die like this. The space was too tight to turn over.

What was I thinking, crawling in here?

Her candle flickered, then went out. She felt like crying.

The stone walls magnified the sound of footsteps on the stairway across the room.

No need to hide, I guess.

"Are you ready to express your undying gratitude?" It was the young doctor from the session; she'd forgotten about him. Relief swept through her body.

He flipped on the lights, saw the stool and the basket on the floor, and quickly figured out what Edie had done.

"As long as it's not dying gratitude," Edie replied.

"Are you stuck?"

"No, I'm taking a nap! Get me out of here."

"Terms first."

"What do you mean, terms?"

"Treat me to a nice dinner before I leave town."

"I'm a happily married woman."

"I'm not proposing, just like to get to know the lives I save."

"OK, OK—get me out."

The student climbed onto the stool and crawled up to his waist so he could reach her feet. He grabbed her by the ankles.

"You may get a few scrapes and scratches from this."

"I don't care," Edie said.

He pulled and inched his legs downward, adding weight to help move Edie along.

"Ouch!" The stones scratched Edie's legs and belly as her uniform skirt slid up, exposing her skin to the rough surface.

"Your underwear is showing."

"GET ME OUT OF HERE and don't look."

When his feet reached the stool seat, Edie's feet and shins were finally out of the opening.

"Now I'm going to pull harder. I'll have you out in a couple more slides."

"If there's anything left of me," Edie muttered.

"I'm Dr. Tharp," he offered.

"GET. ME. OUT. NOW."

Tharp pulled hard. As he leaned back, the stool tipped over, and he fell. Edie was airborne right behind him, landing in a sitting position on his chest and knocking the wind out of him.

"Thanks for the landing surface," Edie said.

Tharp coughed and gasped, struggling to breathe.

Realizing he wasn't breathing properly, she squatted beside him, straddled his torso, and pushed on his chest. "Are you going to be alright?"

When he didn't respond, she pressed her palms into his chest again, harder this time. Not sure what else to do, she placed her lips over his, stuck a finger into his mouth to hold his tongue, and blew.

"It's alright . . . I just need to breathe awhile," he finally managed. "That was nice, except for the finger."

Edie, seeing he wasn't about to die, pointed at herself and said again, "Happily married."

After a while, his breathing steadied. "You're heavier than you look. I think you broke two ribs."

"Thanks. How gentlemanly of you to notice," she replied sarcastically. "I appreciate you coming back. Thank you for the rescue. I thought I was permanently stuck in there."

"Are you alright? You've got an active bleed."

Edie looked down. The torn front of her uniform revealed a superficial gash on her stomach.

She retrieved her wicker basket, took a drink from her goatskin, and handed it to Tharp. Then she ripped two pieces of cloth she had brought to block the carriage windows. She dampened one with water and cleaned her wound.

Tharp found a bandage and some tape in the medical supply cabinet used by the nurses who attended to patients. He gently applied the bandage.

"Good as slightly used," he said.

"You got in here without a problem. How do we get out? And tell me your name again?"

"Tharp. Dr. Arundle Tharp, from the United States—Maine. Nickname's Ary. I don't believe we've been properly introduced. Your name is?"

"Well, Dr. Ary Tharp, I am Lady Edith Black. Edie. Now, how did you get in, and how will we get out?"

"The kitchen staff doesn't question medical staff with keys, which were hanging near the kitchen office. Getting you out, especially in a torn, bloodstained uniform, might be trickier. We need a situation that won't raise questions."

"Got anything in mind?"

"I'm thinking," he said, still rubbing his chest and ribs. Edie hoped he wasn't truly hurt.

"What were you doing in here, anyway?" he asked.

"Trying to save my best friend's life. I'll tell you the details if we get out safely."

DISEASED CORPSE

Tharp, wearing a mask and gloves, approached the kitchen manager in the main kitchen. "Mr. Rice, I've got a little situation and need your cooperation."

Rice eyed him with suspicion—doctors rarely addressed kitchen staff. "What is it?"

"I've been charged with removing a diseased corpse from the research laboratory. During last night's education session, we treated the disease, but the patient's condition was far worse than expected, and she died. We can't leave the body there, and I need to remove it quickly for cremation—it's highly contagious."

Rice's eyebrows drew together. "How can you protect my staff and the food?"

"I'm coating the body in a disease-shield ointment and wrapping it in burial cloth. There's very little chance of contamination if I'm in and up quickly."

"Up?"

"I need to use the lift. That's the help I need. When I'm ready, I'll ring the bell. If you or one of your staff activate the lift, I'll handle the rest."

"Very well. Shall I bring in the nursing staff?"

"No. Nurse Kramer authorized me to deal with this. I don't

want to put the nurses at risk."

The manager was visibly unsettled. He didn't want to be at risk, either.

"Bradley, come here." He summoned a low-level kitchen helper and gave him brief instructions on what to do when he heard the bell—without mentioning the supposed risks. Then he disappeared into his office.

"Bradley," Dr. Tharp said, "it'll be about half an hour before I'm ready. Please be prepared to act quickly when you hear the bell. Wear a mask and gloves, and dispose of them as soon as we're done."

Now Bradley was nervous.

"Don't worry, Bradley. You'll be fine. Just do exactly as I say."

When Dr. Tharp rang the bell, the lift clanked to life and began its descent. He just hoped Rice hadn't talked to any nurses or doctors.

Tharp wrapped Edie tightly in a burial shroud—no part of her was visible. She wore a white cap and a cloth over her face. As instructed, she lay stiff as a board on the metal table.

When they reached the kitchen level, Edie held her breath. Staff backed away from the lift area; Bradley kept his distance, and no one dared come closer. Tharp swiftly rolled the table off the lift, through the double doors, and into the rear storage area. He didn't pause.

Halfway down the storage corridor, Tharp muttered, "Alright, you can breathe now, but we're not in the clear yet."

At the loading dock, he activated the second lift. As it descended from the ceiling, he shifted the lever to the middle slot, hoping it would stop at their level. It did. He rolled the table onto the wooden platform and moved the lever again. The lift descended to the dirt floor. The delivery doors were still unlocked. He rolled the table down the earthen ramp.

"Hold on there."

Under the shroud, Edie froze again. Tharp startled, heart thudding.

"Who are you, and what are you doing?"

It was the caretaker and gate guard, Rodney. He walked up to Tharp and stared him directly in the face. "Well?"

"I'm Dr. Tharp," he began, a little shakily. *Should've made up a name.* "This body is going to the morgue building for inspection by the coroner."

"I've never seen a doctor bring a body out before."

"She was my patient. I feel responsible. And . . . she's contagious."

Rodney studied him. "Has the coroner been notified?"

"It's in process now with Nurse Kramer," Tharp replied, hoping the name-drop would help.

"We use that beige barn over there, past the fever tents when the coroner's needed. Please take the body there." Rodney glanced at the shrouded form and turned away.

Tharp didn't hesitate. Once inside the beige barn, he pulled the doors mostly closed, leaving just enough morning light to seep in. He checked to be sure no one had followed, then began to set Edie free. First, he uncovered her face. She took several deep breaths—though the air in the barn was far from pleasant. Working quickly and with her help, they unwrapped the rest of her body.

"It's going to be broad daylight soon. I need to get back to my carriage on the other side of the central wing," Edie said.

"It will not be easy. The grounds are busy during the day."

They fell silent. A scratching noise came from the back corner of the barn. Edie had abandoned her basket—her only light source. There were no windows. Tharp felt around near the entrance, searching for a lantern. They didn't dare open the doors and draw attention. This place was rarely used, and never by the living.

The scratching came again.

"I hate rats." Edie cringed.

A louder, more forceful—almost angry—scratching answered her comment.

"Sounds like you offended the rat," Tharp said.

Edie checked the pockets of her torn uniform. One match.

Tharp gathered some loose hay from the dirt floor and wrapped it with strips of the burial cloth he'd used for Edie, leaving strands of hay exposed at the tip. "We've got one shot. Let's hope the match lights."

Edie struck the match on a rock by the door. Nothing. She tried again. This time, the match flared. Carefully, she touched the flame to the makeshift torch. It caught, and the space slowly took shape in the dim glow.

The scratching resumed.

They followed the noise to the back corner. There, half-concealed on the floor, was a dirty body bag. Inside, something was moving—and moaning.

Tharp struggled with the drawstring at the top, finally pulling it open to reveal the back of a woman's head. He didn't turn her, afraid of causing injury. Instead, he reached inside, undid the gag, and pulled it away.

The woman gasped for air.

"Betty? Is that you?"

Gasping and sobbing, Betty said, "Untie me."

"Are you seriously injured anywhere?" Tharp asked.

"Just my mouth."

They gently turned her over. Her mouth was bleeding—scraped raw from trying to drag it across the pebbles to make noise.

"Oh, Betty, I'm so sorry!"

"Just get me out," she said.

They pulled the shroud off Betty, untied her wrists from behind her back, and loosened the bindings on her legs. Betty stretched out her limbs and slowly tried to stand. She wobbled and sank back down. Tharp and Edie each took a side, gently helping her to her feet. Once upright, they walked her a few steps back and forth. The torch had gone out; the barn was dark again.

At last, Betty spoke, her voice catching as she told them about her time in the cemetery and trapped in the dark.

"They're robbing graves to provide cadavers for medical students—that must be illegal," Edie said.

"It certainly seems that way," Dr. Tharp replied. "An even bigger issue would be if they are selecting patients—those who won't be missed—for execution and then making them into cadavers."

"Killing them," Betty said. "Now that you mention it, I can recall several instances where pauper or problematic patients vanished and were reported dead." She hesitated, then continued. "Your friend Britina might be in the same situation; she's a threat to them."

"Your experience alone is enough to involve the police," Edie said. "And I recognized the cadaver used last night—it was Heather Stone. Britina could be in immediate danger."

As he listened, Dr. Tharp stood, stunned. His thoughts drifted back to the body Dr. Snow had dissected.

"I cannot go to report this morning. Missing morning meeting is grounds for dismissal. I can't show my face in the asylum," Betty said.

"And from the look of your uniform when we had light, you've got nothing to wear anyway," Edie added.

They shared a nervous laugh.

Dr. Tharp spoke up. "Right now, we need to come up with a plan to get off this property, all three of us, and get to the police."

"Shouldn't we try to get to Britina first?" Edie asked. "I came here to hear her story, to find out what she knows. Now I feel she needs protection."

"If someone exposed our escape from the cellar or if anyone visited the space, the whole asylum will be on alert for an intruder, and for me. It's far too risky," Tharp said.

Edie fell silent.

•

Dr. Tharp peeked out the doors of the morgue building. Seeing no activity nearby, he stepped outside and dashed toward the children's cottages that backed up to the building. He spotted the caretaker approaching—but the man hadn't seen him.

Tharp ducked behind one cottage.

He gave the caretaker enough time to pass, silently hoping he wouldn't discover Edie and Betty. But that was out of his control now.

He needed to make his way past the receiving dock and reach the barn Nurse Betty had described. He had the key to Edie's carriage, and with luck, Snow and Asa wouldn't be there. If they were, he'd have to play it cool—he was a trusted student, unless word had already spread about his efforts to free Edie.

Asa was there, but Snow was nowhere in sight. Asa was organizing the back of the transport wagon, its contents scattered across the floor—including near Edie's carriage. He cleaned every tool as he removed it.

"Hello, Asa. I'm Dr. Tharp, from the class."

Asa startled, but quickly recovered. He stood up straighter, nodded, and said, "Hello."

Tharp wasn't entirely sure which horse belonged to Edie's wagon, but he could guess. "Asa, I need to move some of your stuff to get through. Would you be willing to help me harness up my horse?" Tharp bent and began shifting items from behind the carriage.

Asa glanced all around, but he turned to tend to Elouise. He rubbed the back of his neck, mumbled something, and then obeyed.

Tharp drove Elouise slowly out of the barn, not wanting to appear rushed. But as he rounded the end of the receiving entrance, he nearly ran into Dr. Snow. With no time to hide, Tharp smiled and waved. Snow, startled, responded with a wave of his own, turning to watch him pass.

As Tharp neared the morgue building, he saw the caretaker exit through the barn doors and lock them behind him. He carried a gas lantern.

Either Edie and Betty had hidden well—or they were no longer inside. The caretaker padlocked the door and headed toward the front of the central building, where the laundry was located, disappearing from view.

He probably noticed the body was missing, Tharp thought. *He's likely going to sound the alarm.*

Tharp parked on the far side of the building, out of sight of the laundry. He dismounted, approached the barn doors, and pounded on them, hoping for a response. Nothing. He tried again. Still nothing.

They're either not there, or hiding. Or worse. The caretaker might have captured them.

With little choice left, Tharp climbed back into the carriage and drove toward the gate. The caretaker was still away. *Hopefully, the gate's unlocked.*

Tharp dismounted, pushed the wooden gate open, and drove

out. Pausing just beyond, he stepped down and closed the gate behind him to avoid suspicion.

He needed a plan.

And he hoped—desperately—that Edie and Betty had avoided being seen.

CHAPTER 30

DOUBLE, DOUBLE TOIL AND TROUBLE

"Now what?" Edie asked. "We can't stand out here in the daylight and wait for Tharp or the next person to come along and ask what we're doing."

"I think we're safer inside the building. Follow me. We'll go in through the rear nurses' entrance. We have a couple of options from there."

When the caretaker entered the morgue building and lit his lantern, Edie and Betty were hiding behind storage crates near the entrance. As he moved to the back of the building—where the coroner examined corpses—they quietly slipped out the door, undetected.

•

Thaddeus Snow was worried. The success of the entire operation depended on keeping the body harvests hidden. He couldn't be angry with Asa—it wouldn't help—but the nurse who'd witnessed the disposal of the cadaver had to be silenced. She could destroy everything they had built. His mind drifted to Shakespeare: *Double, double toil and trouble; fire burn and cauldron bubble.* Well, the cauldron was about to boil over.

And now Asa had left his tools and supplies in the cemetery and hadn't even completed the reburial. They had work to do.

"Asa, reload and prepare the wagon. We'll pick up your captive and take her to the warehouse. I'll be back in half an hour."

Snow left the barn and reentered the building through the storage doors, heading for Kramer's office, hoping Dr. Brookfield might be there, too.

Inside, he found only Nurse Kramer at her desk, running her hands through her hair.

"We have a problem," Snow said.

"I seem to have a day full of them," Kramer replied.

"One of your nurses apparently discovered Asa disposing of the remains. He captured her and has her tied in a body bag in the mortuary building."

"I feel a vise closing in, Dr. Snow. We need some serious cleansing of all threats. Camouflage or concealment—whatever it takes. Including disposal." She stared directly into Snow's eyes, daring him to push back. "Where is Asa now? He could be a threat."

"He's with the wagon and horses, preparing to leave."

"You should stay. We may need your help, Dr. Snow."

"We also need to clean up the cemetery before anyone becomes suspicious. Tell me what else is happening."

"One of my nurses just left here—she came from the research laboratory. She found this." Kramer lifted a wicker basket from the floor and set it on her desk. "It's full of suspicious items, including two hand-drawn maps of the exterior grounds and the women's wings. One map shows Britina Myers's old room.

"Upon questioning the kitchen staff, it turns out young Dr. Tharp took a wrapped corpse, apparently female, from the laboratory very early this morning—only there wasn't a corpse there to take. She must have been an unwelcome observer of our training last night, likely with Tharp's help. We must capture and get rid of them all.

"Caretaker Rodney had just left when my nurse showed up. He questioned a young man in doctor's scrubs carrying a mummy-wrapped corpse, which he directed to the morgue building—where your nurse in a bag was deposited. Not long after, he went to check if the coroner had arrived. Instead, he found no coroner, no body, and no one tied up. Just an empty, dirty body bag and a pile of shrouds. It appears, Dr. Snow, that we have infiltrators on the grounds who could jeopardize everything."

Snow sat down and placed his hands flat on her desk. "What do we do?"

"I've instructed Caretaker Rodney to keep both gates locked, with someone stationed at each to keep everyone in—and out. My head of grounds, Attendant Wagner, is assigning search areas to the other attendants. I told him to pull as many staff as we can spare to patrol the women's wards and the grounds until we locate them. We know Britina Myers is beyond reach in the criminal cell—I am monitoring that personally."

"Then what?" Snow asked.

"I don't know." She trembled slightly. "The discovery that we're digging up corpses—especially if they identify this one as Heather Stone—could implicate us all in her murder, at least as accessories. An investigation could go much deeper. I don't know how much our three fugitives know or suspect, but I can't let them just walk out of here."

•

Dr. Tharp watched as the gatekeeper locked the front gate and took his position outside. Surprisingly, the man was armed.

Tharp considered his options. He could try to jump the guard and take the key—but what good would that do, even if he could manage it? He didn't know where Edie and Betty were. There was no way of finding them without being detected. And the guard looked rugged enough to make any attempt risky at best.

My only option is to get help. I have to go to the police.

The activities Edie and Betty described are criminal, he thought. *If they're captured, their lives could be in danger. I can't leave. I have to do something.*

Getting help would have to wait.

CHAPTER 31

CHIEF INSPECTOR McELROY

Chief Inspector McElroy was preparing to leave for Parliament when a messenger hand-delivered a request to meet with Coroner Wallace. McElroy had planned to join Constable Penn to further question Chaloner about his involvement on the night of the orgy. But Edie weighed heavily on his mind. She hadn't been at home or her office, and when he phoned Benji, there was no answer. He hadn't spoken with her in over two days. She should be present for the interview with Chaloner. But first, McElroy had to meet with Wallace.

Coroner Wallace greeted him warmly and ushered him not into a formal office but a casual sitting room. He offered tea and poured for both of them.

"Raymond, I asked for this meeting because something's been bothering me—and still is," Wallace began. "After Heather Stone's death, Dr. Brookfield, Nurse Kramer, and even your boss, Superintendent Cartwright, pressured me to expedite the coroner's inquest. I carried out the investigation and fact-finding as usual, but I took the word of the asylum staff that morphine caused her death. The evidence supported that—an empty vial in Britina Myers's room, a used syringe, reports of morphine missing from the supplies. The evidence convinced me. I filed it away, assumed it was done."

He paused, then leaned in.

"But I couldn't shake it. I woke up two days ago and realized what had been nagging at me. In death, Miss Stone's eyes were extremely dilated. I assumed it was from strangulation, a physical response from someone realizing they were dying and fighting. But the poison was administered first, and she was already comatose. There wouldn't have been a struggle. And morphine? Morphine causes sedation, drowsiness; it depresses the nervous system. It causes myosis."

"I'm sorry, Doctor," McElroy said. "What is that?"

"Extreme constriction of the pupils. Like the way your eyes react to a bright light. But Heather's pupils were the opposite—dilated, bulging, and bloodshot."

McElroy leaned back, absorbing the implications.

"I save body fluids and tissue samples from all my cases, refrigerate them for months. Once my concerns surfaced, I retrieved Heather's samples. I tested them—on a rabbit, a couple of mice, a guinea pig. Not all at once. I observed their behavior, vital signs, and signs of distress. None of them showed the effects of morphine—no pinpoint pupils, no respiratory depression, no sedation."

He took a breath, voice lowering.

"The guinea pig developed a distinct smell. Hydrogen cyanide. A bitter almond scent—commonly associated with arsenic."

"Could that happen with morphine?" McElroy asked.

"No. Morphine has almost no detectable scent. If the dose is lethal, you usually see a bluish tint on lips and extremities. Heather had that, but strangulation—a lack of oxygen, not a struggle—can cause the same reaction."

"Are you certain enough?" McElroy asked. "Do you have the evidence to recommend we reopen the inquest?"

"Yes. I hate putting it like this, but I think you must."

"Will you prepare paperwork for the magistrate? We need to transfer Britina Myers to police custody for renewed investigation—nullifying her criminal insanity commitment."

"I've already prepared it." Wallace handed him an envelope.

McElroy flagged a hansom cab and told the driver to head to the courthouse—fast. Chaloner and his Mace-wielding escapades could wait. Penn would realize soon enough he wasn't coming.

What had Edie written? 'Loyal friends cannot abandon friends, regardless of the risk.' Or something like that.

She meant to help Britina—or try. Could she have gone to the asylum? If so, she could be in danger. His gut told him he had to get there as soon as the magistrate signed the documents.

He leaned out of the cab, urging the driver to hurry.

•

McElroy was furious. Time had slipped away, and he'd been unable to find a single magistrate at the courthouse to sign the release papers for Britina Myers.

Magistrate Carter lived nearby, and they shared a decent rapport. He persuaded an assistant to prepare the documents for Carter's signature. He would take them to Carter's home himself and press for the signature—he had to. Getting Britina out of that asylum, away from Kramer and Brookfield, couldn't wait. And what might they be doing to Edie now, if they had caught her helping Britina?

He didn't have the police carriage—Penn had taken it. He'd need to find another cab.

CHAPTER 32

DR. THARP

D r. Tharp returned to the rear entrance, hoping it was still unlocked. Now, though, there was an armed guard, which meant it was probably locked. He turned the carriage around and started back down the road.

How is this all happening? If my father had only listened to me, I'd have a comfortable medical practice in Maine by now. Instead, I'm outside an asylum trying to save damsels in distress—and possibly risking my license. Oh hell, I always did dream of being a hero.

Rounding the bend at the far end of the institution's rear brick wall, he spotted a wooden cart pulled by two draft horses, laboring uphill with its load. The cart of rough-hewn lumber, with its sides slotted to allow airflow, was barely moving. It had a tin roof and a sturdy frame with iron-rimmed wooden wheels. Inside were four cattle—cows or steers. It was hard to tell.

Tharp jumped from the carriage and flagged it down, leaving his own horse and carriage to drift off.

"What you want?" the grizzled, weathered driver asked.

"Are you delivering these animals to the asylum?"

The man, chewing what might once have been the stub of a cigar, curled his lip, furrowed his brow, and stared at Tharp. "Road only goes one place, and you didn't answer my question."

"For two quid, can I hide inside with the animals?" Tharp hesitated, eyeing the bulky cattle. "Are they safe?" He added, "I need to get inside. I wasn't supposed to leave, and they'll punish me if they find me out here."

"You got money?"

"I do."

The driver grinned, revealing a patchwork of brown and black teeth. He held out his hand. "Hand it over and climb in. Stay low in the front where the cows can see you, and you'll be fine."

Tharp unlatched the rear gates and climbed aboard. He latched the gates through a slat and made his way to the front of the cart, squatting to knee level among the cows, his back pressed against the front wall. The nearest cow bent its thick neck and sniffed his hair, leaving a generous layer of saliva in its wake.

At the rear gate, a guard stopped the cart.

"Hello Bart, new meat for us?"

"Yup. Every month, as long as I can keep a herd growing."

"New procedures today. I need to get permission to let you in."

Bart looked wounded. "You know me, Rodney! You've let me in a hundred times."

"It won't take long; I've got one of the cottage urchins running for me."

Kirb—short for Kirby—took off at a sprint. It took him about twenty minutes to return with the go-ahead. Tharp's knees were screaming, and one cow had nibbled on his hair.

"Said you were to watch the unloading. Make sure no one gets on board to leave," Kirb said.

"I can't guard the entrance and watch the unloading at the barn at the same time."

"I'll do it," Kirb offered, "for a shilling."

He got paid and walked alongside the cart to the cattle barn.

Kirby's mouth fell open when a man in doctor's scrubs, hair slick and shaggy, followed the steers off the wagon. "You can't sneak out," Kirby said.

"I'm sneaking in, not out. Two shillings for you to stay quiet."

Kirby held out his hand. "I'm having a good day! Need any help?"

CHAPTER 33

EDIE AND BETTY

Edie and Betty waited in the dim light of the basement, struggling not to get sick from the noxious odor. Betty had suggested a plan.

"We'll wait until the next laundry collection. That's when the washerwomen come and gather all the soiled laundry here for processing. They come twice a day."

During the wait, staff tossed several loads of filthy laundry into the cellar through trapdoors in the ceiling. Edie and Betty hid in a dark corner near the double doors that led to the laundry yard. At the scheduled time, the washerwomen unbolted the doors and rolled in half a dozen large linen carts to collect the piles. With the washerwomen's backs turned as they gathered laundry, the two slipped quietly through the doors, out onto the lawn, and around the corner, out of sight.

From across the yard, Edie could see that the laundry building was large and imposing, made of stone and brick. The side facing them had wide windows for light and ventilation. Pipes on the roof spewed steam. The laundry building connected to the long kitchen and storage wing, which also contained the carriage barn on the far side.

Betty led them across the lawn and crouched behind a

brick-walled enclosure used for washing laundry carts. They stacked some loose bricks into makeshift seats so they could wait and plan.

"The laundry is huge!" Edie said.

"And full of machinery and pipes and whatever else," Betty replied. "Many of them can be dangerous. Once we're inside, follow my lead and be careful. At the far end of the building, there's a loading dock where soiled laundry from the outer buildings gets delivered and clean linens picked up. It's enclosed by a fence with a metal gate that's kept locked—but I've seen where they hang the keys, so any laundry worker can open the gate for a delivery or pickup. Once we're through that gate, it's just a short distance down the outer wall to the barn where your carriage is."

"Of course, the other possibility is that your ghoul could still be there. That's where they store their wagon," Edie said.

Betty shuddered. "I remember."

Edie paused, thinking. "Betty, I haven't accomplished what I came here to do. I can't leave without at least trying to get to Britina, especially now." Her face hardened with determination. "Her life may be in danger."

"With everything you've seen, and the attack on me, and what I witnessed—that's not enough?"

"None of it proves Britina didn't take Heather Stone's life."

"Couldn't we just get out and have your police friend return?" Betty asked.

"He needs evidence to get her released."

"And how do you plan to get that?" Betty pressed.

"I don't know. You said Britina's room is accessible—if I could talk to her and get her side of the story, it might help. She hasn't even had the chance to defend herself. She could have something—anything—that helps McElroy build a case. We won't know unless we ask her."

"And if you're caught, you might end up in one of those torture machines you told me about, with electrodes strapped to your head."

"Betty, if there's a workable way in, I have to try. I think we should split up. You try to get to the carriage and get out of the grounds—with or without Dr. Tharp. Go to Chief Inspector McElroy and tell him what I'm doing. He'll be furious, and that alone will be enough to bring him back here to protect me. Is there a way in from the laundry that doesn't lead directly into the wards?"

Betty hesitated, then nodded. "There is, but it's still risky. The kitchen and dining areas have a separate deposit and collection point for linens to keep things sanitary. A laundry chute carries soiled linens from the main kitchen floor, and a small rope lift next to it transports clean kitchen laundry to the storage floor above. The chute and lift are on the laundry wall that connects to the kitchen.

"Workers clean, dry, fold, and then return the kitchen laundry to storage. If you take the lift with some laundry, you'll have to exit through the kitchen and follow the map to Britina's room. With a bonnet on and a cart of folded linens, you could pass for someone delivering fresh laundry to the ladies' wing. Meanwhile, I'll try to get out through the loading dock. If I succeed, I'll leave the gate unlocked—or at least leave the keys in the lock."

Edie nodded. "If I make it, I'll try to come back and leave the same way. Tell me about the lift."

"It's simple. There's a platform big enough for a person and two laundry carts. There's a rope on either side. Some system of gears and counterweights make it easy to pull yourself up. One rope releases the brake, and you just keep pulling. The other rope sets the brake when you want to stop—either at the kitchen or the second-floor storage."

Edie thought for a moment. "Are there a lot of workers in the laundry?"

"Quite a few—women and men. But the place is enormous. There are workers twenty-four hours a day, though after the morning shift, there are far fewer than during the midday and night shifts."

Edie listened intently, already planning her next move, though dread crept in with every thought of acting alone.

"Don't worry too much about laundry workers," Betty added. "They're pretty removed from asylum operations. They just do their jobs, and new workers come and go all the time. We don't need to raise any suspicions—but we need uniforms. There are drying rooms filled with clotheslines and radiators along the walls to help with the drying. We'll enter through that door over there; it's a drying room." She pointed across the space. "We'll find some uniforms, change, then head to the kitchen laundry area. If anyone stops us, we say we're assigned to handle that section.

"The drying rooms won't be occupied—we'll be fine in there, unless something goes wrong. I'll leave you at the kitchen ironing station."

Edie clenched her jaw, resolute. "I'll try to get to Britina, find out what I can. If possible, I'll bring her with me. Then we'll try to get back to the barn and wait for you and the police there."

"And if you can't?"

"I'll rely on you and McElroy to find me. Just—please hurry."

"Let's go," Betty said. "Act like we belong. We'll claim the kitchen ironing and folding area as our assignment. If we run into trouble, we'll be firm. We can't show doubt."

CHAPTER 34

LOCKDOWN

Nurse Kramer received the report from an attendant on the search crew.

"Tharp was spotted riding along the exterior wall of the asylum in a small carriage. We found the carriage with a broken wheel and the horse grazing down past the cemetery near the train tracks. Tharp either escaped on foot or possibly caught a train."

"We must assume he's gone for help. He assisted in getting the spy out of the research room. Was he alone in the carriage?"

"My guard said he was, but someone could've been hiding in the enclosed compartment. There were candle fragments and other suspicious things inside. Also, Nurse Robinson's husband came looking for her. I told him she'd been terminated and sent him away, but he threatened to go to the police."

Kramer closed her eyes and thought for a moment. The spy could still be on the property. *Probably is—and probably with Nurse Robinson. And there's no telling what the husband will do.*

"We still have at least two intruders on the property, probably hiding in one of the outer buildings. Find them. Bring them to me."

Kramer was in full panic mode now. Things were unraveling

faster than she'd imagined possible. As far as she could tell, she had a rogue nurse and a spy from the training sessions loose somewhere on the grounds—and a rogue doctoral student with knowledge of the operation, possibly on his way to the police. All of them knew too much.

She needed Brookfield urgently. She'd sent him a message with enough detail to signal trouble and asked him to come quickly. That had been hours ago, and still no word.

Against his orders, she phoned the hospital and left a message: he needed to come now.

•

Dr. Bran Brookfield had no intention of stepping into a mess that might damage his reputation. The tone of the messages made it clear he needed to prepare an alibi and get rid of evidence. Kramer would likely face investigation for her involvement with the corpses, the training sessions, and the experiments on patients. He was confident he could plausibly deny all knowledge, because his direct connection to the murders and corpse harvesting couldn't be proven. Kramer's greed, her executioner Sturgis, and of course Snow and his assistant, could take the blame for that. All his directives had gone through Kramer. The others wouldn't be able to implicate him with evidence.

He wrote a message back to Kramer, sealed it in an envelope, and handed it to the head nurse on his floor, instructing her to send it by delivery service. It read: 'I don't know what problems you are referring to, but I'm trying desperately to save a life.' *My own*, he thought. 'I will come when I can.'

He signed the note formally, careful to show no familiarity with Nurse Kramer.

Afterward, he locked the door to his private office. Methodically, he gathered every file related to the testing, the experiments, and the medical students' training. All of his research was now useless—and worse, incriminating. He needed to hide it until things blew over.

·

Dr. Thaddeus Snow was now certain the activities surrounding the asylum grounds—and his work with Dr. Brookfield—would not end well. He had his own affairs to worry about. It was time to gather his equipment, his wagon, and Asa and get out of Melbourne as quickly as possible. He would need to return to the warehouse, find Henderson, and possibly shut down operations temporarily.

He prepared to leave. As he walked, he ran through a quick mental checklist. *Was there anything in the basement research and training room that could incriminate me?* He wasn't sure. The equipment and the remnants of Asa's work in the barn—and what they'd left behind at the cemetery—certainly needed to be dealt with.

He stopped in his tracks. The realization hit him hard: his greatest threat was Asa himself. Asa didn't understand the threat and would talk under pressure. He wouldn't even realize he was condemning them both. The second threat was more complex—the observer and the nurse Asa had captured. If word got out that he had performed an autopsy on an illegally obtained corpse, his career—and freedom—would be over.

He needed to destroy all evidence, clean out the drug warehouse, and quietly return to Sydney and resume his normal life. He'd deal with Asa there. The fortune Brookfield had promised was clearly not going to materialize.

Kramer would make him the scapegoat in a heartbeat—and so would Brookfield.

How do I protect myself? He knew the answer.

He headed for the exit through the kitchen and its adjacent receiving area; the laboratory was on the way. It was the shortest path to the barn and the one with the fewest people who might recall seeing him. He wouldn't let these amateurs destroy the lucrative enterprise he had built.

In the cellar laboratory, Thaddeus gathered the body shrouds and operating towels scattered around the room, stuffing them into a laundry bag. He placed his personal equipment and supplies into another. He crumpled additional shrouds and wrapping from the autopsy area, including some that had aided in the intruder's escape. Everything went into the bags.

Climbing the stairs back to the kitchen, he made his way toward the storage exit that led to the barn. No one in the kitchen questioned him—he was a doctor, after all.

CHAPTER 35

THE LAUNDRY

Edie and Betty slipped into the drying room just after the first shift ended for the day. They could hear voices from the second-shift ladies—small groups talking, some laughing. Those they couldn't avoid. They'd have to pass as new workers.

They hurried along the clotheslines, searching for uniforms of the right sizes. There were plenty to choose from. Edie found one that was a little damp but not dripping—good enough.

"Find a cloth hat as well," Betty said. "It's required for laundry workers. Hair can get caught in the manglers."

As they stepped into the main laundry, Edie could feel the heat rising from the firepits under the boilers. Two burly, shirtless men were shoveling coal from a large bin into the flames. The massive boilers hid the washing tubs where most of the workers gathered. Steam hissed from joints in the piping, and the air shimmered with heat.

They skirted the low pipes, feeling the warmth radiating from every surface, then crossed to the other side of the building. There, past the ironing and folding tables, Edie spotted the lift—a small, enclosed ramp set back in an alcove about three feet from the laundry wall.

Am I really going to get into that? Her heart raced, and her throat tightened.

The only person who paid them any mind was a large, older washerwoman who rolled over a laundry cart and growled, "More kitchen laundry needs ironing and folding." Then she turned and left without another word.

Leaving Edie to her mission, Nurse Betty timed her exit with a tea break and slipped through the metal gate at the laundry shipping dock. She left the key in the lock behind her. Hugging the walls, she made her way toward the barn. At the open door, she paused, listening.

A kerosene lamp was burning inside—someone was here, or had been. Edie's carriage was gone, likely taken by Tharp. No one was immediately visible, but Betty thought she heard something—movement inside the large, enclosed wagon. The same one in which she had been held captive.

Then she heard a noise. She froze.

"Psst."

There it was again, coming from behind a boxwood hedge across the road. Tharp's head popped up over the hedge. He raised a hand, motioning for her to come over.

Betty scanned the area, checking for signs of movement near the gatekeepers and groundskeeper's cottages. She crouched low and darted across the road to join him behind the hedge, grateful for the familiar face.

There, squatting beside Tharp, was a grinning urchin.

"He's my puppy," Tharp said cheerfully. "I told him to go home, but he said no one was there. He'd rather stay with me. His name's Kirb—short for Kirby."

"Nice to meet you, Kirby," Betty said, holding out her hand.

To her surprise, he shook it firmly, pumping it up and down. "Pleased to meet you, madam."

Betty smiled. "Where are your parents?"

"They're in the fever tents. Not fatal, just the usual fever. I don't seem to get sick."

"That's convenient. What do you do when they're confined to the tents?"

"My mates and I have adventures. This is a good one so far."

"Umm, yes—for you, perhaps. Our lives are in danger, and we need to get out of the asylum and find the police."

"The doctor didn't tell me that. He just paid me to get into the grounds."

Tharp looked sheepish. "Can you get us out of here, Kirby?" he asked.

"Yes, but you never asked. Want to know the price?"

"Tell us about your escape route first," Tharp said.

Kirby nodded. "All the border property along the north side of the asylum is airing grounds—game courts for patients and staff. Lawn bowling, even a cricket oval. They're only used during the day and when the weather's good. The area's surrounded by ha-ha walls, but I don't know why they're funny."

"What are they?" Tharp asked, receiving only a blank look from Kirb.

Betty stepped in. "From outside the asylum, they look like low stone walls, so it doesn't look like a prison. Visitors can see over them to the grounds. From inside, patients can see out to the surrounding area, which seems more humane. But the ha-ha is actually a deep ditch sloped down to the base of the wall, making it impossible to climb. So, it's a trap of sorts—clever and hidden."

"How does that help us get out, Kirby?" Tharp asked.

"My mates and I—we made a tunnel under the wall and up on the outside grounds. We dug from the ditch side at night so no one would see us. Candlelight only. We carried off the dirt every night and spread it in the gardens or along the inner road. We made wooden covers for the holes and laid sod on top. You can't see them during the day at all.

"The tunnel on the ditch side goes away from the wall first, then straight down about five feet. We reinforced it with wood from the carpenter shed, scraps mostly. We even put in small pipes for air, hidden in the grass."

"Brilliant!" Tharp said. "Keep going."

"We angled down toward the wall, and once we were deep enough, we went straight under it. There's a stand of trees about ten feet beyond the wall—we aimed for that. Missed a little, but not by much. Now my mates and I can leave for adventures whenever we want, at night."

"You're one smart kid, Kirby," Betty said, impressed.

He grinned. "I'm going to be an architect. My mother teaches at the children's cottages. My dad's got a memory problem now, but he was an engineer."

A promise of two pounds sealed the deal—an absolute fortune in young Kirby's eyes.

•

Edie, dressed in her uniform and cap, pushed a tiered cart half-filled with folded laundry through the kitchen, into the dining room, and out toward the women's wing—exactly where Betty had marked Britina's room on the map. She passed two nurses along the way, but they didn't pay her any attention.

She found the door, glanced up and down the corridor, and quietly slid open the bolt latches.

"Britina, it's me, Edie," she whispered.

She pulled the door open. It was dark inside, and there was no response.

They've moved her.

Voices echoed down the hall. Edie stepped back, heart pounding. At the far end, she saw the two burly nurses she recognized from the dissection in the basement. They were walking toward her, talking.

I need to disappear.

Grabbing her cart, she turned and rolled it quickly in the opposite direction. When she reached an intersecting aisle, she abandoned the cart and half-ran down the corridor.

"It must be the spy!" Ralphine shouted.

"Stop if you want to live," Ashley bellowed.

Edie yanked open the nearest door and slipped inside. A stairwell. She descended quickly, hit by the same noxious stench she and Betty had endured while waiting for the laundry workers. It must be the same space. The laundry exit would be locked. The entrance might be open—but maybe not. There was no time to weigh options.

She bolted down the stairs and dove into a nearby pile of laundry, burying herself in soiled bedsheets.

The door creaked open behind her, and heavy footsteps hit the top stair.

"Go get Sturgis. Come back quickly," Ashley ordered Ralphine. "There's no way out at this hour. I'll handle her. I'll enjoy it."

Ashley struck a flint and lit a candle lamp hanging by the doorway. She stood at the top of the stairs, casting her eerie silhouette into the dim cellar.

Ralphine's footsteps echoed as she sprinted toward Kramer's office.

Edie yanked a sheet over herself—foul with excrement and vomit. Swallowing her gag reflex, she crawled low across the floor, keeping to the dark side of the stairwell.

Ashley's voice rang out—loud and cruel. "You're our spy,

aren't you? Trying to save that nun? Since you were in her old room, I know. Well, I've got news for you. You're too late. And if you want to live, I suggest you give yourself up now."

She descended a few steps.

"If you don't cooperate, you'll be the next cadaver on the table—for the good of medical science—right after your nun friend. What do you say?"

She paused, waiting for an answer.

Silence.

"I could protect you," Ashley offered, her voice dripping with false sweetness. "If you cooperate."

Three more steps. Edie thought.

Edie tensed, counting. Just two more . . .

"Come on now," Ashley said. "I don't want to hurt you, but I will."

One step. A pause. Another.

Now.

Edie sprang from beside the staircase enclosure, leaped, and slammed a bundle of soiled linen over the nurse's head, pressing foul-smelling excrement into her face.

"Bitch," Edie muttered.

Nurse Ashley lurched back, gagging, and fell onto the stairs. Edie stepped past her, planted a foot on her shoulder, and shoved—sending the nurse sliding on her back down the remaining stairs, still choking and retching.

Edie bolted up the stairs. At the top, she checked both directions. Turning back briefly, she saw smoke—then the flicker of flames. The candle lantern had tipped and caught the sheet on fire.

There was no time. No chance of finding Britina now, not with fire and the alarm about to be raised. She had to make it back to the barn unseen and pray for rescue.

She darted off in the direction she guessed led toward the dining rooms and kitchen. It was late for meals—hopefully, fewer people would be around. She recognized the layout now. She cut through a communal ward filled with voluntary patients. They stirred as she passed, some agitated, some rising to follow her.

At the far end, she spotted the dining area. Just to the right, Kramer and Sturgis were entering Kramer's office. They hadn't seen her, but her position was exposed, and the patients behind her were attracting attention.

She dropped back and allowed a few patients to surround her like a loose, moving curtain.

Ralphine burst into Kramer's office. "Ashley has the spy trapped in the laundry cellar."

Kramer turned, gazing at Ralphine. "What are all those patients doing out of bed? Where are the attendants?"

She remembered—the attendants were still out, searching the outer buildings.

"Ralphine, handle the patients. We'll help Ashley."

They headed down the corridor toward the women's wing. Ralphine moved toward the patient group.

Edie knew it was now or never. She sprang forward, pushing through the patients, sprinting straight at Ralphine.

"Here she is!" Ralphine shouted, pointing.

Kramer and Sturgis turned, eyes locking on Edie.

Just then, a nurse came running toward Kramer and Sturgis, shouting, "Fire—there's a lot of fire!"

Smoke followed her like a trailing cloak.

Ralphine turned toward the sound. The moment's distraction was all Edie needed.

She rammed into Ralphine with full force, knocking her flat, and fell on top of her hard. Rolling off, she scrambled to her feet and sprinted toward the kitchens. Ralphine grabbed her foot but couldn't hold on.

Edie flew down the length of the dining room and into the kitchens. Ralphine scrambled up and gave chase, joined by a couple of others, while the rest of the staff swarmed toward the fire.

Edie sped toward the exterior wall, near the stairwell leading to the basement and upper storage. She spotted the chute—the one for soiled linens—and lunged for it headfirst.

Please let there be a cart in place, she prayed.

The chute was steep, and the ride fast. Her hands hit first, her head tucked instinctively. She slammed into a small pile of dirty linens in a waiting cart. The impact tipped it over, spilling her to the floor.

She scrambled to her feet, breathing hard. She shoved the cart out of the way. If Ralphine followed, she'd have a harder landing.

But Edie heard nothing. No one was coming down after her. Not yet.

Edie didn't wait—she tore through the laundry, heading for the far end. The workers on duty turned to watch, stunned, but no one moved to stop her. She reached the loading dock door, where the keys should have been hanging. They weren't. Her heart pounded. She couldn't stop now—if she had to climb the wire gate, she would. She ran out onto the dock and jumped. A four-foot drop. She landed hard and rolled through the gravel, the sharper stones tearing at her skin. Gritting her teeth, she scrambled to her feet and sprinted to the gates. The keys hung in the lock.

Betty! Please be at the barn. Please have Eloise ready. She flung the gate open and kept running, breath burning in her chest, legs straining. She pumped her arms harder.

Behind the hedge, Betty, Tharp, and Kirb watched. They'd been planning their escape when Edie appeared, running flat-out down the road. She hadn't been inside long enough. Something was wrong.

"Edie!" Betty shouted, panic breaking in her voice.

Edie reached the barn, turned the corner—and stopped. Her hands flew to her face, barely stifling a scream.

No Betty. No carriage. No Eloise.

Only Dr. Thaddeus Snow—Rohwedder—waiting to greet her, his ghoul of a sidekick at his side, the body wagon hitched and ready to go.

Snow recognized her at once from their dealings during the *Ferret* theft.

"Hello, Edie."

"Rohwedder," she gasped.

"Grab her, Asa."

She tried to fight, but she was in shock, too slow. Asa seized her easily. At Snow's command, he gagged her and bound her hands and ankles. Edie thrashed as they went to the back of the wagon and slid out a casket.

Not another one. Please, no.

•

Betty, Tharp, and Kirby watched helplessly as Asa and Snow nailed the lid shut, lifted the coffin, and slid it into the wagon's shelf. They packed the rest of their gear, climbed aboard, and drove off toward the back gate.

Snow turned towards the asylum, where smoke coiled into the sky from the women's wards. Flames licked out the windows.

Betty, Tharp and Kirby stared as well. All three froze. Disbelief rooted them to the spot.

"There's no way to rescue Edie—we'll have to get help if we can. Let's go," Tharp said.

"And Britina's trapped in the building," Betty added,

voice breaking.

Kirby led them silently, weaving behind cottages and fever tents, staying hidden. Flames now ripped through the roof of the women's refractory ward, distracting most people. Staff guided dazed patients down the steps and out onto the lawn.

•

Snow slapped the reins and steered the wagon toward the gate. If the gatekeeper gave him trouble, he was ready—he had a key of his own. He spotted the man standing by the gate. Handing the reins to Asa, Snow jumped down and charged.

The gatekeeper met his eyes, then shook his head. *Not letting you out now, I have orders*, the gesture said, loud and clear. Snow yelled, arms raised in an attack position. The gatekeeper turned and bolted toward the burning building.

Many others were running in that direction as well. *Perfect*, Snow thought.

He fished out the stolen keys, unlocked the gates, and swung them open. Asa drove the wagon through, then paused while Snow relocked it behind them to prevent others from following.

•

From their hiding place near the morgue barn, Betty, Tharp, and Kirby watched him go.

"If he leaves it unlocked, we can just walk out the gate," Tharp said, hopefully.

But Snow shut the gates tight. They waited for the wagon to disappear down the road, then Tharp sprinted over and tried the gate.

Locked.

He jogged back, shaking his head. "No luck. It's back to the tunnel."

CHAPTER 36

HOT

Nurse Kramer was terrified. She needed Brookfield, and it was becoming clear he wasn't coming. An investigation was now unavoidable—if the facility survived. She turned to face Sturgis.

"If we're going to salvage our enterprise, we must eliminate any implicating threats. That means the laboratory, the spy, Tharp, Betty Robinson . . . and Britina Myers must sustain a fatal injury during evacuation. Purely accidental, of course."

"Any suggestions?" Sturgis asked.

"She's weak. A broken neck from a fall down the stairs could work."

"We could let her burn," Sturgis offered.

"We would be charged with negligence. And there's no guarantee she'd die."

"There's no guarantee she'll die from a fall, either," Sturgis argued.

"That's your job. But we must at least appear to be trying to save all the patients," Kramer said firmly. She handed her a ring of keys. "Make the accident look real—make it work. I'll deal with the laboratory. There's a fire, and if it somehow spreads to the central building . . . not so far-fetched. The lab would go up. I'll just speed things along after removing any incriminating evidence I can."

Kramer turned sharply and hurried to her office.

•

McElroy's meeting with Magistrate Carter did not go as planned. He had the cabbie wait in front of Carter's house on the outskirts of Melbourne. The magistrate was already waiting on the screened-in porch.

"Raymond, I got a call from the courthouse alerting me of your arrival. Then, another call from your station. The phone is an amazing tool—you should try it sometime. I would have come to you."

He stood, arms crossed. "First, Nurse Betty Robinson's husband came to see you. She left home in the middle of the night and left him a note. It seems she's been helping Edie Black investigate activity at the asylum. She hasn't returned home. He got worried and went to the asylum to check on her. An armed guard stopped him at the gate. He said the asylum was on lockdown. No one in or out without permission."

"Permission from whom?" McElroy asked.

"Head Nurse Kramer. He requested seeing his wife, and the reply came back: his wife wasn't there, and she no longer worked there. He told the guard he was going to the police. Said he knew his wife wouldn't stay away unless she was being held—and he was angry with you for letting her get involved in police business."

Carter took the papers from McElroy and signed them. "I'd hurry if I were you."

•

Betty, Tharp, and Kirby reached the far side of the vacant grounds near the ha-ha ditch and lay in the grass. To their left, flames and smoke rose from the asylum wing, burning out of control.

Betty hoped the patients—all of them, including Britina—were being moved to safety. But now she knew Edie wasn't safe, and they needed help to save her. The ghoul and his doctor boss certainly would not let her live.

Kirby instructed, "Stay low. Run for the ditch and dive or roll in—it doesn't matter which. Once you're in, you won't be visible, but I think everyone's too distracted by the fire to notice us."

He felt through the grass until his fingers found a pull ring, which he hinged upright. Taking a jackknife from his pocket, he measured out from the ring to the tunnel door's edges, then quickly cut through the grassroots along the perimeter. Grasping the ring with both hands, he leaned back and popped the lid free. The grass and sod held firmly to the lid.

"The grassroots seal in the door quickly," he explained. "That helps keep it hidden. We'll have to pop the door on the other side with brute force," he added with a smile.

A box attached to the side wall beneath the door held a supply of candles and a container of matches to keep them dry. But when struck against the lighting strip, several matches were too damp to catch.

"You two go first. Wait for me," Kirby instructed his troop. "I'll make sure the door's properly back in place. Take more candles and a box of fire sticks with you. The air supply is spotty, and the candles might go out. Once we get to the flat, the air pipes will give us a bit more air, and they should stay lit."

The tunnel wasn't tall enough to stand in—not in the first section. Tharp went first, and Betty followed, moving in a duck-walk through the angled section away from the wall. At the drop, there was no ladder or rope; they had to jump. Both Tharp and Betty landed in a squat, then fell face-first into the dirt.

The straight section beneath the wall was just tall enough to stand hunched at the waist. The air felt fresher here. They lit a second candle so each could carry one.

Kirby soon joined them. "Neat, isn't it?" he said. "I might specialize in tunnels and bridges when I'm an architect."

They agreed the tunnel was impressive. This section had wooden supports along the walls, with beams crossing overhead every five feet—but a few chunks of dirt lined the path ahead, doubtless fallen from above. Tharp glanced up at the ceiling, hoping it would hold.

•

Britina was thirsty—hungry too, but mostly thirsty. They hadn't given her food or water for over two days, punishing her for refusing to swallow her pills. She'd rejected all oral medication after slipping into a stupor following that first meal. When she swallowed, she forced regurgitation as soon as she was alone. The injections she couldn't avoid; they held her down and filled her with something that knocked her out. She didn't resist, knowing resistance meant the straitjacket or, worse, the body containment bag—sealed tight with only her face exposed.

Sometimes—perhaps the injections were less potent without the pills—she'd pretend to be asleep whenever Kramer's freaks came into her cell. A few days ago, she'd overheard a conversation about over-harvesting patients. Someone—it sounded like Sturgis—said Britina shouldn't be harvested. Not yet . . . it was too risky. Harvesting her would raise too many questions; they needed someone less visible for the moment.

"Harvesting patients" didn't sound good to Britina, but for now, it seemed she was being spared.

Britina could feel Edie's presence nearby. She didn't know how this was possible, but she knew it was real—and that Edie was in danger. It wasn't her imagination, just as she'd known the presence in her previous room wasn't her imagination. Putting her hands together, she prayed—for Edie and for help. It had been a long time since she prayed, but it made her feel better.

Then she smelled smoke.

•

Kew's prominent hilltop position overlooked Melbourne, nearly four miles from the magistrate's residence. The asylum was visible from all east-facing observation points. By now, the entire city knew Kew was ablaze. As McElroy exited the magistrate's home, he glanced toward the Kew promenade and saw smoke billowing. His concern deepened. He hurried back to the magistrate's door.

"You said you had a telephone."

"I do. What's wrong?"

"Kew is on fire. Call my office and have them alert the Melbourne Fire Prevention Society to head to the site if they haven't already done so. Let them know that any available personnel should proceed to Kew immediately with buckets and protective gear. May I borrow your horse and carriage? I'll dismiss the cabbie."

Carter made the call and helped rig up the carriage. "I'm coming with you," he said. He drove fast, at least until they reached High Street, which was jammed with carriages, including police vehicles, gawkers, and presumably some fire society volunteers.

"Take the tram—Number 75—it'll be faster. I'll keep going through the traffic until I reach the asylum. I'll look for you," Carter said.

McElroy jumped off the carriage and ran toward the tram stop. Tram 75 would take him to the base of the hill just below the cemetery.

•

The traffic hadn't reached Kew yet, but it would soon. Snow could see carriage lights on the road below. If the authorities stopped him for any reason, they would arrest him. Getting caught with a living woman confined in a coffin wasn't something he could explain.

He couldn't allow Edie to stay alive. She knew who he really was. She might not know about the Sydney operation, but she had seen the dissection—she knew too much. With her gone, he could save himself.

As he descended the long hill toward the cemetery, he made a sudden turn and slipped into the grounds, heading straight for the paupers' graves.

Once there, out of sight of the approaching traffic, he and Asa gathered the buckets, tarp, and other materials Asa had left behind after capturing Nurse Betty. Asa shoveled in the last of the dirt and patted down the unmarked grave that now held Heather Stone's remains.

•

McElroy exited the tram. Seeing the flames rising from the asylum, he began running toward the hill. Within three minutes, he was breathless. Smoke was settling into the lower ground while more billowed up from the fire. He slowed to pace himself. The first of the firefighters were just passing on the road.

He broke into a run again, and as he neared the entrance gate to the Yarra River Cemetery, a large black wagon drawn by two powerful stallions burst through the gate, swerving toward him. It nearly ran him down. He fell backward into the roadside ditch.

There was no time to investigate. He had to save Britina—and Edie, if she needed saving. He flagged down the next water wagon, heading uphill, and begged for a ride. His badge paid the fare.

•

Sturgis wasn't concerned about killing. She enjoyed it, was skilled at it, and was well-compensated for it. However, how could anyone guarantee a person would break their neck and die from a fall down a small set of stairs? She needed a better plan. She had no intention of sticking around for any investigation.

•

Kramer took all their cash and valuables and placed them into a medical bag, adding incriminating files and evidence. She left her office and ran to the laboratory. Smoke had seeped into the space, but no flames were visible yet. Down the corridors to the women's wings, there was bedlam. She grabbed a tin of lamp oil and matches at the kitchen entrance, then found an empty flour sack in storage.

She unlocked the door and turned on the electric lights. One of the steam dynamos hissed and began generating electricity, bringing the lights to life. Kramer closed the door behind her and descended the stairs. First, she placed the skulls in the empty flour sack. Fire wouldn't destroy them—she would have to bury or dispose of them some other way. She doused the equipment and combustibles with kerosene. Then she grabbed her bag of valuables and evidence and the sack of skulls and climbed halfway up the stairs. She lit a match and tossed it into a small puddle of the flammable liquid. Instantly, it burst into flames. She felt the whoosh of warm air and pressure strike her. Turning quickly, she climbed the remaining stairs and opened the door.

Sturgis stood there, a crazed look on her face. She grabbed a bag from the startled Kramer, tossed it behind her, and shoved Kramer with both hands. Kramer fell backward, arms flailing, landing at the foot of the stairs. Flames engulfed her. Sturgis closed and locked the door, slid the locking bar into place, picked up the bag, and left to find Snow—her next victim. He knew too much.

Sturgis assessed her situation. The risk of killing Britina was too great—she might fail, and she might be seen. She ruled it out. Instead, she would focus on protecting herself from those posing a genuine threat. She preferred a quiet, simple extermination. Britina, if she remained alive and coherent, had no concrete evidence against her. If the current crisis spiraled and threatened Dr. Brookfield, he could sacrifice Sturgis, but he knew she had evidence she could use against him. She had a plan. She left Britina in the care of others, to survive or not.

Sturgis gave the keys to a trusted attendant and told her to gather as many employees as possible to evacuate the refractory ward's cell patients—including Britina—to the back lawns. Others were handling the paupers' wards, and many of the medical and voluntary patients had already made it out; those who were able had exited on their own. Other than Snow, who had his own cover-up to deal with, Brookfield was the only one left aware of her actions—and he had ordered them. He would deny any involvement and could likely get away with it. Kramer was out of the picture. Brookfield owed her for that. Snow first.

•

McElroy jumped off the wagon. "I'll get the gate," he said. It was the first fire pumper to arrive. The wagons carried their own water supply, but would tie into the fire pond on the property when needed.

The gate was locked, and no attendant was there to unlock it.

He returned to the wagon. "Try the rear gate. If it's locked and unattended, use your axes—you have my permission."

From their position, they could see heavy activity on the lawns and feel the heat of the flames, even from a distance. The fire appeared to be confined to the middle section of the facing wings for now. McElroy hoped Edie and Britina weren't in those areas.

"Quickly!" he shouted, pointing toward the rear gate. "I'll direct the following wagons." He began ordering non-essential vehicles to pull off the road to clear a path for firefighting and official vehicles. He quelled a few objections with a flash of his badge and the threat of arrest. Anxiousness grew in him—he feared for Edie and Britina.

•

Going against the traffic, Snow and Asa could move quickly, though a few bold vehicles—likely news reporters—tried to bypass the congestion by driving up the right lane. They veered off the road quickly when they saw the big black wagon barreling toward them at full speed.

"Asa, I'm headed for the warehouse. We'll dump the coffins and tools, load all the medicines, drugs, and stored supplies into the wagon, and fill it to the roof if we have to. We're shutting down the Melbourne operation. If we find Henderson, he comes with us. If not, he'll have to catch up. We'll torch the warehouse when we leave. All the firefighters are up at Kew—it'll be a total loss. No evidence left."

"Yes, sir." Asa was at a loss. This man had once been his salvation, but now he seemed scared—and that made Asa scared, too. Worse, he feared Snow. The man who had cut people up, who nailed people alive in coffins—what might he do to Asa because of the nurse who got away?

•

Betty and Tharp, with Kirby in tow, pulled themselves up out of the exit door from the tunnel, took deep breaths, and covered the door with sod.

"We have to find help," Betty said.

Kirby took off his pageboy hat and held it out. His hair looked like he cut it himself. "Can I get paid?" he asked.

"Fact is, Kirby, neither of us has two pounds on us. But we'll pay you extra as soon as we can. Why don't you stick with us, and we'll get you paid soon?"

"I should've asked for money in advance!" he said. Then he smiled, dimples showing. "But I'm having fun—I'm sticking with you." He carefully smoothed the grass around the edge of the tunnel cover.

The three of them started down the road, heading down-hill. More fire pumpers were just entering the back gate of the property, with other vehicles following behind. Looking over the ha-ha walls, they could see many patients scattered on the grounds—some sitting or lying down, others wandering without supervision.

They rounded a curve and approached the front gate. Betty spotted someone directing traffic. She recognized McElroy from the inquest and ran to him.

•

As the bucket brigade and the pumpers attacked the flames, Britina lay in the chilly grass. The fire alert had interrupted evening medications, and the earlier drugs were wearing off. Her head slowly cleared, and her body felt less numb. She thanked God for getting her out of that building. Left alone, she stared at the stars, the moon, and the flames.

•

Betty didn't explain everything to McElroy—just that Edie had been nailed in a coffin and carted off in a black hearse wagon, pulled by two large stallions and driven by Dr. Snow.

McElroy recognized the wagon; it had nearly run him over when it exited the cemetery.

He spotted Magistrate Carter's carriage about a quarter mile down the hill, stuck in traffic. The fire vehicles bypassed the congestion and followed others to the rear gate. Some volunteers had abandoned their vehicles and run ahead on foot.

"I'm going to find her," McElroy said.

"We're coming with you!" Tharp and Betty said. Kirby nodded, joining the conversation. McElroy didn't argue. He reached Carter's carriage and quickly explained the situation, handing back the papers.

"We can't do much until the fire is contained," Carter said. Just then, a loud explosion rocked the area—the steam tanks in the research facility had blown. They all flinched, startled.

"Which will be quite a while, I'm guessing," McElroy said. "I must try to save Edie. Will you look for Britina the best you can? We'll go after the corpse wagon."

Carter agreed and took the papers.

McElroy needed a faster wagon than Carter's. He selected an abandoned one with two strong-looking horses. "Climb aboard and hang on!"

He stopped at the entrance to the cemetery. "You three split up and question the vehicles stuck in traffic past this point. Ask if they've seen the black hearse and where it headed. I'll check the cemetery in case they dumped the coffin. If I don't find Edie, I'll pick you up in a few minutes."

Kirby ran past many vehicles, working his way back. Tharp went halfway and did the same. Betty started with the nearest carriages and worked toward them.

McElroy drove the wagon into the cemetery and around the cart paths between burial sections, looking for Edie's body or an abandoned coffin. When he discovered no sign of either one, he returned to the road and found Betty.

"Everyone saw the black hearse speeding away, but couldn't tell where it was headed—only that it was moving away from the asylum."

Kirby had better luck. One witness had narrowly avoided a collision when the hearse cut in front of him, turning onto Flinders Lane.

•

Meanwhile, Snow and Asa reached the warehouse after a fast and dangerous escape from Kew. Asa jumped down and unlocked the two large entrance doors. Snow took the reins and snapped the horses forward into the warehouse.

Too late. Someone had emptied the warehouse; all the drugs, supplies, and patent medicines were gone. The safe stood open and bare. A fortune, a year's worth of production, vanished. Asa stood frozen, hoping Dr. Snow wouldn't blame him. "Henderson! I'll find him and kill him!" Snow roared.

Snow realized there was nothing left of value. Worse, the shattered bottles of patent medicine and open vials of morphine would implicate him.

"Asa, unhitch the horses and take them to the stable. Sell them for whatever you can get. We're taking the next train to Sydney."

Asa unhitched the horses and left. Snow gathered all the remaining combustible fluids and doused the perimeter of the space thoroughly, especially anything incriminating. At the door, he lit a fire stick and tossed it into a puddle of lamp oil. Flames caught instantly. He turned and hurried off to meet Asa and get to the train station.

•

McElroy assumed from the route that the most likely destination was the train station. The wagon was hard to miss—they still had time. He was determined to catch them and rescue Edie. He slapped the reins to go faster.

McElroy yelled, "Another fire." Betty, Tharp, and Kirby looked up; they could see the glow over the trees before reaching the central train station. They galloped toward it. The warehouse was ablaze; townspeople were tossing pails of water at the flames, but it was no use. All the pumpers in the region had gone to Kew.

They tied the horses and wagon across the street and ran toward the crowd. Some of the idle bystanders said the black hearse wagon had entered the property. The stable manager confirmed it—he'd just bought the horses and had asked for additional tack, which a boy had fetched from the warehouse before the fire.

"Got them cheap, too," he added.

"Good God," Tharp yelled. "There's a woman in that wagon—alive—in a coffin!"

The stable manager called to some of his friends. "Focus on getting the doors open. There's someone in there." He ran to his stable and grabbed supplies.

The firefighters quickly doubled their pace and turned their efforts to the doors. The stable manager, Hal, took charge. With blacksmith tongs he retrieved from his stable, he gripped the door handle and pulled it open. He immediately stepped back as a rush of hot air and flames burst from the building. Tharp started after him and grabbed some leathers from the ground, but Hal waved him off.

"Stay there for now. Take this rope—pull me out if I get in trouble."

After the initial blast, the flames encompassed the perimeter of the building. The wagon had just begun to smoke, its wood moister than the building's timbers. The sudden rush of fresh air fed the fire, and the blaze inside intensified. But the smoke thinned, and the flames turned inward, revealing a path to the back of the wagon.

Hal went to the well, soaked some cloths, and dumped a bucket of water over his head, then another just to be sure. He filled the bucket again, returned to the doors, tied the rope around his waist, and repeated his instructions: if the rope wasn't moving or tugging, they were to pull him out. He covered his head and face with a wet cloth, crouched low, and duckwalked into the warehouse, dragging the bucket of water behind him. Everyone watched, tense and silent. The bucket brigade kept working, focusing now on Hal's path.

By now it was clear—the warehouse was going to be lost.

Hal reached the rear of the wagon and splashed water on the small flames licking at the door, then cooled the metal handles. The heat was crushing, the air thin. He felt sick but kept going. Pulling the cloth back from his face, he opened the door and climbed into the hearse. Coffins lined the left side, and one by one, he yanked them down. The lids slid off as they hit the ground. He hadn't been gentle, but there'd been no weight— every one of them was empty.

Staying low, he crawled out of the wagon.

"Pull!" he shouted.

They hauled the rope, and Hal stumbled into the open air, collapsing as soon as he crossed the threshold.

"No one in there," he croaked. "I need water."

Betty ran for water and returned quickly to his side. "There was someone—she's just not there now. Thank you for your bravery."

"Did the young man who sold you the horses say where they were going?" McElroy asked.

"He said he was from Sydney and was heading back for good."

•

Edie tried to control her breathing. She didn't know if the coffin was airtight. She slowed her breath, but her heart kept pounding against her chest. Asa had sealed the lid with just a few nails, no straps. Maybe she could force it off.

•

The three mounted the wagon and raced back toward Kew. McElroy clutched the reins tightly, his breathing quick and shallow. Where was she?

He drove the wagon into the cemetery at too high a speed and had to correct the course to avoid tipping. "She is here somewhere, or they dumped her—or heaven forbid, they drowned her." He shook as he said this aloud.

At Betty's suggestion, they drove the wagon down to the Yarra River access just outside the area for pauper graves, recalling her earlier experience in the cemetery. They spread out, exploring the shoreline. Tharp found a broken shovel, and McElroy picked up splintered wood shards that looked like they could be from a coffin. Betty reminded them she'd seen Snow's assistant placing body parts into the river to float toward Melbourne. Near the boxwood bush Betty had hidden behind, there were skid marks they believed were from a coffin being pushed into the river.

"Oh God, no," Betty exclaimed. "Would a coffin float?"

McElroy was about to answer when he heard a splash. Tharp

had taken his boots off and dived into the river, searching the bottom.

He surfaced. "Not here," he yelled.

"Betty, you and Kirby run to the tram stop and head to the police station. Find Penn if he's there, gather any help you can, and start working the shoreline back toward us. Tharp and I will work it from here toward Melbourne. We've got at least four or five miles of twisted shore to cover, perhaps more so. It's a race against time; if she is floating, she won't forever. Check every nook, both shores—it could be anywhere, it could have sunk," McElroy ordered. As they ran off, he shouted, "Get whistles and torches!"

Tharp pulled on his boots. McElroy removed the two carriage lamps from their brackets, and handed a lamp to Tarp. They headed into the bushes along the shoreline.

•

Edie could breathe, but she felt the weight of the dirt and rocks Asa had shoveled into the coffin through a hole smashed in the lid. His shovel had broken, or he would have done more. Water pooled around her feet and legs, rising steadily. The coffin sat lower now and would soon take on more. She fought to hold her panic at bay, breathing deeply—*there was still hope*, she told herself, just not much.

•

Magistrate Carter gained access to the property by abandoning his carriage and hitching a ride on a pumper wagon, flashing his credentials at the driver. Hundreds of patients were gathered on lawns across various courtyards and the open gaming field. Only the wings in immediate danger were being evacuated, and the process continued. The fire in the central building seemed to have ignited at the center and hadn't yet reached the men's wings, though a large section of the kitchen was already ablaze. Carter was relieved to see that someone had evacuated the confined and immobile patients—or, at least, some of them.

Carter began a methodical search of the grounds, questioning both patients and staff about Britina Myers—though many didn't know names. He added she was a woman from Jamaica with brown skin. He also asked after Nurse Kramer, but no one had seen her. Then, he spotted a woman descending the stairs near the central building. He recognized her as the person who had had authority over Myers at the coroner's inquest and moved to catch up.

Sturgis was carrying a leather bag and a heavy-looking sack. She was some distance ahead, but Carter kept his eyes on her as she headed to the far side of the central building, walking briskly.

She knew Snow kept his wagon in a barn and was hoping to find him. One threat had been dealt with—now she meant to eliminate another. A hypodermic was ready in her bag. She had been disappointed to find the sack she grabbed before pushing Kramer down the stairs into the fire held not valuables from the safe, but skulls. Planted on Snow's body, they would draw all suspicion toward him.

But the wagon—and presumably Snow and his companion—were gone. Her plan unraveled. She would have to deal with Snow later. She wished there were a horse or carriage left, but the stable was empty.

As she turned to leave, Carter stepped into the barn. "May I have a word? I've forgotten your name, but I saw you with Britina Myers at the coroner's inquest. I'm Magistrate Carter."

The introduction triggered alarm bells for Sturgis—another threat. Her senses sharpened. "I'm Sturgis. I was trying to track down Doctor Snow. It's come to my attention that he's seriously violated both the law and the integrity of this institution. He may have set the fire. But his wagon is gone . . . I assume he is as well."

"I saw his wagon race away from the grounds some time ago. What can you tell me about his violations?"

"He's been teaching anatomy to medical students from various hospitals—but I suspect the cadavers weren't all obtained legally. I think he and Nurse Kramer had a partnership going. I found this in his possession." She dropped the sack and spilled the skulls across the barn floor. "I was going to confront him with these."

Carter, his guard lowered, bent down to examine the skulls. Sturgis moved quickly, jabbing the hypodermic into the back of his neck and pushing the plunger in one swift motion. Carter's hand shot up, striking hers. She let go. He grasped at the syringe and tried to pull it free—but then collapsed to the floor, the hypodermic still clutched in his hand.

•

Betty followed Penn across the lawns leading down to the riverbank. He moved quickly, and she kept her eyes on the flickering torchlight ahead. Just as she caught up to him, Ralphie and Sammy appeared, running from the river's edge.

Since discovering the severed leg, the boys had taken on several scouting errands for McElroy and were eager for any paying assignment.

"Got something for us, Officer Penn?" Ralphie asked.

"It's Constable Penn, Ralphie—and yes, a very serious assignment. You need to move fast and be thorough. You're looking for a floating coffin. There's a woman inside, alive, bound and gagged. You could save her life."

The boys immediately grew more serious.

"Geez," Sammy exclaimed.

"Take these torches and start towards Kew Asylum. The coffin may be partially sunk or stuck on a log or rock—it could be on either side of the river or even completely underwater. Don't miss a single spot. But hurry. We'll take the tram halfway downriver, split up and work in both directions. Chief Inspector McElroy and a young doctor are already searching from the cemetery end. Between us all, that's over five miles of riverbank to cover. Take this police whistle—if you find the coffin, blow it and don't stop. Try to get it to shore and open the lid. We'll do the same if we find her first. Let's hope it's still afloat. Now go!"

The boys dashed off. Penn and Betty ran for the tram stop.

•

Edie drifted in and out of consciousness. Time had passed. The water inside the coffin had risen, bitter cold now, though she was still afloat, moving slower. She'd bumped into several things and stayed motionless for long stretches. Wet sand had packed around her feet and legs, pinning them. Breathing only through her nose, short of air, she occasionally choked as water splashed into her nostrils. Hope was slipping away.

She thought of her past, of Benji and Britina and the other stall ladies, of Betty and Ruth and Elizabeth, and said a brief prayer. Saying goodbye.

She closed her eyes—then heard a youthful voice shout, "There it is!"

•

Sammy and Ralphie had been making their way upriver for about three quarters of an hour when Sammy spotted the coffin bobbing and tipping in the current, mid-river, where the current was strongest.

"Blow the whistle and don't stop. I'll have to swim to it. It's half sunk, and it's going to be hard," Ralphie said.

•

Penn and Betty had just split up when they both heard the whistle. Betty caught up, running, before Penn even got started. They ran through brambles and brush along the wooded bank.

•

McElroy paused, listening. "Did you hear that, Dr. Tharp?"

"No." He stopped, then caught the sound.

They started running along the riverbank.

•

Penn and Betty saw torchlight up ahead, the whistle still sounding. When Penn reached Sammy, he quickly assessed the situation: Ralphie had reached the coffin, nearly submerged, and was clinging to the top, kicking but making little progress. He was clearly exhausted.

Penn kicked off his heavy boots and dove into the Yarra.

"Any strength left, Ralphie?"

"Yes, sir—a little."

"Let's both kick. I'll try to steer it toward the shore."

Progress was slow. They paused often to catch their breath, and the coffin continued to sink deeper. They were halfway to shore now, drifting downstream with the current. Both were nearing their limits.

"We have to keep going, Ralphie," Penn urged.

Ralphie didn't answer, but managed a few more feeble kicks. Then his hands slipped from the coffin, and he went face down in the water. Penn lunged, grabbing him under his right arm.

With one hand on the coffin and the other around Ralphie, he struggled to stay afloat, but they weren't making progress. The current was pulling them back toward the center.

"To hell with this—I can swim," Betty said, diving into the river.

"I can't!" Sammy shouted from the bank.

Betty reached the front of the coffin and secured a weak grip, but it wasn't enough. She swam to the back, taking position on the far side of Ralphie.

"Just keep kicking, Penn. We can make it."

They drifted with the current, pushing hard to cross it and reach the shore. The coffin wouldn't steer. Betty and Penn were near exhaustion, Ralphie barely conscious. They still had three hundred yards to go. Ralphie wasn't kicking—his head rested on the coffin, adding dead weight. Again, they were being drawn toward the central current.

Suddenly, three new figures appeared in the water, approaching the coffin. Penn nearly cheered. He released his spot on the casket, wrapped one arm across Ralphie's chest, and began paddling in a one-arm backstroke, aiming for shore.

Sammy had run to the street and came across a small group of university students celebrating. After a rushed explanation, they didn't need convincing—young men with a few beers in them welcomed the chance to be heroes.

The students reached the coffin, paddled it towards shore, and, with some effort, dragged it up the muddy riverbank. They were fresher than the exhausted trio and finally slid the casket onto a patch of lawn. Ralphie, Penn, and Betty collapsed beside it. The students grabbed the coffin's top through the broken opening and yanked and pulled until the top released.

As soon as Edie was visible, Betty pulled herself up and knelt beside the coffin. Edie's eyes opened—and lit up at the sight of her.

Betty tried to untie the gag but couldn't get a grip with all the water and mud around Edie's head. "We have to get you out of this coffin, Edie. Is anything broken or injured?"

Edie gave a small shake of her head before slipping into unconsciousness.

"Quickly, carefully—move the mud away and lift her out onto the grass," Betty instructed. The students obeyed, Penn assisting.

Chief Inspector McElroy and Dr. Tharp arrived, but there was little left for them to do.

Penn, regaining some strength, said, "Sammy, run for help. We need a vehicle to get Lady Black and Ralphie to the hospital—and we need water and blankets, lots of blankets."

"I'll go too," one student offered. Another followed, eager to help.

"Go to the desk constable at the station," Penn said to the remaining student. "Tell him we need blankets, water, and help. Tell him the message is from me, Constable Penn, and let him know what's happening here."

Edie was unconscious, her body convulsing.

LOOSE ENDS

Britina knew Kew's property well from her days as an attendant. All around her, staff were still frantically evacuating patients or battling the fire. No one stood guard. Weak but not confined, she slowly rolled over a few times, then a few more, edging away from the other patients in her section of the courtyard. She got to her knees and paused there, breathing hard. After a few moments, she drew in a deep breath, pushed herself to her feet, and shuffled unsteadily toward the fever tents. She fell once, but rose again.

Behind the fever tents, she could see the rear gate. She leaned against a tree to rest and caught sight of Sturgis hurrying past the end of the central building toward the gate. She was carrying her leather bag and a cloth bag that looked heavy.

Axes broke open the gate, but now a replacement guard watched it. The guard was letting in fire wagons and monitoring anyone trying to leave. Britina watched as Sturgis approached him, said something, and walked past, but he turned and grabbed her arm from behind.

Dropping the medical bag, Sturgis swung the cloth case up over her head with both hands and brought it down hard on the guard's skull. The strike was so swift and forceful that he collapsed to the ground. She walked out the gate.

Britina could hardly believe her chance had come. She waited a few minutes—she certainly didn't want to cross paths with Sturgis—then made her way cautiously to the gate. She stopped to check on the guard; he was unconscious, breathing, and bleeding only slightly from the head. "You'll be okay. Just stay still." Britina stood tall, lifted her chin, and walked through the gate toward whatever fate awaited her.

•

Sammy and the student soon commandeered a carriage and driver. The other students returned with blankets. Penn wrapped a blanket around Edie. Betty, though shivering, refused to leave Edie's side. Penn helped both women into the carriage.

Inside, Betty sat with Edie's head on her lap. Edie stopped shaking and twitching once several more blankets were piled on top of her, but she remained unconscious.

"I'll change into a dry uniform at the station and have someone call the hospital to let them know you're on the way," Penn said. "I'll get a police carriage and join you shortly." The carriage departed for the Royal Melbourne Hospital.

Confident Edie would soon be in professional care, McElroy and Tharp headed back to the asylum. Kirby ran to catch them before they boarded the tram.

In the emergency room, a young doctor and a nurse met Betty. Penn had alerted them that this was police business, and they acted swiftly, carrying Edie into the bustling hospital and placing her on a cot. The doctor checked her heart rate, breathing, and eyes. The nurse removed her dirty, wet clothes, cleaned her, dressed her in a gown, and covered her with warmed blankets.

Later, with Betty now under a blanket wearing clothes a nurse had lent her and Penn beside her, the doctor explained,

"From examining her and hearing what you've told me, I believe she's suffering from shock. Since there's going to be a police investigation, we'll move her to a private room. We'll monitor her through the night—I expect we'll know much more by morning. She may need to stay a few days."

Penn wrapped Ralphie in a blanket and drove him to the hospital, with Sammy beside him on the driver's bench of the police wagon. Ralphie was recovering quickly, but Penn insisted he get checked. After a brief exam and a donation of dry clothes that were way too big, Penn arranged a hansom cab to take them home and paid the driver. Never having ridden in a cab before, the boys were thrilled.

With the doctor's assessment complete, Penn turned to Betty. "There's nothing more you can do tonight. I have a police carriage waiting—why don't I take you home? Your husband already filed one complaint; I imagine he'll be relieved to know you're alive. No need for him to file another. You were heroic tonight. We'll check on you tomorrow."

She nodded in agreement.

•

A few vehicles were still arriving as Britina walked out of the gate. She took to the woods and fields, heading away from Kew, instead of navigating the crowded road and facing people she might not want to encounter. *I could just walk away—and maybe disappear.* It was still dark, but the rising sun lit the horizon, and a quiet warmth spread through her chest. She didn't know if it would last, but for the first time in months, she felt alive.

After about an hour of walking, though, her strength waned. She needed water, food, and sleep. In the distance, she spotted a farmhouse, a barn, and a small orchard. The orchard had been picked clean; not even rotting apples littered the ground. She approached the barn from the rear and cautiously followed the wall to the front doors, which were unlocked. Across the cart path, she checked the house for any sign of activity. It looked quiet, unoccupied for now.

She opened one of the barn doors just enough to slip inside and closed it gently behind her. A strong, slightly sour, slightly sweet aroma permeated the space. She could hear bubbling. A lantern hung by the door beside a box of matches. It could be risky, but she couldn't hide in total darkness. No light would make it through the barn walls. She lit the lantern, turned the flame down low, and swept it slowly from side to side. The barn was clean and tidy—no animals, just barrels of bubbling apple cider. *That's where the damaged apple drops go*, she thought. Several barrels of bruised or rotting apples stood nearby, waiting to be mashed. She picked a few that weren't too damaged. They'd make a fine breakfast.

At the back of the barn, she saw a ladder leading up to a hayloft. She fixed the picture in her mind, extinguished the lantern, and hung it back on its hook. With one hand stretched out and the other cradling her apples, she walked straight ahead until she bumped into the ladder. She climbed the twelve rungs awkwardly, her limbs trembling with fatigue.

At the top, she dropped to her hands and knees and crawled toward the far back corner. There, she arranged some bales and loose hay into a nest. She curled up inside the wall of bales and covered herself with all the hay she could reach. She ate three apples and, with a full belly and a flicker of peace, she fell asleep the instant her eyes closed—more content and safe than she had felt in months.

•

McElroy and Tharp looked up at the Kew facility as they climbed the hill. Kirby ran ahead to check on his parents.

The flames had diminished, but thick smoke still rose from two parts of the complex. Reaching the back gate at last, they passed through without resistance. There was no guard. A few exhausted fire crews were pulling away, though many remained active across the grounds. Patients were everywhere: lying on the grass, resting on cots, or wandering in confusion.

McElroy had three goals: confront Kramer if she was alive, locate Magistrate Carter, and find Britina. He didn't see anyone clearly in charge—just a handful of attendants and nurses caring for patients. The back wing of the women's ward had collapsed into the cellar, a complete loss. The central building had a gaping hole in the roof, its walls charred black, but the fire seemed contained there.

He dreaded learning how many lives had been lost. Had Carter gotten to Kramer and escaped with Britina? McElroy scanned the chaos for a sign of the magistrate but saw no trace of him amid the scattered crowds on the lawn.

They made their way toward the central building and to the loading dock. Two doctors in scrubs were bent over a patient on a folding cot. McElroy recognized the patient— Magistrate Carter.

"We found him collapsed on the stable floor. He's alive, but not in good shape. His breathing's shallow and strained. We've kept him warm and tried to get fluids into him, but he's not conscious enough to swallow. We're headed out to find transport to get him to a hospital."

"What happened to him?" McElroy asked.

"Oh—sorry. Someone attacked him. He had a hypodermic needle in his hand. The injection site was at the back of his neck, so it wasn't self-administered. He must've pulled it out. Half the dose was still in the syringe, luckily. Judging by the color and smell, I believe it was arsenic. A full dose would've been fatal. This one still might be. He needs to get to the hospital immediately."

That matched the coroner's description of the poison used on Jane Doe.

Kirby returned, reporting that his parents were safe.

"Kirby, we need to get someone important to the hospital. Are there any carriages or horses left we can commandeer?" McElroy asked.

"Everyone avoids the coroner's barn. There's a wagon that transports corpses to the cemetery. I can fetch one of the plow horses still in the farm stable."

"Go. We'll get him onto the wagon while you bring the horse."

The fire would likely burn for another day, McElroy figured, but the firefighters had gained ground. It was no longer spreading. Now he had to find Kramer. Papers or not, he'd remove Britina from the facility himself—if she was still alive.

"Tharp, I officially deputize you."

Tharp stood taller.

"Take Magistrate Carter to the Royal Melbourne Hospital. Bring the syringe and tell them this is a police matter—possible attempted murder by poisoning. Substance unknown, but possibly arsenic."

McElroy noticed a set of stairs still in use, where workers were moving in and out with cloths tied over their mouths. He pulled his own handkerchief up and stepped inside.

A large, tough-looking woman in a torn, soot-streaked uniform stepped in front of him, holding up a hand. "Where are you going?"

"I'm Chief Inspector McElroy, Melbourne Police. And you are?"

"Nurse Ralphine. I'm acting Chief Nurse right now. I'm in charge."

He flashed his badge and leaned in, exerting his authority. "I need to speak to Nurse Kramer immediately, and I need to know where patient Britina Myers is. Can you help me with either?"

"Well, Chief Inspector, doesn't seem to be your lucky day. Britina Myers, I suspect, is burned to a crisp. And you can't talk to Nurse Kramer because she's in little pieces, scattered all over the research laboratory under the kitchen. We think the fire reached the auxiliary steam boiler—it blew, and so did Kramer."

"Nurse Ralphine, I realize you have your hands full, but we're investigating at least one murder—maybe more. I need your full cooperation. If not, I will have you cuffed and taken to the lockup for obstructing a police investigation. Your choice."

Her mask puffed outward as she let out a shocked breath. Her voice rose. "You can't do that . . . can you?" Her eyes widened.

"I believe I can," McElroy growled. "Now take me to what's left of Kramer. Then I want to see her office if it's still standing. In the meantime, assign someone to locate the remains of Britina Myers—if she is, in fact, dead."

•

"Wake up," a gravelly voice demanded.

Britina brushed hay from her eyes as her thoughts scrambled to come together. As her vision cleared, she saw the double barrels of a rifle pointed directly at her head.

"You escape from the asylum?"

She couldn't find her voice.

"Never mind. Obvious. You're still in your patient garb."

The man had a dark, matted beard and a nearly bald head. He wore a dirty plaid shirt and coveralls.

"You were snoring so loud I could hear you from my porch."

"I'm a nun," she managed to say.

"Yeah, and I'm the King of England. Get up!"

She tried, but collapsed back into the hay bale. "I need water."

"They'll give you water back at the asylum."

That, at least, reassured her she wasn't about to be shot or assaulted. She tried again and got to her feet, unsteady.

"Now, down the ladder," he said, swinging the gun toward it.

"The asylum burned," Britina said.

"That's what I smelled!" He wrinkled his nose. "If that's true, I'm takin' you to the police."

Britina quietly thanked God as she climbed down the ladder and stepped into the bright sunlight streaming through the open barn doors.

•

The remains of Nurse Kramer were not as scattered as Nurse Ralphine had suggested, but there was no question she was dead. The research laboratory contained some charred, water-damaged treatment materials and equipment that would need further investigation. Smoke and steam filled the flooded room. An unchecked water supply from the laundry was still pouring into the space.

McElroy ordered the room sealed and locked. He would send an investigative team along with the coroner to inspect and collect the body. He instructed Ralphine to dispatch another employee to locate and shut off the water valve. She complained, but one look at McElroy's eyes and she held her comment.

The inspection of Kramer's office yielded little except for a calendar book with a page labeled "Class Schedule" and a list of names—McElroy noted Tharp's name among them. No one had found Britina Myers's remains, and, surprisingly, they recovered no bodies except Nurse Ashley's nearly unrecognizable remains. All patients had been successfully evacuated and were scattered across the outdoor spaces, including the men's courtyards.

The volunteer fire crews dealt with the building's smoldering ruins. They were exhausted, soot-streaked, and soaked, but other than a few minor injuries, the firefighters emerged unscathed.

McElroy gave Nurse Ralphine strict instructions: if Britina Myers was found alive, she was to be brought directly to Central Police Station. He warned her that this was now a police matter.

The cloth around her face didn't hide the way her lips curled into a snarling frown.

"Failure to comply—or any interference—will result in your arrest."

He turned and walked to the main entrance, exited, and walked down the hill just as the sun began to rise. It was going to be a beautiful day.

He hoped Edie was doing well and that Magistrate Carter was recovering. There was only one way to find out. He made his way to the tram stop and waited for the first tram of the morning. He needed sleep, a wash, and clean clothes—but that could wait.

McElroy summoned Penn to his office as soon as he arrived at the station.

"She's going to be alright, sir. I stayed at the hospital overnight."

McElroy's face betrayed his relief and gratitude. "And Magistrate Carter? Any news?"

"Nothing new, sir. Still unconscious. They're forcing fluids and hoping it helps. I took Nurse Betty home—her husband wasn't pleased. My explanation of what had happened didn't help. Betty just sent me away and said she'd deal with him. I paid the boys—probably too much—but they took serious risks to help. I also gave some cash to the university students. They went off to find a pub with a fireplace. And I have more good news, Chief."

He never calls me Chief, McElroy thought.

"Cartwright fired Kernot for botching the asylum investigation, based on your report. I think he needed to appease the higher-ups, and Kernot made for easy scapegoating."

McElroy nodded and inwardly smiled. He stood and walked over to the chalkboard near his office door. Penn followed, peering over his shoulder as McElroy picked up the chalk.

He began writing.

Who stole the Mace?

He glanced at Penn.

"From the interviews and Lady Black's notebook, it looks like Donavon removed the Mace from Parliament on Chaloner's orders—meant to return it after the orgy. At least, that's Chaloner's story. Lady Black noted Donavon's dodged multiple interview requests. We may need a warrant," Penn said.

McElroy nodded again.

He wrote: *Who attacked Heather Stone?*

Then: *Who killed Heather Stone?*

"She left the orgy with Chaloner, but the man could barely stand," McElroy said.

"And Estelle said it wasn't unusual for Madam Wilson's girls to escort visiting Parliamentarians back to their rooms if they were too drunk or drugged to manage. It wasn't Chaloner's first time. I don't think he had the strength to start anything—even if he wanted to," Penn added.

"From what you've pieced together in the timeline—and the comments from your publican witnesses—it seems the attack likely happened as Heather was returning after helping Chaloner to his quarters to sleep it off." McElroy cupped his chin and continued. "If we line up the timeline with the witness testimony, the assault was underway just as the second-to-last guest was leaving the orgy, carrying a wrapped object about five feet long over his shoulder."

"The drug dealer—Henderson," Penn said, putting the pieces together.

"Right. And apparently, he interrupted the attack, threw the assailant into the road, checked on Heather, took his parcel, and carried on. But was it already too late for Heather?"

"She was still alive when the brothers got her to the hospital," Penn said.

McElroy began pacing. "Alive as in breathing, but never to wake up again." He turned and faced Penn. "We need to find Henderson, but I think we can rule him out as the attacker—and I'd say we can rule out Chaloner, too. Let's recheck the notes."

They both reviewed their notebooks, then swapped and read each other's.

"Our notes show all of Chaloner's guests paired up, and we have accounted for Henderson. We've got conflicting accounts for Donavon, but one of those comes from Chaloner—not the most reliable source. Two unidentified men also joined the orgy," Penn said.

McElroy hesitated. "Still too many unknowns. We had one more person tied to the event. When Donavon returned with the wand—or Mace—the electrician, Chester, joined him."

"But Chester didn't stay," Penn replied. "He left almost immediately after fixing the gramophone and being rejected by Estelle. I think he approached Heather Stone after that—Estelle mentioned something. Two rejections, and he walked out."

"Right," McElroy said, "but let's walk through the scenario again. When Edie and I interviewed Chester and his wife about the Mace, he admitted he doesn't react well to alcohol or drugs. That might make him an excellent candidate for our assailant."

Penn pushed his cap back and scratched his head. "But his departure time would've been before Heather was bringing

Chaloner back to Parliament, and Edie has him taking the tram to his home stop, with a parcel, around ten. Now, we're pretty sure it wasn't the Mace, but the timeline doesn't work."

"Penn, how else could it have happened? Let's move the pieces around."

Penn paused, then paced the room for several minutes. Picking up a piece of chalk, he sketched a rough map on the chalkboard—boxes for the bordello and Parliament, the alley, and the bar. He added a tram line and Chester's stop. Then he started drawing stick figures and labeling them as he talked.

McElroy watched, quietly impressed.

"That's it," Penn said. "Chester leaves Chaloner's rooms after whiskey and who knows what else, obviously impaired. According to the tram operator's report, he manages to get home, wrapped parcel and all. Because of his condition, his wife locks him out of the house, which I suspect happens often; we'll have to verify that.

"Chester then returns to Parliament for the night, as he often did, and in time to accompany Donavon to the bordello, perhaps less impaired than he had been. He fixes the gramophone, but then Estelle and Heather Stone reject him. He leaves, sulking, and makes his way back to Parliament again. Probably has more to drink. Then Heather shows up with Chaloner and puts him to bed. Chester follows Heather when she leaves and attacks her on her return trip."

"Good work, Penn. I think it's a workable scenario; he wouldn't tolerate being rejected a third time. He just jumped to the top of my suspect list. We'll follow up by checking that he didn't sleep at home that night and that his wife sent him away soon after he arrived."

"Chief Inspector," the desk constable interrupted.

"Yes, Constable?" McElroy was mildly annoyed—their

momentum was building.

"There's a farmer downstairs with a woman. Her hands are tied with hay bale rope. He says she escaped from the asylum and broke into his barn. Wants her charged. She asked for you by name. Her name's Britina."

McElroy smiled. He and Penn didn't need to say a word—they both turned and headed straight for the stairs.

•

Britina started crying the moment she saw Raymond descending the stairs. He opened his arms and wrapped them tightly around her.

The farmer looked uncertain about what to do next, but Penn stepped in quickly. "This is in police hands now. Thank you. You may go."

"Edie?" Britina asked through her tears.

"I'm told she'll be alright. She's at the Royal Melbourne Hospital."

Britina leaned her head back and looked into Raymond's eyes. "She isn't safe."

"Britina, Kramer is dead. You need to tell me everything."

She nodded, her head drooping. "Just protect Edie, please." She looked utterly spent. "I'll tell you all I've learned."

•

Sturgis had to plot her moves carefully. She had intended a long career in discreet eliminations and cadaver brokering. They might still resurrect some version of the trainings. She was a professional.

Kramer had treated her as a servant, but, through Kramer, she had access to a storehouse of potential bodies. Brookfield would deny all wrongdoing and protect her, she was sure. He

319

would claim that he'd had no knowledge of any illegal activities. All the blame would rest on Kramer's shoulders.

Edie Black, however, was now her immediate concern. She had seen far too much. Once Sturgis heard she'd been located and was at the hospital, she added her to the extermination list. She didn't know exactly how much Edie had figured out, but she had observed the dissection, and it was clear she'd recognized the body as Heather Stone's. That, alone, was enough.

She sat on the edge of her hotel bed across from the hospital entrance, sipping brandy and smoking a cigar. *I should have been a man*, she mused, *but I get away with so much more as a woman.* She glanced in the mirror. She knew Edie was in a private room, courtesy of the Melbourne Police. How convenient.

Sturgis shaved her hair, scrubbed off her makeup, and waited until past midnight. She dressed in a doctor's uniform, added gloves, and pulled a white surgical cap low over her head to partially conceal her face. In her right hand, she carried her leather medical bag. She would avoid contact if possible—she needed to remain undetected. There were others yet to be dealt with.

Crossing the road, she kept to the hedges that lined the drive leading to the receiving docks. The night had turned cold, and she shivered slightly before shaking it off. She crouched in the shadows and waited. She had already observed the pattern of the night guard who patrolled the building's perimeter alone. After about twenty minutes, he came around again, checking doors and windows. He paused on the dock and lit a fag. The sight irritated her—she wanted to yell, "Move on," or slit his throat—but she waited. Finally, he rose and resumed his patrol. She estimated it would be thirty to forty minutes before he circled back.

She tested the doors—locked. From her pocket, she unrolled a small leather wrap and selected a hook pick. Inserting it into the keyhole, she twisted and pulled slightly. The lock was simple; it clicked open. She repacked the pick set, tied the wrap, and slipped it back into her pocket. With her bag in hand, she stepped inside, locking the door behind her.

She was on the floor below the first patient level, in the building's storage and utility wing. Several staircases ran along the corridor. Edie's room was two floors above, near the far end. The area was empty at this hour, allowing her to move quickly to her chosen staircase.

Finding herself at the first patient ward, she scanned carefully for any signs of movement or noise. Before she reached the stairs to the second patient ward, she saw a nurse attending to a patient on a trolley. She ducked into an empty room and waited. When the hall was clear, she stepped back out and found the connecting stairwell.

Entering Edie's room, she kept her head lowered in case the patient was awake—but Edie appeared to be sleeping soundly. Sturgis placed her bag on the bedside table and opened it. She removed a pillow from the empty bed nearby, just in case. Then she took out a vial and syringe, preparing the injection.

She bent over Edie, positioning the needle near her neck.

Edie's eyes sprang open. Her hand shot up and grabbed Sturgis's wrist.

Sturgis gasped, startled.

The door burst open—McElroy and Penn rushed in.

"Drop the syringe!" McElroy commanded. "We've been waiting for you."

Sturgis glowered; she yanked free of Edie's grip and backed away. Penn stepped toward her. In one swift move, she dropped the pillow and jabbed the syringe into her own neck, pushing the plunger down. She collapsed to the floor.

Edie stood up, clearly feeling stronger, and wrapped her arms tightly around both McElroy and Penn. "You were right," she said, voice trembling. "My life was in danger."

Sturgis was pronounced dead by the head night nurse and removed to the morgue.

"Thank God you were here, Raymond—and you too, Penn. I'd be dead now." Edie gave Penn a warm smile, and he turned red.

"It's not God you need to thank, Edie—it's Britina. After she arrived at the station, she told us a great deal about what was going on at the asylum. She's lucky to be alive."

Edie had already been told Britina was in protective custody at police headquarters, receiving special attention. *I'm so pleased she's safe and well. I can't wait to see her.* "Oh, and I'm fine—just two sprained wrists and a bump on the head where I hit that laundry cart. Nothing serious. But I've been in one too many coffins for one lifetime."

"I'll need a full report on all your activities—many of which should never have happened," McElroy said. "You don't take orders well."

Edie looked a little chastened, but inside, she knew she had done what she had to.

A young doctor entered the room. "I have news on Magistrate Carter. We've started treatment that should help him recover. The vial that the woman was using contained arsenic—a fast-acting poison, rare in hospital use. We're administering fluids and activated charcoal to dilute and absorb it. Thankfully, he received less than half the intended dose. Hopefully, he'll regain consciousness in a couple of days. Hi, Edie."

McElroy hadn't looked directly at the doctor. Hearing Edie's name, he did a double take.

"Hi, Tharp," Edie said.

Tharp turned to McElroy. "The hospital hired me for temporary assignments—staff's stretched thin. I'm waiting to hear about positions in the US. Maine—Portland or Bangor."

McElroy shook his hand. "You were a valuable deputy; Edie might not have made it without you. Thank you for your help."

"You're still underestimating me, Raymond," she said, "but Tharp, thank you. Raymond may be right."

•

Edie regained her strength and energy quickly at home, helped by Bart's hearty dinners each evening and short walks around the neighborhood twice a day. Benji was returning home from Adelaide and would arrive in a couple of days. She'd have to tell him everything herself; if she didn't, Raymond surely would.

She invited Britina and Betty over for lunch. Bart made his Guatemalan borracho cakes with rum sauce and sliced guava for dessert. Afterward, they sat on the porch, sipping tea well into the late afternoon.

Betty had secured a position at the Royal Melbourne Hospital. It was too far to ride her bicycle, so she now commuted by tram. Britina had chosen not to return to religious life; instead, she was working as an assistant teacher at Sacred Heart Industrial School for impoverished girls and had found an apartment nearby. She taught reading, the Bible, and stall trade—though she left out the parts about stealing goods.

•

Edie had made an appointment and visited Raymond's office the day before Benji was due to return.

"Raymond, I hope you won't make too much of my adventure when Benji gets back—he's arriving tomorrow."

"Edie, you could have been killed—either in your escapades or in that floating coffin. You should never have been there. That's my professional reprimand."

"And Britina would probably be dead by now," Edie said.

She shuddered and took a sip of her tea. "I survived, and I'm perfectly fine now. I've learned some lessons, and I'm ready to return to work."

"You know I care for you. But I can't, and won't, be responsible for you being put in danger. You were supposed to conduct interviews only—which you did commendably—and they led to solutions."

"Thank you, Raymond. But in this case, my best friend and confidant was in danger. I couldn't just sit back while she suffered under false accusations."

"You didn't know they were false."

"Yes, yes, I really did. I was the only one outside the asylum who knew that. Will you stop lecturing me and bring me up to date on the case? What's done is done."

Raymond took a gulp of his tea and looked into Edie's eyes. The look she returned told him he would not convince her to give up—or give in.

"Okay, Edie. But from now on, you clear all actions with me before running off. I can't have a civilian put in danger on police business—and, personally, I want you safe."

"Fine. Tell me."

"You already know Sturgis is dead—took her own life, caught trying to kill you. Most likely, trying to prevent you from testifying about what you saw in the research facility. Your testimony helped secure Britina's release and the warrants for Dr. Brookfield and Dr. Snow. We believe Sturgis locked Kramer in the research lab during the fire and was responsible for Heather Stone's death. The fire in the research facility was separate from your fire. There was no path between them."

"Can we call it something else besides my fire?"

McElroy smiled. "Of course. The fire inspectors found

evidence Kramer or Sturgis deliberately set the laboratory fire. Their deaths eliminate two suspects from prosecution and prevent them from testifying against others."

"Unfortunate, in some ways," Edie said, her voice softer. She looked up. "What about Snow and his ghoulish friend?"

McElroy scratched his mustache. "You were a victim of Dr. Snow and his assistant. When they're arrested, we'll prosecute them for kidnapping and attempted murder."

Edie shuddered, remembering being nailed into the coffin and pushed into the river.

McElroy continued, "Betty Robinson's testimony on her observations in the cemetery and Asa's assault of her will be critical in their trial as well. The illegal exhumation of bodies involves all the parties. It will come together in trial, I believe."

"When will you arrest Snow?" Edie asked.

"Snow is no longer in our jurisdiction—he's in Sydney. The authorities there have him under surveillance. His assistant seems to have disappeared. Dissecting a cadaver for medical training isn't illegal as long as the cadaver is obtained legally. But if he was involved in what Britina called 'patient harvesting' with Sturgis or illegal exhumations, then we have grounds for additional charges. Sydney police can pick him up anytime. They are trying to gather more information and are hoping Henderson or the assistant will reappear. They will soon arrest Snow.

"Dr. Brookfield is free pending arraignment, but he's on leave from the Royal Melbourne. I don't believe we have enough to convict him. The only witnesses we have to testify are Britina, who had brief contact with Brookfield while confined and drugged, and you, who were trespassing illegally. Snow could turn on him, but I doubt it. What crime can we definitively prove was committed? I suspect Brookfield was the brains behind the entire operation, but how do we prove that?"

"I saw him torture a patient," Edie said.

"Torture or treatment—hard to prove. And with all the equipment destroyed, there's little to examine. The treatments may have even been legal. A parliamentary committee is being formed to investigate, and Brookfield will be a focus. We'll both be called to testify, and they'll determine if any illegal activities are to be prosecuted.

"Edie, what's still open is the attack on Heather Stone and the missing Mace. We're pretty sure Thomas Chester followed Stone back into the Lon after she returned Sergeant At Arms Chaloner to his rooms. We spoke with Chester's wife. She confirmed he became violent after consuming even a little alcohol. She'd banned him from the house many times, including the night of the assault. He often slept at Parliament. His wife kicked him out for good after our first visit, and now he's disappeared. There's a warrant for his arrest and wanted posters at every station in Victoria. He'll turn up, eventually."

Penn's witnesses had confirmed that the police artist's poster rendering matched Chester, the man they'd encountered at the bar the night Stone was attacked.

"That leaves the Mace," Edie said.

"We don't know where it is, but our witnesses saw a man pass the scene of the attack. He dropped a five-foot parcel, threw the attacker into the road, checked on Stone, and left with the parcel—leaving behind an emerald. Your work, pairing orgy attendees with Wilson's ladies, helped us find our suspect."

"Henderson," Edie said.

"Precisely." Raymond nodded.

"Let me guess—no idea where he is or where the Mace is."

"You're right. But Chaloner and Donavon will have to answer for the disappearance. Both are suspended and awaiting arraignment. We've never been able to interview Donavon. No one has seen him at Parliament since the orgy. He has no family, so he might've taken off—or he could be another victim."

"Police work is frustrating!" Edie said.

McElroy smiled and refilled the teacups.

TIED ENDS

Asa had become a liability. His withdrawal and sulkiness since returning from Melbourne had culminated in his missing a scheduled laudanum production run the night before. Thaddeus no longer trusted him. Asa had served him well, but if questioned and frightened, he would talk.

In the lab, Thaddeus kept a safe with quantities of poisons. He had a few clients who occasionally needed a lethal dose. This time, he chose an extract of castor bean waste, left over from castor oil production—an extremely poisonous substance, hard to detect, and without a known antidote.

He had to be cautious. He took the bottle and a syringe to one workbench. Mask, gloves, apron—he suited up with care. He uncorked the bottle, poured a small amount into the syringe barrel, sealed it with the plunger, and then placed the prepared syringe in an airtight case.

As he moved to put the poison away, Thaddeus glanced at the cabinet where he kept four notebooks—formulas for everything they produced and a fifth that listed shipping customers and sources. The door hung open. The cabinet was empty. The notebooks were gone.

Panic rose. He snatched the syringe case and made for Asa's

shack. In his rush, the case clipped the bottle of poison, tipping it. The cork popped free. The liquid spilled across the table, down the front of his apron, and into his boot, soaking his sock. His raw wounds—his shin and feet—burned where the fluid touched them.

He would be dead in two to three days, if it took that long.

The cold realization settled over him. His composure cracked. He sank to his knees.

It had all been for nothing.

•

Asa sat beside Henderson, enjoying the open air. He trusted this man. Henderson had always been kind to him—and now, he was offering Asa a future: a junior partnership in a new operation, with Asa in charge of production in a new city.

Henderson had just made a very lucrative deal: he'd sold off the entire Melbourne inventory to the Fitzroy Gang, one of his most eager customers. They'd jumped at the deep discount. The Mace was already safely stowed in the wagon, serving as extra capital for the next move. The notebooks with everything he needed to make a fortune were safely stored in his trunk.

Adelaide was young and full of promise. The drug trade there was barely off the ground; alcohol still ruled as the poison of choice. Henderson intended to change that. He had the experience, the formulas, the sources, the capital—and now, the assistant—to do just that.

THE END

AUTHOR'S NOTES

While the events and the stories in this book are fictional, I used actual events and locations as creative inspiration. The theft of the parliamentary Mace really happened, although I may have manipulated the timing a bit. Chester, the electrician, was a suspect (I changed his name and some details). The first tram ride he takes comes from published tram driver interviews. The theory that the Mace ended up at a brothel as part of an orgy was one of the public's favorite speculations. To my knowledge, no beating related to the alleged orgy took place. My research revealed no solution to the Mace's theft, and it remains a mystery today. Last I knew, there is still a reward.

Severed limbs were found in and around Melbourne, near the same time as the Mace's theft. I discovered this while conducting newspaper and magazine research, which did not reveal their origin. The connection between the two events is purely my own.

To my knowledge, Kew Asylum never experienced a devastating fire. While there were several investigations of inappropriate caretaking and actions at the asylum over the years, I found no evidence of murder or "body harvesting." That is purely a construct of my imagination.

MICHAEL G. COLBURN

2025

INSPIRATION AND ACKNOWLEDGMENTS

As I was completing book one of the Lady Black Mysteries, *Stolen Brilliance*, I read a biography of Eliza (Lizzie) Agnes Merritt (née Dimsey), researched and written by Linley Walker, a descendant of Lizzie's. The story is told through Lizzie's own accounts of her struggles and the recollections of her daughter and estranged husband, according to the author's acknowledgments. The title is *Lizzie's Journey to Yarra Bend*.

Lunacy was a crime when Lizzie arrived in the new colony of Victoria (Australia) in 1855. The harrowing and tragic events of Lizzie's life affected and influenced me. Her struggles landed her in jail and in Victoria's first mental institution, Yarra Bend Lunatic Asylum, where she spent the last four decades of her life.

Asylum Murders is not about Lizzie or her story, but my characters had already set foot in Victoria, and an asylum seemed a perfect setting for a mystery. Because of the overcrowded conditions of Yarra Bend, the government constructed a second more modern, state-of-the-art facility across the river. The overcrowding at Kew Asylum quickly caused a decline in the quality of care. It became the setting for the struggles of my character, Britina.

None of the true events of Lizzie's life are part of my narrative, at least not intentionally—but her incarceration in Yarra Bend was the inspiration for Britina's harrowing experiences.

I want to acknowledge Celia Johnson of PubPros for creative editing. It didn't hurt that Celia was born and raised and in around the Kew district of Melbourne, Australia. Thanks also to Alisia, for a pre-publication edit, and to Books Forward and Books Fluent for their help and representation. I have received so many positive comments for the covers of Lady Black's novels: thank you, Karl Spurzem.

The final critical edits of *Asylum Murders* have been conducted by Emily Colin of Books Fluent and have, in my opinion, made this book far more readable.

I acknowledge and thank my wife, Mary Esther Treat, who reads the terrible drafts and makes gentle suggestions, edits my spelling and grammar, and suggests some changes because "that's not really needed." All my love, dear.

I'm pleased to have received great reviews for *Stolen Brilliance*. I set out to write novels where a few characters have their own stories highlighted in a series of books. Yes, it's Lady Edie Black's series, but I felt I needed to develop her more deeply in book one and then spend more time with Britina in book two, and Benji in book three, tying them all together just like the multiple themes in my stories. And don't be surprised to encounter Jack Cramer again.

Thank you, readers.

Mike

CHAPTER 1

R.M.S. Quetta

Benji stared at the leftover glow of another sunset spectacle. The high shoulders of Mount Bremer rose from the dusky landscape, its rounded summit catching the last copper light of the day. Lower ridges unfurled beneath it like rumpled cloth, the edges of Pudding Pan Hill rounding off into the scrub-covered slopes below as they caught the last blush of sunlight to the west. *It's like burnished gold*, Benji thought. A hilarious name, Pudding Pan Hill, but also very romantic. The only thing missing was Edie.

Benji sipped a ginger seltzer and Bundaberg rum. He liked the effervescence from the seltzer that tickled his nose, the bite of the ginger, and the caramel sweetness added by the rum. As the light faded, stars appeared but were not yet fully visible.

He turned his attention from sky-viewing and glanced around the first-class deck. The style and design of the RMS *Quetta* impressed him, accommodating passengers while also functional for cargo and mail handling. He sniffed the salty sea air as a squadron of pelicans flew overhead, completing a day of fishing and eating, heading for their night on some beach or lagoon until dawn.

Although he would prefer not to be alone, he couldn't help

but be in awe of the islands, the beaches, and the landscape. This was his first trip sailing back to England along the east coast of Australia. *It's my last trip alone. Once I complete this trip, all travel will be the two of us, or perhaps someday with children, who can tell. Hell, I'm lonely.*

Enough self-pity, Benji thought. *I can't plan our future alone. I've got a first task, and that is to complete this sale of the farms, processing, and distribution business in London and return to life with Edie in Melbourne.*

"What are you drinking, mister?"

Startled, Benji snapped out of his thoughts. He looked up into the bright blue eyes of a young girl, perhaps around eight, with a ribbon in her golden-brown hair, wearing a frilly white dinner dress. She was barefoot but standing very erect and proper at the end of his lounge.

"It's a seltzer," he said, his voice hedging a little.

"I'm very thirsty. Can I have a swallow?"

"Ah . . . no, sorry, it's a strong seltzer."

"Alcohol?"

"Yes. Just a-a little," he stammered. "I'll signal a deck steward and get you a water or a sweet drink. Would you like to take a seat?" He gestured towards the lounge to his left, away from his drink table.

"That would be nice." She went to the lounge chair and, smoothing the back of her dress, sat down.

Benji looked up and down the deck, looking for a steward to summon. No one was visible. "I'm sorry, but there doesn't seem to be a steward available. They're probably all engaged in saloon activities now."

"That's all right. It's almost my dinnertime. We dine at six; my father thinks that dining at the early seating will leave my sisters and me tired and ready for bed, but what happens is he puts us to bed, we pretend to be asleep, then he goes to socialize in the saloon and we get up and play games or explore the ship. I'm the youngest, so my sisters pick on me sometimes. I still love them." She paused. "It's just nice to get away by myself for a little while. Would you like to join us for dinner? My father would welcome new company, and my older sister would probably get a crush on you."

"I would be delighted, with your father's approval, of course. What's your name?"

"I'm called Matty. It's really Mary Edie, my first name, both parts, but my friends shortened it to Matty. What's your name?"

"Benji. My wife's name is Edie, short for Edith, but like a part of your name."

"Benji's a funny name. Are you famous or anything?"

Benji laughed. "No, afraid not. I'm just a farmer, at least for a while longer."

Benji's heartstrings were being pulled in this young girl's direction. It felt good to have a conversation with someone so young. He and Edie had tried to have children, but hadn't yet been successful. Perhaps there would still be time.

"Well, finish your drink then, and I will take you to our table. My father has a cocktail before dinnertime and will be at the table with my shoes."

The evening saloon meal was extensive and elaborate, even the early serving, which intended to accommodate the children and older adults. Benji enjoyed the company of Matty and her family. Boogaard was their surname, and their father told story after story of his adventures. His name was Cornelius. He was a physician and self-titled master explorer. He puffed his chest as he made this declaration and glanced at the girls. They all giggled, but Benji observed his eyes light up when he told of his adventures.

Benji leaned in towards Cornelius, waiting for the next piece of each adventure, like a chapter in a book. The family was originally from London, but they now lived in Edinburgh, Scotland. His wife, the girls' mother, had died just a few years earlier, and he'd moved them back to where he'd grown up. They were returning from a month of exploring Tasmania, living in tents, cooking over open fires, foraging for food and hunting. "Builds character," Cornelius said as he passed the cheese plate to Benji.

"I couldn't take another bite of anything," Benji moaned, rubbing his tummy. The girls giggled some more. But he drank the port intended to accompany the cheese.

The roast beef and Yorkshire pudding, peas, and mashed potato main course, which was preceded by a potted shrimp appetizer, was more than he would normally eat. He would have liked to loosen his belt a notch, but that wouldn't have been proper. He enjoyed a mild glow from the wine at dinner and the port that followed.

The three girls seemed to get along fine. As they left the dining room, headed for an evening deck stroll, the sisters skipped ahead. They had taken their shoes off, carried by the two older girls, each of whom held one of Matty's hands.

"*Oranges and lemons,* say the bells of St. Clement's. *You owe me five farthings,* say the bells of St. Martin," they sang in unison, their voices high and sweet. "*When will you pay me?* say the bells of Old Bailey."

"When I grow rich." Matty took the line alone, and they all laughed.

The waning moon hung brilliantly in the eastern sky, casting a silver sheen across the restless waters of the Torres Strait. Following the girls at a more leisurely pace, Benji and Cornelius paused, leaning on the bulwark to watch the moonbeams catch the ripples on the water, flash briefly, then disappear into the waves.

"It's beautiful," Benji said. "It's my first trip up the east coast of Australia." *I may have mentioned that at dinner.*

Faintly, the haunting last verse to the girls' song echoed from somewhere toward the stern.

"Here comes a candle to light you to bed . . ." Mattie sang.

Then the voices of the two older sisters, first one, then the other:

"Here comes a chopper to chop off your head!"

"Chop, chop, chop, chop—the last man's dead!"

Their voices faded away with laughter.

The moon bathed the water and land in crisp clarity. The air was still warm, salt-laden. Cornelius was describing aspects of their adventures in Tasmania, as he had most of the evening. Benji was still interested. He hadn't yet visited and realized there were so many places that he and Edie might travel together. They agreed to meet for dinner again the next evening, unless Benji would like to join Cornelius later for drinks and cigars, perhaps some cards with a group of friends. Tired, Benji begged off.

As they resumed strolling, a fearful crash and a horrific ripping noise split the air. The vast ship shuddered as if cold and stopped dead in the water. The men fell forward, first to their knees, then to their stomachs. All went quiet; then pandemonium broke loose as panic set in among the passengers.

Benji lifted his head and looked in the direction the girls had skipped. How frightened they must be. He was frightened, as well. The fear sobered him instantly. He needed to save them.

People lay face down in all directions, some crying, many shrieking, frantic. A voice, probably the captain's, yelled, "All that want to be saved go aft." As the hysterical screaming intensified, many women and children headed aft. Benji got to his knees, stumbling forward, looking for the girls.

The stern rose as the bow of the ship went under. Water rushed by his legs on the decking. He fought to stay on his feet as people washed toward him. As the *Quetta*'s bow submerged, the stern lifted and the ship split in two, swallowing bodies and wreckage alike. The ship disappeared from beneath Benji; he was one among hundreds of others, washed over the bulwark into the ocean waters. Saltwater forced its way into his throat.

He kicked, clawed with his arms, forcing his way to the surface. When he got his head above water, he began coughing; his eyes burned with saltwater and oil. The surrounding sea frothed with planks, crates, pigs squealing, bales of cotton, and human limbs. Sensing a pulling drag on his body from the sinking ship, he swam as hard as he could, aided by a riptide coursing through the strait like an invisible river. He had to distance himself from the debris and the sinking, pulling feeling.

Countless passengers and crew were in the water, crying or shrieking at a deafening, heart-wrenching decibel. A dozen women were tangled in the canvas awning from the aft deck. No way to help them. He swam harder. Using one foot, he pushed off the shoe on the other foot, then repeated with the other shoe; they were too heavy.

A sucking sound filled the air behind him and he flipped onto his back. To his horror, a large, swirling black hole had formed around the sinking stern. The vortex was sucking in people and remains—whatever was near—and taking everything to the ocean bottom. Benji had escaped this grisly death. A shape drifted near—a woman, face down, her dinner skirts spreading like the oil on the water. He closed his eyes momentarily.

Safe from the vortex, he treaded water and turned in multiple directions to search for fire or lifeboats. He saw only one lifeboat, capsized, its white hull belly-up; it soon submerged.

He could see heads bobbing everywhere. It could not have been more than ten minutes since they'd been walking the deck, perhaps much less, and the ship had completely disappeared, leaving a hole in the water.

He thrashed toward a floating form and grabbed a wooden deck chair; he was floating away from the scene in the current, pushed by the turbulence of the sinking ship. In the distance, he thought he could make out the shadow outline of one lifeboat, but wasn't sure. He tried to kick at the water in that direction. The noise of so many people in various stages of distress and panic was overwhelming. All grabbing for anything, desperate for help.

No lifeboat came near. After some time, he'd drifted farther away from other survivors. All that had found a float were on their individual journeys. His lips were bleeding, eyes screaming with pain, and his body near exhaustion. He put his head on his floating chair and tried to rest, waiting for a rescue opportunity. One never came.

When he opened his eyes again, he was alone in the vast blackness of water and waves around him, nothing in sight. He had lost all sense of time. The fatigue overpowered him; he shivered uncontrollably, not from cold. The water was very warm; he reasoned, as best he could, that shock or fear was causing it. He mentally tried to control his reactions. The chair was breaking up. Soon it wouldn't be large enough to keep him afloat. He knew there were many small islands in the Torres Strait where they had been sailing. *Hang on and wait for morning*, he told himself. If his chair would stay afloat, then he would assess his options.

The morning brought blue sky broken with tall, dark cumulonimbus clouds, promising inclement weather later in the day. It was the wet season and isolated squalls were frequent and sometimes violent. The wind aloft was audible. His shivering had calmed. He could barely feel his legs. Very far away, he spotted the shape of a ship he thought might search for and rescue passengers from the water. He was too far away to get their attention. He knew the island he could see near the ship was Mount Adolphus Island, but it was too distant to swim there.

Behind him were smaller islands, some just rocks, but some with palm trees and vegetation. Surveying the surface, he spotted a flat plank as it poked an edge over a wave. Visible in the moonlight, it was bigger and much more buoyant than the chair planks. *I'll have to abandon the chair if I try to reach it.* Letting go, he tried to kick. At first, he sank. His legs were not responding; he struggled with his arms and commanded his legs to move. *It means survival.* Eventually, they responded. He kicked and flung his arms towards the plank riding the current's waves. Grasping its edge, he pulled his upper torso onto its width. It supported his weight; he worked his left leg onto its surface. Except for one leg, he had a float. He passed out.

He woke in darkness; the sky above was visible, but he could see nothing around him. The moon had vanished behind a towering mass of cloud; the sky split with a ragged bolt of lightning that tore across the blackness. The wind started hissing along the surface of the water, spraying the tops of the waves. Then pellets of rain fell as if propelled from a cannon, drumming on the plank and his body, stinging his skin like needles. Waves pitched higher as the gusts tore across the currents, the plank bucking and twisting like a trapped animal.

Benji held the edges, his fingers locked, aching. He was long past fatigue. Flashes of light illuminated the darkness, thunder encompassed him, and the rain fell sideways. The waves surged to a towering height. One rose out of the darkness like a mountain moving toward him, giving him only a heartbeat to brace. The plank beneath him surged upward, catching the wind like a sail. It and Benji were airborne—lifted, flung like a rag into the blackness. Debris circled him as the plank flipped, smashing into his skull.